NATURAL BRIDGES

by

Debbie Lynn McCampbell

THE PERMANENT PRESS
SAG HARBOR, NEW YORK

Library of Congress Catologing-in-Publication Data

McCampbell, Debbie Lynn.
    Natural Bridges/by Debbie Lynn McCampbell.
        p.   cm.
     ISBN 1-877946-79-6
     I. Title.
     PS3563.C3347N38   1997
     813' .54--dc20   96-19007
                                        CIP

First editon, 1500 copies, February 1997.

THE PERMANENT PRESS
Noyac Road
Sag Harbor, NY 11963

This book is dedicated in loving memory of Grandma Pasley and Tasha for their inspiration. And to some of the delightful living: Mom for her love, Erik for his laugh, Uncle Jay for the lore, Aunt Glenda for letting in strays, Kurt for the loading the software, and most of all, to Johnn and his family for lending their steadfast encouragement.

This book was also written with the wish that all strays, human and canine alike, find loving hearts or homes.

1. Three Garage Sales

It was the Saturday before Florabelle's wedding, and Momma had sent us out to find Florabelle a wedding gown. She already had a real nice one that Momma made out of taffeta two years ago when Florabelle was supposed to marry Skeeter McCoy who died of rabies before they got around to it, but now with Florabelle seven months pregnant, that dress wouldn't fit her. We'd only thought about it a week before when I was letting the waist out of the yellow gingham she wanted to wear to her wedding/baby shower.

We took Daddy's Ford pickup, and of course with Florabelle as big as she was, I drove. Birdie, our little sister, rode in the back with the pups. I had my window down, looking for numbers on mailboxes. It was a real hot day, and we'd stretched a worn potato sack out over the vinyl seat in the cab so we wouldn't have those little seam patterns on the back of our thighs when we got out to shop. Florabelle should've been watching out for house numbers on her side, but instead, she was digging through the glove box for change.

"Ain't nothing in here but tobacco and nails," she said, slamming the glove box door. "Don't you think he'd carry quarters for pop?"

I looked over at her and shrugged. She was slumped down in the seat, knees wide apart, feet on the dash, thick white calves jiggling to the rhythm of the motor. Her belly puffed out and sagged between her thighs. She was carrying low and was so big that we couldn't even tie an apron around her. Grandma Trapper Feezer was predicting triplets. Florabelle was hoping to God Grandma'd be wrong.

"Sit up," I said.

"What?"

"Sit up. Or you'll have a crooked baby."

Florabelle shifted her weight, straightened a little, smacked gum.

"Look for numbers," I said, "two-one-one-six. Should come up a little ways past the Whistle Stop."

Florabelle suddenly sat up. "Honk."

"Where?" I accelerated.

"Honk when we go by the Whistle Stop. Jason'll be there drinking. They're off today. Factory's closed weekends. Honk."

"Too late."

Florabelle jerked around to look for Jason's truck.

"Face front," I said.

"Why didn't you honk?"

"You're going to twist that baby."

"Mind your own business, Fern."

"Mind yours. Look for numbers."

She turned around, slumped back down, folded her arms over her belly. "I don't know why anybody'd even *have* a garage sale. Hell, we don't even have a garage. Seems like if folks had stuff worth selling, then it'd be worth keeping. Especially a wedding gown; you could make it into fancy table napkins or something."

"This is Bowen; more folks live here, and they have garages. If we have to, we'll head into Stanton. Momma says some of the wealthier folks there decorate their houses every other summer and sell their old things in garage sales."

"Not big wedding gowns."

"We'll find you one," I said. "The kind with the drop waist. Now keep watching for numbers. Here's the list. There's a few here in Bowen, one on up in Rosslyn."

Florabelle took the list, counted the addresses, spat her gum over me out my window.

I ignored it. Whether we found her a gown or not didn't make much difference to me. I was more worried about the other reason we'd driven this far out of Leeco.

Heidi, Daddy's blind blood hound, had given us another

litter, and we weren't allowed to keep them. Daddy claimed they cost too much to feed, and he didn't want them running around tearing up the garden. Last winter, when she'd had her first, we'd tried giving all the pups away to neighbors, but no one else could really afford to keep them neither. So Daddy had ended up disposing of them—said he took them down to the *pound.* Florabelle said it was the *pond.* Says he drowned them. Buried them for fertilizer near the tomatoes.

This time, though, Momma had come up with a different plan to get rid of the pups that Daddy knew nothing about. I still looked at it as something next to murder, but Momma said it was part of life and looked at it more as charity. "Everybody this side of the gorge should have a good bloodhound," she'd said. "For protection."

I glanced in the rearview mirror and saw that Birdie was holding one of the pups. She sat against the spare tire, her bare legs stretched out, pinking in the afternoon sun. Wind brushed brown hair across her little face so I couldn't see her expression. The other two pups had slid and were huddled together against the tailgate. The water bowl that Birdie and I had put back there had spilled over, and rivers ran down the grooves of the truck bed.

"Now *you* ain't watching numbers," said Florabelle.

"Am too."

"No you ain't." She grinned. "I know you ain't because we just passed two-one-one-six."

I slammed the brakes, forgetting about Birdie and the pups, and turned the truck around in the road. "You want a dress or not?"

Florabelle snickered. "Three houses back on your left."

I stopped the truck in front of a small red shotgun house. There was no garage, but the yard was full of furniture and other household things piled high on oil barrels and card tables. Two skinny boys in overalls ran around, picking up things, playing with them, and putting them down in the wrong places. An old woman sat in a yard chair near the door to the house, watching the boys, suspecting.

"You and I will ask about the dress," I said, still eyeing

the woman. "Birdie'll do the other thing."

"Why don't you just go on up there and ask? I'll wait here," suggested Florabelle. "I'm aching." She held her stomach.

"Get out," I said.

Florabelle squirmed. "That old hag ain't going to have no wedding gown. She probably ain't never been married. Let's just leave."

"We can't. The pups."

Florabelle sighed, opened her door.

I went around to the back of the truck to lower the tailgate. Birdie was struggling to tie a rope leash around one of the pups that kept wiggling. I didn't offer to help her; she'd see that I had the shakes.

"You ready?" I asked.

She nodded and climbed out.

"Sorry, Bird."

She frowned up at me.

I laid my hand on her bony shoulder.

"Let go," she said, shrugging my hand away, and led the wobbling puppy up the gravel driveway.

As we approached, the old woman stared right at Florabelle, then rose from her chair. She was large-busted; a faded floral duster hung loosely over her body, and matched her faded, yellow terry cloth slippers. Her face was puffy and pale, aged.

"Afternoon," she said. "Don't got no baby clothes or bassinet if that's what you're after. Even the grandchildren are all growed up now. Do have some nice quilts though." She waved a fleshy arm. "Made them myself."

"What we're after," said Florabelle, "is a wedding gown."

The woman raised her brows, rendering judgment, and shuffled over to us. "A weddin' gown?" she asked.

"That's what I said." Florabelle waited.

The woman then looked at me. "For you?"

"No, for me," said Florabelle. "I'm getting married this coming Friday night." Her face beamed.

Mine flushed.

The woman padded back across the yard about ten feet from us, steadied herself against a wooden chest of drawers. Her face, suddenly, was as red as her house. "Whore." The word cut through the thick air like a buzz saw.

Florabelle stepped back.

The skinny boys ran off.

I turned and motioned for Birdie, who was still standing in the driveway, to move along. "Oh, no, ma'am," I lied. "See, this is going to be my sister's *second* wedding."

Florabelle poked me in the back, hard.

"Her first husband," I continued, "this baby's Daddy; he died a short while ago. What we need now is a bigger dress than what we already have."

"Hogwash," said the woman. "Ain't a vessel of truth in your story. I know sorrow when I see it, and this girl ain't grieving over no dead husband."

I dropped my head.

"Then you got a dress or not?" demanded Florabelle, hands on her hips, stomach pointed accusingly at the woman.

The woman stood there, lips pursed, scowling at us like we were stains on a rug. Then she spoke, voice quivering. "Do you know why I'm selling all my things today?"

"You're redecorating," said Florabelle.

The woman frowned and stepped back up on her front stoop. "My husband built this house forty-two years ago. We worked hard to make this a home, brought four children into the world, taught them how to work hard, too. Now Delmar's gone, passed on in his sleep a month ago. I can't go on living here with all the memories. Look around. He still sits on the chair over there, still eats off that table, and he still wipes his boots on this here rug. His ghost won't leave this house, so I got to." She took a deep breath and with a slippered foot, straightened out the rug on the stoop. "That, missy, is grief. And there ain't no sign of it in your eyes. Shame neither." She took a crumpled handkerchief out of a torn hip pocket and dabbed at her forehead.

"Let's get out of here," said Florabelle, turning to leave.

9

I looked around the yard and saw Birdie still wandering around the side of the house. We couldn't leave yet. I grabbed Florabelle's arm. "Go look at them quilts," I told her. I had picked up an old dust broom to take down to the service station where I worked half-days. Clem Proffit, the owner, didn't worry too much about cleaning the place, and it needed it badly.

I paid the woman fifty cents for the broom. She took the coins and rubbed them between her fingers. She stared down at them; her eyes were red, near tears. Then she went to her chair, sat down, got up again, cleared her throat. "How old are you?" she asked Florabelle.

"Twenty," said Florabelle.

Florabelle was nineteen; I was twenty.

"When do you drop?" asked the woman.

"Two months."

"Been to a doctor?"

"I ain't sick." Florabelle started back to the truck.

I squinted and looked for Birdie again. She was already back in the truck. Job done.

"We have to go," I said.

The woman nodded, stuffed the damp hankie back in her pocket.

"I got no wedding gown to sell," she said. "Passed it down to my oldest daughter. That's where I'll be going. To live with her in Dayton."

"Dayton's supposed to be nice," I offered. I wondered if this was something like what Grandma Trapper Feezer had gone through when Grandpa had died. Finding words to soothe this kind of pain, I learned back then, was futile.

"Miss?" called the woman.

I turned back.

"Here," she said. "And get that girl to a doctor. Preacher, too. She ought to be praying."

"Yes, ma'am, " I said, taking the quilt. "Thanks."

Walking back towards the truck, carrying my broom, she must have seen us as three witches, straight out of Salem.

The sun was so bright that I could see the heat waves over the hood of the truck. It was August, and we'd had a two-week dry spell, which was unusual for that time. Dust from the road powdered the windshield. On both sides of the road were open fields. Grazing heifers looked like black blurs. Tobacco rows browned in the sun, dry and brittle, ready to be cut.

I thought of stopping the truck and setting the pups free in the open pastures, letting them choose their own fate. But I was afraid they would end up joining the pack of strays that was always pestering folks' hen houses and then getting shot at, or getting run over in the road. Plus, I couldn't risk having Birdie recognize them and see them run loose like that, all skinny and mangy, or rabid like that one that killed Skeeter.

We were heading south on 15 towards Rosslyn, which was mostly oil fields, tobacco farms, and the Tennessee Gas Transfer Company where Daddy worked, repairing pump machinery. I looked down at the gas gauge and noted we still had almost a full tank. Daddy never let it go dry; in fact, I doubted he'd ever even let the needle go below the halfway mark. He was peculiar that way, always on the safe side, going to all measures to avoid a hassle. Like lubing belts and hoses on the cars so they wouldn't crack. Like sharpening hunting knives all the time so they wouldn't go dull. Like killing dogs so they wouldn't starve.

About ten minutes after being back on the road from the old woman's house, Florabelle finally spoke.

"Why'd you lie for me back there?" she asked.

"I lied for me."

"So you're ashamed of me, too."

"Didn't say that."

"Momma, Grandma, and now you." She stomped the floorboard. "Well, *I* ain't ashamed. Me and Jason love each other, and people in love get married and have babies. Don't matter which order you do it in neither."

"Guess not." She and I didn't see eye to eye at all on this matter, and there was no use, this late in the game, saying anything more about it. Get Florabelle up against any talk about morals, sin, penance, anything at all along the lines of righteousness and faith, and she'd flare up like a hell-cat then go on like there was no tomorrow about God being vengeful and merciless. She'd start citing Bible verses about God's retribution upon Cain, Moses, and Lot's wife until she'd run out of passages, then she'd conjure up another account of His merciless wrath, and it would have seven heads. No, I wasn't going to say one more word about it. The baby, Jason, nothing. Let the sleeping dogs lie, as Momma would say.

After a lull, I asked, "You love Jason?"

"Sure I do."

"You love that baby?"

Florabelle shifted, looked behind her, lit a cigarette. "Shit."

"What?"

"Oh, it's Birdie. She's back there whimpering, I can see her."

"She ain't crying," I said, looking in the mirror. Birdie was sniffling, cradling both pups. "What did she do with it?" I asked.

"Tied it to a spigot on the side of the house. Woman's probably found it by now." Florabelle blew smoke out in the cab, clouding my vision.

"It's not right," I said, shaking my head.

"Why not? That old biddy could use the company."

"I mean making Birdie do this."

"I don't see nothing wrong with it. All she's doing is giving folks a free hound. So what if it's a surprise to them."

"No telling, though, what folks will do with them."

"You mean kill them like Daddy did?"

"He didn't kill them."

"Yes, he did. Drowned them, saw him do it."

"No you didn't."

"Well, anyways, giving them away to strangers is much better, the way I look at it. Can you think of something else? Maybe we could stew them like rabbits; the Chinese do." She smirked.

I shot a look at her. "Birdie wants to keep them."

"Can't. They dig up the garden. Besides," she added, "them dogs stink."

"You don't give something away just because it smells bad. What are you going to do when your baby craps his diaper?"

"Tie him to a spigot at some old woman's garage sale." Florabelle threw her head back and laughed.

"Give me the list," I said, pointing at the dash.

She handed me the list, still laughing.

"Next one's two-one-eight," I said. "Start looking."

My left arm was starting to freckle from the sun, where it rested on the door of the truck. We were beginning to see more houses closer to the road and a few businesses now that we were nearing Rosslyn. We passed a monument company and the Leggatt Platt bedspring factory where Jason worked. Leeco, where we lived, was set in the curve of a foothill, with nothing around but a few houses, trailers, hollows, and rocks. Where we lived, there were no street names, and few last names. I figured Birdie was at least enjoying the new sights.

Florabelle had switched her cigarette to her left hand and had her right arm out the window, bouncing it against the wind, counting. "Two-one-two ... two-one-four ... two — there it is."

About a half a dozen cars and trucks were parked alongside the road in front of the house, so I had to drive a little farther up. The house was much bigger than the old woman's. Junk spilled out of the garage into a paved driveway. The garage looked big enough to store ten John Deere mowers. People hovered over tables covered with glasses, costume jewelry, and rusted-out countertop appliances. There was a couch for sale that folks kept sitting down on and getting up, trying it on for size. Birdie would have to be careful with her charge this time, with so many people around.

She carried a pup in her arms and walked ahead of us. We couldn't tell whose house it was, so Florabelle and I just started looking for a dress by ourselves. We browsed through some clothes that hung from a rope tied from one end of the garage to the other. We found mostly men's slacks and women's blouses and stretch pants.

"Momma'd like these pants for gardening," said Florabelle.

"Hardly ever worn," came a voice from behind the clothes. Then a man's head appeared between two corduroy jackets. "Frank," he said, offering his right hand, "Frank Murray."

Florabelle shook his hand. "Florabelle Rayburn," she said smiling. "This is my sister, Fern."

The man that came out from behind the clothes was tall with jet black hair and dark brown eyes, and suntanned skin. If it weren't for the fact that his nose formed kind of an arrow, he looked right out of Hollywood, especially with his sensual smile, under a thin mustache, that sort of lured you in and washed you over. The bright-colored polyester shirts he had stepped out from behind draped him like stage curtains.

Florabelle stared at him like she was in some sort of trance. "If them pants never been worn," she challenged, "why are you selling them?"

"They belonged to my mother-in-law, who recently lost a lot of weight on one of those protein milkshake diets. They're practically new."

"So you're married then," said Florabelle, starting to flirt.

"Yes." He smiled again. "You must be, too." He patted her stomach, hand lingering.

"No," she said, "but Fern here is getting married soon, and we're looking for a wedding gown. Would your wife by chance be selling hers today?"

"Congratulations," he said, I guess to me, but looking at Florabelle, still laying on the charm.

Of the two of us, it always seemed, Florabelle attracted more men. She had a welcoming look of intent about her, always quick to warm up to strangers, while I would stand back, measuring people up. And as far as looks went, even pregnant, Florabelle had a figure that curved in all the right places, and I was as skinny as a beanpole. I was flat-chested, bony at the knees and shoulders, and though there was quite a distance between them, my hipbones protruded. No one in the midwest could have a more fitting name than I did. Silver Fern. Just like the one on Momma's kitchen table. Wide at the base, narrow at the top, with studded stems.

Florabelle's skin was fair, much smoother than my darker, drier, quick-to-bruise, prone-to-freckling complexion. Her hair was thick and ash blond, and she could wear it in all sorts of styles. My hair was blond, too, but with more of a honey gold cast from the sun; it hung straight and limp to my waist. Momma and Aunt Hazel had once given me a Lilt perm in the basement, but it didn't take. Aunt Hazel said it could have been defective chemicals or too large rollers, but Momma argued that it was just my bad luck to have hair as fine as a frog's.

It wasn't five minutes after standing there making small talk, that Frank put his arm around Florabelle, just as if he'd known her forever, and led her over to a table covered with books and record albums.

"I'm going to find Birdie," I said, and left them alone. I squinted in the bright sun and looked around. She wasn't in the garage, driveway, nor yard, so I figured she must already be back at the truck.

In the street out in front of the house, a boy and a girl were fighting over a bicycle for sale. Two women hollered at them from the curb, threatening to count to three and get their daddies. The boy pushed the girl down, then both kids started screaming.

As I got near the truck, I could see Birdie's small head over the edge of the tailgate. Her hair, which was unfortunately taking on my hair's traits already, hung over the side, tangled from the wind. She was going to need my help with the snarls later.

"Hi," I said.

She didn't sit up. Her eyes were shut so I thought she might be sleeping. I leaned against the side rail of the truck. I'd parked under an oak tree, and the shade felt good. I shut my eyes, too, and waited.

"I put her in the desk drawer," said Birdie.

I turned around and looked at her, but her eyes were still shut.

"What?"

"That desk they was selling. I put her in the bottom drawer when nobody was looking and left it open some."

I looked at the remaining pup. It was snuggled up between Birdie's legs with its head resting on her crotch.

"Is that one there male or female?" I asked.

"Boy." She opened her eyes. "This one's Jimmy."

"Jimmy," I repeated, reached in and scratched his ears.

"He's the smartest," said Birdie.

"How do you know that?"

"Cause he keeps trying to hide. Climbs in the tire. He knows."

"I wish you could keep him, Bird. But you know Daddy—"

"He should just drown *Heidi*. That way we won't have to kill any more of her puppies."

"Oh, no, Birdie, it's not Heidi's fault. She doesn't understand. She just has pups because God wants her to."

Birdie sat up, glared at me. "God don't put no babies here just to die."

"No, you're right," I said. "Just bad luck I guess." I couldn't think of how to explain ill fate or neglect to an eight-year-old. "Birdie," I began, "Clem Proffit down at the station has an old retired friend who used to doctor race-horses. He would know how to fix dogs where they don't have any more litters. Doesn't hurt the dogs any. We'll have Clem check into it for Heidi, see how much it costs. How's that sound?"

Birdie moved Jimmy from her lap, set him down in a shady spot. "He's thirsty," she said.

"We'll see about some water at our next stop."

"Florie ain't found a dress?"

"Not yet."

Florabelle, just then, was walking back up the road, swinging her arms, carrying what looked like an old tennis racket.

Florabelle didn't play tennis.

Birdie settled back against the tailgate. "Fern?"

"Uh-huh?"

"This thing Clem's friend can do to dogs to make them not have babies. Can he do it to humans, too?"

"Well, yes, I suppose so. But it's a whole different kind of thing."

"They should do it to Florabelle."

We rode in silence for quite a while, then about a half mile past a No Shoulders sign, I hit a pothole and Florabelle said, "So you done turned Birdie against me too, now."

"Have not."

"She's being a pissant."

"Don't call her that."

"She hasn't spoke to me all day."

"It ain't you she's worried about," I said, glancing in the mirror at Birdie once more. "She named them pups, you know."

Florabelle turned and glared at me. "I don't see what the fuss is over them damn dogs. Nobody seems too concerned about me finding a wedding gown. Anyways, if I was Heidi, I'd be glad to be getting rid of the things, saves her from having to take care of them." She lit another cigarette. "You see them two fighting over that bicycle back there? I wanted to smack them both. Seems like kids are always running around, getting into things, making noise and messes." She blew smoke into the sunvisor mirror and checked her lipstick. "Frank agrees with me."

"You shouldn't be having that baby," I said.

"Got to."

The next garage sale wasn't too far up the road from the last one. It was off a side street, right outside of Stanton. Florabelle got out first this time and said something to Birdie that I couldn't hear.

The house wasn't a whole lot bigger than the tool shed Daddy had built behind Grandma Trapper Feezer's. A few pieces of furniture crowded the small yard, and dishes, pots, utensils, and toys balanced on an old cedar chest.

A girl sat alone on the front stoop. She looked about eighteen and had a small frame like mine, but petite rather than scrawny. Her hair was black and shiny, and her eyes were tiny, round, and chestnut-brown. If it weren't that her face was so pale, she could have passed for Cherokee. Her whole complexion lacked luster, and she looked almost scared of us as we walked up.

Birdie was the first to speak. "This is Jimmy," she said, holding up the pup, way over her own head.

Florabelle grabbed at the pup and yelled for Birdie to put it down. But Birdie quickly pulled Jimmy away from her and hugged him close. The startled pup let out a yelp and wet all over Birdie's T-shirt. Birdie looked embarrassed.

"It's okay, Birdie," I said.

The girl stood up and disappeared inside the house.

"What are you doing, Birdie?" Florabelle snapped. "Now's she's going to notice if we don't leave with it."

Birdie stared at her, not answering.

The girl came back with a towel. "Here," she said and started wiping Birdie's shirt off.

"I'll do that," I said, taking the towel.

Florabelle walked away and started looking through the stuff.

"Jimmy's very handsome," said the girl, squatting down to Birdie's level. "Can I?" She gently took the pup from Birdie's trembling hands and sat back down on the stoop. "Bloodhound, right?"

Birdie nodded.

"My Daddy raises these on his farm in Carrollton," said the girl. "He'd be real proud if one of his turned out looking like this one." She handed Jimmy back to Birdie.

Birdie smiled, pleased.

The girl took the damp towel from me and set it aside. She smiled up at me but didn't speak. Her beady eyes, nearly lost in her colorless face, made me think of brown M & Ms.

Florabelle hollered from where she stood by the dishes and toys. "You got a kid?"

The girl hesitated, smile suddenly fading. "No."

Florabelle walked over. "Whose toys then?"

"They belonged to my little boy. He died, though."

Florabelle stared at the girl a moment. "But you're married, right?"

Again, the girl hesitated. "No. Was for a while, but—"

"The reason my sister's asking," I began, glaring at Florabelle, "is because what we're looking for is a wedding gown. For *her*."

The girl stood up and walked over to the cedar chest and began taking everything off of it. Birdie followed her and helped, still holding Jimmy. They worked silently while Florabelle and I stood watching.

The girl opened the chest. "Here," she said, lifting out a full, rustling dress. The dress was eggshell white, sack style, and although it was wrinkled, the lacework and sequins still looked good. The girl held it against her, smoothing out the creases. "This was mine," she said, handing it to Florabelle. "It might fit you, I was bigger then. You can go inside and try it on."

"It's pretty," said Florabelle, studying the detail. She took the gown into the house.

We waited by the door a few minutes, not speaking. Birdie played with Jimmy around the hedges. I gave up hope on getting rid of him here.

When Florabelle came back outside, she was smiling. The dress was a little snug around the middle of course, but because of the style being low-waisted with a sash belt, it did at least fit around her. Even with her blue sneakers and her shirt collar showing underneath, the dress looked fine. She looked real pleased with herself as she paced in front of us for approval.

"Fits," I said and looked over at the girl for her to agree.

But she had no expression on her face whatsoever, just sat there staring at Florabelle, her eyes all glazed over as if she'd left us there, alone for a moment, to revisit something. "Looks nice," she said at last.

"You think so?" asked Florabelle.

We nodded.

Florabelle strutted up to the girl. "Your husband die, too?" she asked, softly this time.

"No. He left." She hesitated, looked at me as if for consent to go on. "Left when Michael was born. Married me when we found out I was pregnant, left soon as he was born. Got scared, I guess."

Florabelle stopped pacing, considered this. "You miss him?" she asked.

"Not much." The girl shrugged. "Just my baby." She sat back down, head bowed.

Florabelle sat down beside her, lit a cigarette, offered one to the girl.

The girl shook her head.

"What happened to him?" asked Florabelle.

"Pneumonia. Had it bad last winter. We both had it."

"How old was he?"

"Eight months."

Florabelle exhaled, long and slow. "Miss him bad, huh?"

The girl frowned.

"I mean it's not easier now, after some time's gone by?"

"Does it look like it got easier?"

Florabelle glanced around at the few things cluttering the yard.

"Where you going?"

"Home. To my Daddy's. Selling my things for the bus fare."

"Can't he pay?"

The girl looked away. "He don't know I'm coming."

I felt desperate, regretted even having stopped in. I was suddenly disgusted with our whole mission. "Florabelle, Birdie, let's go."

They both stood up. Birdie was clutching Jimmy and sobbing. I put my arm around her.

"How much you want for this gown?" asked Florabelle.

The girl puckered her lips, tilted her head to one side, calculated, candy eyes shifting. "Twenty dollars."

I looked at Florabelle.

"We don't have but eighteen," she said flatly.

20

We'd come with twenty-five dollars that Momma and Grandma had pulled together and given to Florabelle to hold. I couldn't imagine the tennis racket costing much more than two bucks and wondered what she'd done with the rest.

The girl looked at Birdie, who had her face buried against my legs. I could feel Jimmy's wet nose against my thigh.

"Or," said the girl, "you can leave me that pup."

Birdie stiffened.

Florabelle looked down at the gown and pressed it against her swollen stomach. She dropped her cigarette, put it out with her shoe, looked up. "No deal," she said. Then slipped the dress off over her head, balled it up, and gave it to the girl. She turned to me and fixed a stare. "That pup belongs to my little sister." Her face was red.

I lifted the quivering pup from Birdie's cradled arms and handed it down to the girl. I felt like a coon, stealing an egg from a bird nest.

Birdie screamed.

The girl, again, offered the dress.

Florabelle just kept her piercing eyes on me all the while.

Everyone waited while I gazed down at the ground, sweeping gravel back and forth with my foot. Birdie kept on crying. I stood motionless, looking down at the girl cradling Jimmy.

"We're going on to Stanton," I said, finally. "We'll look for a dress there."

Florabelle kicked at the driveway like a scolded child, and headed for the truck.

"He needs water," I said to the girl. "It's been a long ride."

The girl shook her head. "Here," she said, holding Jimmy out to me. "Keep him; that little girl needs him more than I do. Make her quit that crying. Anyhow, my Daddy's got a bunch of them running around the farm for me to pick from."

I looked at the girl. Her eyes had welled up; I could tell she was fighting an urge. One tear broke free and slid down her cheek. I held her eyes, though. M & Ms melt, I remembered, if you hold them for too long.

"Please, Fern," pleaded Birdie, "I'll take care of him. Please."

I just stood there, not knowing what to do or say, thinking about the pond. It was always up to me in these circumstances, to know what to do. To have the right answer and do the right thing. No matter whose business it was, it always ended up being mine. My head hurt from hunger and the heat. My heart hurt from heaviness.

I heard the truck door open, and Florabelle came strutting back, swinging her purse, stomach way out ahead of her. She snatched Jimmy from the girl and shoved him in Birdie's hands. "For God's sake, Fern, will you just come on?" she hissed. "I'll take him with me this weekend; he can stay in Jason's backyard." At the last minute, she opened her purse and threw two ten dollar bills down on the ground at the girl's feet next to the wadded up dress. Then she dragged Birdie by the hand back to the truck, lifted her with great effort into the cab, got in, and slammed the door. When I didn't come right away, she laid on the horn.

It was a loud horn, loud enough to summon up a demon. And the noise blared out, declaring our offense.

At last, I said good-bye to the girl, who said absolutely nothing, just watched me with her hands clapped over her ears. She never heard me go. I never looked back.

2. Hearing Rattles

The rain finally came on the trip back to Leeco, washing away the dust. Florabelle snored the whole way. Birdie was wedged between us, holding Jimmy. We had the windows rolled up because of the rain, and the cab smelled like dog breath.

Even if we'd had enough money left, we wouldn't have been able to find a dress. It was late, the sky was clouding up, and as we drove back through town, people had their garage doors closed and were out taking their signs down off the telephone poles.

Florabelle had finally admitted to having two dollars and fifty cents left in change, and we'd stopped for some burgers at a White Castle. Then I'd run into Ewen's Grocery and bought a six-pack of Almond Joys for me and Birdie. Later, my stomach felt full and bloated from the burgers; I wondered if that was the way Florabelle's felt all the time, except without the grease.

"Is Daddy going to shoot Jimmy once he sees him?" asked Birdie.

"No, he won't see him," I said, looking down at her. "Florabelle's promised to empty out the sewing basket in our room and hide him in there until Friday when she moves out."

Birdie stuck her thumb in her mouth and sucked hard.

"Cut that out," I said. "You want buck teeth?"

"I don't want Daddy to kill Jimmy."

I looked down at the chubby brown pup. "Birdie, quit thinking about it," I said, but I couldn't help worrying about it, too. "Jimmy will be okay," I said, patting his head.

We were nearly two or three miles from home, and I turned on the brights so I wouldn't miss our turn. I didn't get out driving much, except for the tractor mower around the yard, though I always wished for a car of my own. A convertible. I'd always had a thing for cars and enjoyed working on them down at Clem's.

I drove slowly through the darkness. We lived on four acres owned by the Tennessee Gas Company where Daddy worked. Our backyard dropped down into a hollow, and at the bottom of it was a pump that Daddy was paid extra to watch.

Once, our neighbor Bud Fowler's cow wandered over the property line and got herself caught under the well while it was pumping. Cracked its skull and killed it. Since then, if Birdie so much as got a bicycle wheel in Bud's yard, he'd bawl her out.

Our house was big, with three bedrooms upstairs and two down. It had a really large living room, a good size eat-in kitchen, a screened-in front porch, full bath with a tub downstairs, and a basement for laundry and storage. The proprietors kept the house up real well, treated and painted the wood every other year. We all liked it, except for Daddy, because he didn't own it.

Ever since we had to sell our farm in Franklin three years back, Daddy hadn't been the same. All three of us girls were born there, and we'd really settled in. Daddy had tilled most of the land and had kept dairy cattle. One year, Momma and Daddy received a certificate of achievement for producing seventy percent of the family's food. We loved it there, regretted leaving, but the upkeep just got to be too much. The corporate farms pushed us out, and we had to foreclose. It just killed Daddy, now, to pay rent instead of mortgage. He was one of these who believed a man wasn't worth a cent if he didn't own land.

I nudged Birdie. "Wake up Florabelle."

"Don't bother," said Florabelle, hoarsely, sitting up, "I ain't asleep. Who could with that dog panting like he's got asthma. I told you he'd stink, too."

I looked over at her.

"You promised," said Birdie.

"Just take him right on upstairs while I stall Daddy," I told Florabelle.

"Hey, he'll fit in your pocket book," said Birdie, spirits rising. She squeezed the confused pup into Florabelle's vinyl purse.

Florabelle frowned. "Daddy'll be asleep. It's Momma I'm worried about. What are you going to tell her about not finding a dress?"

"Just tell her we'll talk about it tomorrow," I said. "And Daddy will be up; we have his truck. Maybe Aunt Hazel can make you up a dress."

"In less than a week?"

"We'll figure something out. Help Birdie for now."

When we pulled in the driveway, it was ten o'clock. I turned off the headlights and cruised slowly up the gravel. Heidi ran around from behind the shed and barked at us. Everyone always had to be careful not to run into her since she couldn't see. The kitchen light and porch light were both still on. I was tired, and my bottom was sore from sitting so long.

Birdie was trying to zip up Florabelle's handbag, but Jimmy kept poking his head out. "We better hurry," she said, "or he'll suffercate."

"Is he in?" I asked, shutting off the engine.

"He sure as hell better not bark," said Florabelle. "Or piss in my purse."

"Let's go," I said. "Birdie, you keep still. Go in and tell Momma you had a nice day and you're tired and just want to go straight to bed. Don't mention the dress, Jimmy, the burgers, nor the candy, hear?" Momma hated us buying fast food. She claimed it was undercooked and overpriced.

Birdie nodded.

We climbed up the porch steps quietly, though Heidi was still barking at our heels, and opened the storm door. Daddy was lying on the couch in front of the TV; he was still in his work uniform. Momma was sitting at his feet, in her housecoat, snapping beans. The channel six news was on.

Momma saw us and looked up. "Well," she said, almost shouting like she did whenever she was nervous. "We was beginning to worry. Your Daddy was fixing to go out hunting for you, in Hazel's Dodge. Thought maybe you had a flat or the gears in the truck were missing again. Did you find Florie a nice dress?"

Florabelle was already heading upstairs with her purse. "We'll talk about it in the morning, Momma," she called. "We're just so exhausted, ain't we, Birdie?"

"Any trouble shifting?" Daddy was awake.

"No, Daddy," I said. "Truck rode fine. Rattled a little, though. Something up under the hood squeaked every time I drove over a bump. Could be the shocks."

"Must be the way you was braking. What bumps are you talking about? Between here and Stanton?" He scowled.

"Birdie, Honey, come back down here and tell Momma what pretty things you seen," said Momma, setting down the colander.

Birdie looked down at me from the staircase. "I'm

tired." She faked a yawn. "I want to sleep and talk tomorrow. I had a nice day."

"I'll get her bath," I said.

"I saved you girls some dinner," said Momma.

"What bumps?" asked Daddy.

"Potholes, Daddy."

"You have on the headlights?"

"Yes. But it was still dark and it's raining. The truck is okay. I'll take a look at it down at the station Monday."

"What time is it?" he asked Momma.

"It's just a little after ten," she said.

"What business you girls got out gallivanting around after ten o'clock? Where all did you go, Fern?"

"Stanton, Daddy, we were home by ten."

"We sent them, Raymond," Momma reminded him.

Daddy sat up, pulled his shirt down over his stomach. "We did," he said, yawning. "You get rid of all three of them?"

I nodded, looked back towards Momma. It was Daddy's belief that we went into Stanton to take the dogs to a county shelter where he claimed he had taken the first litter. But we knew the consequences there, so that's why Momma had suggested the charity thing.

"Any trouble at the pound?" he asked. "Paperwork?"

"No, I'm going to bed now. Thanks for the truck." I headed upstairs.

"That roast'll go to waste," said Momma.

"We'll heat it for lunch tomorrow," I said from the top of the stairs.

"Fern, I want you to show me what you're talking about tomorrow with them rattles," called Daddy.

"Yes, Daddy," I said.

"Good night, Birdie," called Momma. "Fern, scrub her good. Especially if she used them public commodes in Stanton."

3. Threading Needles

Sunday afternoon, after supper, when Daddy left to go check on the pump, Momma sent Birdie to go get Hazel to come over and talk about the dress. We'd told Momma that we hadn't been able to find a thing to fit Florabelle at the garage sales.

Hazel was Momma's younger sister who lived in a trailer on our lot. Until last year, she lived in Dayton with her husband who was an executive for some big computer company, but he had come home from what he'd called a business trip one weekend and announced that he would be moving to Florida with his secretary. Hazel was a certified beautician and had had her own shop in Dayton called "Hair by Hazel," but now she claimed the chemicals were getting to her and only did perms and color jobs for the old women in a nursing home in Clay City. Her charge for a permanent wave was only three or four dollars, depending on how much hair the ladies still had. She also worked in the kitchen there, four days a week, and helped administer medication to, and bathe, the residents. She made just enough money to pay Daddy some rent for the trailer and a small amount for utilities.

"You expect me to be able to whip up a wedding dress in four days?" Hazel was a chain smoker, unlike Florabelle, who only smoked for attention. Her teeth were yellowed, tobacco-stained, noticeable when she talked. "That's hardly enough time to pin down a pattern and cut it." She blew smoke, hacked.

We were sitting around the kitchen table, still in our Church clothes, except for Hazel, who didn't go, trying to devise a plan.

"Fern said she'd pin, cut, and hem," said Florabelle.

Hazel scooted back her chair, sipped coffee, propped her feet up on the counter. She had a habit of this, putting her feet on the furniture, and Momma just fumed whenever she did it.

"Hazel, get your feet down off my countertop. We're going to pay you for the material and threads, all you got to do is sew. We don't have no other choice. Some of our relations are coming in from Ohio, who we ain't seen in ages, and Florabelle's got to look decent."

"*Decent*?" Hazel winked, then pretended to peek under the table at Florabelle, and we all knew what she was meaning to imply.

"We've all gotten used to that, Hazel," said Momma, who tried never to judge. "What's done is done. Now what's it going to be? You going to help?"

"All right," she said, bringing her feet down. Her rubber soles screeched as they hit the kitchen floor. "But you got to help, Fern." She looked at me. Then Momma too.

"Fern's good with the needle," said Momma, smiling. "She's the one who fixes my sink when it backs up, she can handle a tractor, and she's definitely the one who ended up with the family sewing talent. She can put a button on a blouse faster than a hare hops."

It was true that I was as handy with the needle as I was with a torque wrench, but I never liked sewing. Just did it when it had to be done. Momma's hands weren't so steady any more, and Florabelle just didn't have the patience. I looked at the scraps of roast fat still lying on the plate in front of me, and realized I had no choice other than to help on Florabelle's dress.

For the next four days, instead of helping Clem out down at the station, I sat cooped up in Hazel's dusty, smoke-filled living room, pinning down taffeta and lace. It rained for three of those four days, and the violent torrents that thrashed down the hill through the trees shook the trailer.

The dress took over five yards of material, and that was without a train. The style we'd decided on was straight, drop-waist, a sash belt at the hips with two tiers of lace falling from there to midcalf. It was beginning to look a lot like the M & M-eyed girl's dress, from Rosslyn.

Florabelle, standing up on the coffee table, with Hazel

holding the pin cushion and me measuring the hem, had changed her mind at the last minute and decided to go with cocktail- instead of floor-length to save time and money. She had told Momma she'd lost that twenty-five dollars in a restroom in Stanton last Saturday, and not only was Momma mad and disbelieving, but would only give her ten more for the fabric. I paid the difference.

As for Jimmy, things went rather smoothly with no real close calls. We kept him shut up in our room at night, and Birdie kept him in her room during the day, pretending to be playing a lot with Waylon Jennings, her Cabbage Patch doll. She would sneak Jimmy downstairs and let him pee whenever Momma went to the basement to check the wash, and Daddy was working a lot of overtime, so neither one of them had caught on. Momma just mused a little over Birdie not wanting to play outside much, which she usually did.

Birdie was content to be alone, just as long as she was outdoors. She had some imagination and could entertain herself for hours, climbing trees, naming rocks in the creek, teasing frogs, collecting all sorts of things like pinecones and dead bugs, or chasing Heidi around the pond. Birdie was kind and patient with Heidi, in spite of her age and blindness. She'd tease and play rough with her sometimes, but she'd protect that old dog with all her little might.

Daddy's other dogs, the blue ticks he kept for coon hunting, stayed in pens all day, and Daddy would come home from work at night and let them run. Birdie would pay attention to them, too, talk to them through their cages and bring them table scraps. She had a gentleness about her, calming and thoughtful, a quiet little spirit that we all loved. She embraced her small world, as sheltered as it was, and loved everyone back.

The rest of the week, we were busy with all the wedding arrangements. We were preparing the reception food ourselves and most of the decorations. Since Hazel and I were pretty much tied up with the dress, Momma made almost all the food. She fried nearly two hundred chicken wings, using every skillet we had. She made egg salad finger sandwiches, pickled some cucumbers, marinated other raw vegetables from our garden, fried up some of her famous apple dumplings, baked a couple peach cobblers, did those little hot-dogs-in-a-blanket, deviled four dozen eggs, baked seven or eight pans of cornbread, and stuffed mushrooms with pork dressing. We ordered a wedding cake from a bakery in Bowen, three layers of chocolate because that was the only flavor Jason would eat, and we were making peach sherbet punch.

Florabelle stayed up late every night making centerpieces for the tables. She was sticking peach-colored candles in the glass hurricane lamps we kept in the shed for emergencies, and wrapping crepe-paper flower wreaths around the bases. Then she made a peach hairpiece for Birdie and me and matching bows for our dresses. We were the only bridesmaids, and we already had dresses that we were supposed to have worn in Florabelle and Skeeter's wedding, and they still fit.

Thursday afternoon, we finished the dress. Then Hazel drove Florabelle and Momma downtown to set up the church and the fellowship hall for the reception and to pick up the bouquets. I stayed home to clean up the fabric scraps and keep an eye on some food in the oven. It seemed, by then, the whole downstairs of our house had taken on a peach cast.

Reverend Whitaker called twice that day to confirm the time of the wedding. He was the preacher at the Full Gospel Pentecostal Church in Bowen, where we were members. It was a big church, with a congregation of about seventy-five, over a hundred on holidays.

We were expecting sixty to seventy guests, counting our family, a few neighbors, a couple friends of Daddy's from work, Jason's family, and all his buddies from the bedspring factory.

That night, the eve of the wedding, I lay in bed a while, thinking about it being Florabelle's last night living in our house. It wasn't that we were close and I'd miss her, she and Jason would be living only about ten minutes away, but it would seem strange, especially at night like this, when we both lay in bed in our room upstairs and talked. I'd usually share something from a book I was reading, like a funny passage, or something profound or inspirational, and she would find one thing or another to groan about. She'd rag on Daddy, complain about Jason's work schedule, or make a fuss over Hazel's meddling in her life. Florabelle could bitch for an hour and never come to her point.

She wasn't at all like Birdie, who was accepting and grateful. No, Florabelle assumed things and expected them. She was stubborn and compulsive, but at the same time, she stood her ground on some issues and was loyal to those she respected. For a select few, she would fight a running sawmill, but cross her, and she'd just as readily drive a railroad spike through your skull.

Tonight, though, Florabelle lay speechless and restless; tossing and turning in her bed. As I lay listening to the frogs and the creeping Charlie vine that forever scratched our window, I wondered if she, too, realized the finality of our late-night exchanges, and whether it mattered. This ritual was ceasing. To me, it was an empty feeling, almost threatening. Her being gone, I knew, would bring peace. Silent nights. But I'd grown so used to the complaining; it reassured me.

"Fern?" she whispered.

"Yeah?"

"You reckon Jason ever reads at night?"

"I don't know, probably the sports section of the paper, or maybe the comics."

"Maybe," she said after a short while, and rolled over.

I gazed out our window at the moon, and pulled the sheet up over me. I'd miss her, too.

4. Finding Jimmy

Friday morning, the day of the wedding, we woke up at 6:00 a.m. to Daddy's hollering in the kitchen. I sat straight up in bed and saw Birdie crouched under Florabelle's vanity dresser, hugging Waylon Jennings. She had her own room next to ours but came in our room when she had nightmares.

"What's wrong, Bird?" I asked.

Birdie pointed to the sewing machine beneath the windowsill.

I frowned, not understanding what she meant. "Come out from there. Did you have a bad dream?"

"Listen," she said. "To Daddy."

I sat silent. Daddy was screaming about some puddle on the kitchen floor and I could hear Momma telling him it was probably only the refrigerator leaking again.

"Since when did the fridge leak yellow?" bellowed Daddy.

"They're just having an argument," I told Birdie. "Everyone's just tense over the wedding. Come get in bed with us."

She shook her head. "No." She pointed again at the sewing machine. "Jimmy's out." The lid to the basket seat was flapped up.

I jumped up and pulled on some shorts. "Where is he?"

Birdie shrugged.

"Florabelle, get up." I yanked the sheets off her and shook her. She was sleeping naked, which she knew annoyed me.

"What?" she asked, stretching out full length.

I had my head turned away so I wouldn't have to look at her. "The pup's out. And Daddy's down there yelling about a puddle on the floor. Get up," I said. "We've got to find him."

We both dressed quickly while Birdie searched for Jimmy upstairs. We heard Daddy slam the door and leave the house. We listened until he got down the porch steps.

Birdie came back into our room, sobbing.

"Momma may have already found him and be hiding him," I said. "You just go climb back in bed; we'll find him." I tried to smile. I knew I'd be blamed for this.

When Florabelle and I got downstairs, Momma was on the couch, crying.

"What is it, Momma?" asked Florabelle. "He call you a name again?"

Momma shook her head.

"What's wrong?" I asked.

"Fern, you lied to us," said Momma, not looking up. "He found it. He's got that dog."

My stomach dropped.

"Where'd he go?" asked Florabelle. She kicked the back of the couch and ran to the screen door.

"Florabelle, sit down. Don't be getting yourself all upset," said Momma, pointing at Florabelle's stomach that poked out of a Cincinnati Reds T-shirt. An iron-on baseball centered her navel.

"Where did he go with it?" I asked Momma.

She pointed at the door. "Leave him be, Fern. He's mad as a hornet and he's made up his mind."

I ran out the door with both Momma and Florabelle calling after me. I headed down the path through the field towards the pond. The sun was just beginning to come up and the sky was peach and blue like the icing we'd ordered for Florabelle's wedding cake. I could see Daddy's silhouette as he headed down towards the bank of the pond. Jimmy was wiggling down from Daddy's right hand like a puppet. I wiped dust from my eyes and started running.

"Daddy!" I called. I was about thirty feet behind him.

He didn't turn around, just kept right on going.

"Daddy, wait up!" I was right on him, and he quickened his step. "Please, Daddy, stop." I was out of breath.

He whirled around. "Liar," he said to me, stopping. "When I give you a job to do, you do it and you finish it."

I was standing right in front of him, and his large frame made me feel small and defenseless. He glared down at me. His face was rough; he hadn't shaved yet, and his stubble looked like black nylon threads. He turned around and continued climbing down towards the pond. The pathway was rocky and steep, and it was hard to keep my footing. But I followed along behind him. We were only a few yards away from the pond.

"Daddy, let us keep him. We got rid of the others."

"I told you to get rid of all three of them," he said without looking at me.

"I know, but Birdie wanted him real bad; she got attached to him during the ride. I just couldn't give him away. And Florabelle, she said she'd keep him up at her and Jason's."

We were at the bank of the pond. The water looked calm, a cool green. Daddy squatted down with Jimmy and pulled a bandanna out of his back pocket. "We can't keep it. And you know your sister won't either. Not now. It'll be nothing but a hassle." He stared out at the water a few seconds, wiped his brow. "This is painless."

"Daddy, please, you just can't do this." I pleaded; dust was mixed in with my tears. My stomach was in knots.

He started tying the pup's paws together with the bandanna. Jimmy squirmed under Daddy's firm hold. I watched his busy hands. The water rippled over the bank and Jimmy lapped at it.

"I'll take care of him," I said trying to recompose myself. "I'll pay for his food and train him to hunt." My words choked out. "Daddy, please, don't. Florabelle can take him with her tomorrow."

"They're going to have a young one to take care of; they don't need no dog. Now sit still," he said to Jimmy, who was now yelping.

The puppy struggled. Birdie was right, I thought, Jimmy was the smartest. Maybe he did know. Exasperated, I turned to go.

Then, suddenly, I hadn't taken three steps back, and I don't know what came over me, but something did, an urgency, something powerful and determined. I lunged at the shore and snatched the bandanna out of Daddy's big hands. "No," I shouted, "I promised Birdie!" I had lost all control, and there was no taking it all back. I stiffened, flinched, waited for his blow.

But minutes went by and he never struck. And he never spoke. At last I opened my eyes, afraid of what I'd see, or not see.

Daddy was kneeling, head down, still holding Jimmy,

but more gently now, not so forceful. He looked up, gazed across the pond.

I wiped my face on the bandanna, took deep breaths, and sat down behind him. I didn't speak; nor did he. We both just sat there waiting for the sun to come up and maybe shed some light on what had just happened. And finally when it was up high enough to cast its own image in the pond, Daddy spoke. "What's Birdie want with a mutt like this? There's no guarantee this one can see anything either. Blindness is hereditary in dogs, you know. Heidi was born blind."

"*He* can see," I said, quietly. "He climbed in the tire in the truck. Birdie wants to take care of him. She wants to raise him up and have him as her friend. Heidi's getting old." I was sitting on the bank a couple feet away from him and was beginning to calm down.

Daddy turned the pup over in his big hands and studied him. "He's a sturdy one. Probably grow to forty, maybe fifty pounds."

"We'll feed him."

He set Jimmy down and turned him loose. The pup shook himself, waddled towards the water, and licked the mud.

"His name is Jimmy," I said. "That's what Birdie calls him."

Daddy nodded and tossed a pebble at Jimmy. "Yep, Jimmy's going to be a big one." He turned and stared at me.

I looked down and dug in the soft dirt, with my fingertips.

After what seemed like an hour of silence, us just sitting there watching the day break, he finally said something. "Where'd you get that spitfire? Sure wasn't from your Momma. More like your Grandma Feezer." He grinned.

I shrugged. Daddy had three daughters, but he expected us to be tough and controlled. Whenever we let our emotions show, it made him nervous. He wanted us to be strong. Brave and wise. Restrained.

"I'm going to go on back up," I said. "Momma's probably got breakfast ready, and there's a lot to do with the wedding." I picked up Jimmy, who was chewing on a twig, and turned back towards the house. After a few paces, I turned back. "You coming?" I asked him.

He shook his head. "No, I'm going to stay down here a little while, you go on up. I want to check on the pump. It's been doing an average of twenty a day, but it's been slow this week. Tell your Momma to keep my eggs warm."

I nodded. The sun was all the way up now; once it got going, it always seemed to shoot up fast like a balloon let loose at kickoff. I stretched Jimmy across the back of my shoulders and scratched his hind. "Come on, boy," I said, "we're going home."

5. Taking Vows

The ceremony was going fine and just as planned until Florabelle leaned over to whisper in my ear that Grandma Trapper Feezer, who was sitting on the front row next to Momma, was staring at the preacher. We had been afraid of this and had hesitated about bringing her to the wedding in the first place, but I argued that Florabelle would be her first granddaughter to get married, and if she'd been well enough to have known this, Grandma would have been disappointed for missing all the celebration.

All this had Florabelle worried sick, and she had threatened several things and hurled some rather obscene intentions at us if we dared let Grandma come to the ceremony, but I'd insisted and Momma had proposed maybe this would be one of her "good" days, promising she'd keep an eye out for trouble.

Early that afternoon, when we'd gone over to Grandma's to get her ready, Hazel and Momma figured out that Grandma hadn't been to church for thirteen years. Grandpa Trapper, Grandma's first husband, Momma and Hazel's daddy, had been a Church of God minister, and when he had died, Grandma had lost some mental faculties and couldn't ever attend services without thinking all preachers were Grandpa. What it really was, was that hardening of the arteries and the bad circulation caused her mind to slip, but her health didn't really start failing until Grandpa passed away.

Three years back, Grandma had eloped with Elmer Feezer, who bagged produce down at Mac's Market, but a cashier found him dead in the parking lot, not a week after he and Grandma'd run off. Drank himself to death, they said. No one even knew they had gotten married until afterwards, which Momma thought was foolish and resented to no end. Out of spite now, Grandma still kept Elmer's things around her house, like his bathrobe and bowling trophies, and she still had the pillowcase, unwashed, that he last lay his head on and a half-drunk Pepsi bottle in the refrigerator that he'd opened the morning of his death.

These habits of Grandma and all the leftover remnants infuriated Momma and Hazel like nothing else in this world. When they went up the hill on Saturdays to bring her prescriptions and clean her house, they'd try throwing that stuff away, but nothing got by Grandma when she didn't want it to, and she'd go dig everything out of the trash can and pout a few days before speaking to us again.

Momma called Grandma's condition "going senile." Daddy said it was selective listening. Hazel claimed Grandma was devil-possessed.

Now, standing before the altar, Florabelle kept turning around and watching Grandma's every move. I glanced over my shoulder. Momma was dabbing at her own eyes with a Kleenex, but Grandma looked okay to me. "She's just listening," I whispered back to Florabelle.

But Florabelle shook her head. "It's happening again," she muttered. "She's started her swaying; get her out."

Reverend Whitaker seemed a little distracted or curious at Florabelle and me up there talking during the vows, but he kept right on going. "Let us therefore reverently remember that God has established and sanctified marriage. . ." He paused when he got to "reverently" and said it louder than the other words.

I tried to ignore Florabelle and smiled down at Birdie

who counted the syllables in "reverently," got four, and let go of my hand long enough to hold up four fingers. She was standing unusually still, though, and being good for the most part. Even the peach carnation bouquet she was holding was still in its upright position.

I leaned back a little to let some weight off my feet because the high heels I was wearing were squeezing my toes like a vise. I was surprised to see that Grandma had put her hat back on. Wearing hats in buildings had always been against Grandma's principles; she'd taught us never to do it, said it wasn't any more ladylike than shooting craps. Some of Momma's distant cousins, whom I didn't know, craned their heads and moved back and forth in the row behind Grandma, trying to see around the large, olive-green brim with peach plastic flowers.

"Get her hat," I mouthed and signaled to Momma who frowned because she couldn't understand me and so wrote "WHAT?" real large on an offering envelope and held it up.

"Her *hat*," I mouthed, again, pretending to adjust Birdie's hairpiece, trying to clue her in. "People can't *see*."

Florabelle, too, had noticed the hat, and started tugging at her own veil, glaring at Momma to do something.

Jason stood there, scowling, and his brother, Dwayne, who was standing up as Jason's best man and whom I despised, was grinning; he kept winking at me.

Reverend Whitaker looked perturbed at us and all our interruptions and started speaking louder and louder, voice tremoring. "Forasmuch as these two persons have come hither to be made one in this holy estate, if there be any present who knows any just cause why they may not lawfully be joined in marriage, I require him or her now to make it known, or ever after to hold peace."

Just then, Momma figured out what I'd been trying to tell her, snatched the hat off Grandma, forgetting to take out the bobbypins first, and Grandma hollered.

She yelled loud enough to startle a scarecrow; several gasps came from the congregation and Reverend Whitaker stopped preaching.

"Now you did it," Florabelle hissed at Momma, not bothering to whisper at this point.

Momma, embarrassed and more than likely disappointed that things were no longer going like she'd planned, jammed the hat back in Grandma's lap and hung her head. Daddy, who was sitting on the other side of her, did nothing more than shake his head and shrug his shoulders at us. Everyone else just waited.

"You can go on, now, Reverend," I said, trying to break the silence. "She's all right." I was worried about Momma, though, her being so sensitive.

The Reverend didn't look convinced, but he had a duty to perform, and preachers always seem to pull themselves together. Even in those most trying moments, when someone's in need of healing or saving, or just some reassuring that a Holy Spirit's looking out for the lost souls.

I had by then earned a record of perfect Sunday school attendance growing up and never missing a church service, even with the mumps once, and could rightly testify that when preachers are in the presence of God and an assembly of God-fearing, miracle-expecting people, they stand firm. They possess all strength and know all wisdom, and they own up to it, time after time.

I realized, right then, standing there in the presence of God the Father Almighty, face-to-face with a man of God, and a large wood-carved cross hanging over my head, which always reminded me of two of those Little Debbie Nutty Bar waffle bars, that I could never be a preacher. Not with my wavering in standing firm lately. Not with my mind on candy bars.

Reverend Whitaker, though, was a good man, ordained, one of unfaltering faith and the power to stand solid as a rock. He respected our family in spite of the obvious, and he finally got his sermon going again.

But there wasn't two, maybe three, sentences out of his mouth, when all of a sudden, Grandma, just as loud as she could, started reciting Grandpa's favorite Bible verses from the King James edition of Proverbs, then humming "The Old Rugged Cross" in A major like she had done almost forty years ago as a choir leader of Grandpa's church. And when the Reverend finally pronounced, "Man and Wife," Grandma yelled, "Praise the Lord!"

6. The Icing On The Cake

The receiving line was set up in the church lobby as people filed out to cross the street to the civic hall for the reception. The Bowen Civic Hall was nice and roomy with terazzo floors and a paneled wall. Folks in four surrounding counties used it for square dances, auctions, 4-H club meetings, agricultural conventions, and Tuesday night Bingo. We had rented it for the reception as opposed to using the church fellowship hall so we could dance. The Full Gospel Pentecostal believed dancing summoned the devil.

As the guests filed by us, kissing Momma, shaking Jason's and Daddy's hands, and congratulating Florabelle, Birdie, who'd been the one to leave the altar to take Grandma out, looked up at me and said, "Grandma had Grandpa's supper planned out on the back of her hymnal. Pork chops, fried potatoes, okra, and creamed corn."

"Is she okay?" I asked.

"Yeah, she's sitting on that bench just outside the door, resting."

"Grandma never did handle a crowd real well," I told Birdie. "And she never did forget to include a vegetable, either."

The reception, unfortunately, went no smoother than the ceremony itself. The deejay, another one of Jason's brothers, played good music that seemed to suit everyone's dancing tastes, and he was good with the microphone when it came time to announce the dollar dance and the garter toss. The room looked nice with the crepe streamers and bells draped from the ceiling, and the food was delicious, went real fast. Momma was proud.

It was the cake, though, the fifty-five dollar-and-thirty-two cent cake, that caused the ruckus. Evidently it was delivered while the ceremony was going on, so the bakers from Woody's had just dropped it off and left. They'd set it up on the table with the presents, and it looked extra nice how the icing matched some of the gift wrap. The cake was chocolate, three tiers, just as we ordered, and the icing was the right colors, peach and blue. Even the wording was right; the names were spelled correctly. It read: "Congratulations Florabelle and Jason."

But the topper; it threw a left curve. Where any bakery could ever have found a cake top like the one on Florabelle and Jason Crabtree's cake, I'll never know.

And naturally, Florabelle was the first to spot it. I had just come back from taking Grandma home and had been in the bathroom changing Birdie's dress because Momma didn't want her running around getting the nice one dirty, when Florabelle grabbed me by the bow on the back of my dress and dragged me over to the cake.

"Look," she demanded. "Look at that." Hands on hips, she stood scowling at her own wedding cake, face flushed.

There it was. Two, maybe three feet above our heads, situated between a plastic bride and groom all decked out in formal wedding attire, was a little plastic baby, about an inch high. But it wasn't just a regular baby, though, with a rattle and bonnet, standing there in diapers holding its Momma and Daddy's hands. It was a *black* baby.

The fact that it was black and Jason was white had all sorts of implications, so I could imagine Florabelle's shock and humiliation and understood why her temper, no doubt, was starting to flare.

"I'll get Momma," I said and left Florabelle standing there, mad as a wet hen.

Momma was serving punch and I walked right up to her and just came straight out with it. "Someone's put a white couple with a black baby on top of the wedding cake, and Florabelle's fuming."

For a moment Momma didn't say anything, just stood there trying to register what I'd said. Then she excused herself from some folks waiting in line and charged towards the cake. I followed along behind.

By this time, Florabelle was balanced on a folding chair,

with the front of her dress bunched up in one hand, leaning over the cake, trying to remove the ornament.

"Go grab her," said Momma. "She's liable to fall into that cake."

I rushed over and steadied the chair.

"Jesus," said Florabelle, climbing down. "Do you think I got it in time?" Holding it in her fingertips, as if it were some evil token, she handed me the wicked little family greased with icing. "Get rid of it."

I carried the topper to the bathroom in the lobby of the hall. When I got inside the rest room, no one else was in there, and I was half tempted to lick the icing off it before throwing it away. But the principle of it, the sight of it, the very semblance of Jason, killed my craving. I wrapped it real well in toilet paper, and buried it in the bottom of the wastepaper basket.

When I came out of the bathroom, everyone had gathered around the cake. I guess Florabelle had figured with the top layer all messed up, it was as good a time as any to go ahead with the cake cutting. Guests clapped, encouraging mischief, and flashbulbs blinked like fireflies. Birdie stood in front of me, her heels on my toes, trying to see over the crowd. She had her fingers crossed, hoping for a piece with a rose.

"You having fun?" I asked her.

She shrugged. The room was full of people, but mostly grown-ups, many of whom Birdie didn't know, and some she'd only seen once at our Uncle Emul's funeral. She watched as Florabelle and Jason smeared cake all over each other's face. "Momma's gonna say something to Florabelle later about using forks," she said, frowning.

I smiled. "No, Bird, that's tradition."

"Like having a wedding when you're pregnant?" she asked.

"You want to go outside for a while?" I asked.

She nodded. "Okay, but I want a piece of cake."

"Go on and get in the line then," I said.

"Want a piece, too?"

"Sure. You know me and chocolate. Meet me back here."

When Birdie came back with our cake, I handed her a napkin and led her outside. It was a nice evening, not too humid; a breeze was blowing. It wasn't nightfall yet, but you could see the moon coming up. Someone had turned on the floodlights, so the yard was pretty well lit up.

We walked down the brick sidewalk that led out back. The path ran between little shrubs and flowers protected by two-foot-high lattice fencing. Most of the flowers were in bloom, but Birdie couldn't name any except roses, and picked me one. At the end of the path, I sat down with my thorny treasure on the edge of the fountain and breathed in the night air.

I stuck my hand in the water; it was cool and felt good. The spotlight made the water appear aquamarine like the ocean looked in Key West postcards.

The brick rim around the fountain was only about a foot high and a few inches wide. Birdie climbed up on it, carefully balanced herself, walked all the way around, then sat down beside me. Listening to the music coming from the hall, we ate our cake.

"Don't get that dress wet," I warned.

The dress I had changed her into was new; her bridesmaid dress was hanging safely in the bathroom. One of the night nurses where Hazel worked had given her some of her own daughter's clothes to bring home for Birdie. The dress was orchid eyelet with a full skirt trimmed in a darker purple satin, pulled tight at her waist with a matching purple sash. Her long sandy blond hair hung in curls below the bow. She was still wearing her white lacy tights and patent leather Mary Janes.

She looked real pretty; I was proud of her that night. It always worried me that with my influence, she'd grow up being too much of a tomboy and not ever want to put on a dress or curl her hair, or play with dolls. But so far, she seemed to be as much interested in playing Momma to Waylon Jennings as she was in chasing Jimmy around the field.

Standing on the edge of the fountain, Birdie spotted a little girl playing on the swing set, in the backyard of a house next to the civic hall. Birdie jumped down, darted to a tree, crouched and spied.

The girl looked about Birdie's age, maybe a little older. She was wearing a frilly blue dress and was swinging high in the air, singing. Each time she swung forward, her chubby little legs poked out from under her netted crinoline, and pointed in our direction. She pumped her little legs, swinging with all her might.

Suddenly, the girl let herself fly out of the swing to land in the yard.

This startled Birdie, and she drew back quickly and ducked down.

"I saw you!" shouted the girl.

Birdie looked at me, crouched lower.

"Today's my birthday," the voice came again.

We could see the girl more clearly now; she was standing at the fence.

"I'm nine!"

"Go on," I motioned Birdie, "go on over there and talk to her."

Slowly, Birdie moved out from behind the tree. She walked to the fence, faced her opponent.

"What's your name? Mine's Cynthia. Cynthia Louisa Wingate." The girl smiled.

"Mine's Birdie."

"Birdie? Is that your real name?" Cynthia frowned.

Birdie nodded, lowered her eyes, and stood quiet for a moment, pulling at her sash. "Today you're nine?"

"Yep. August ninth. How old are you?"

"Eight. But almost nine," said Birdie.

"I'm taller and older," said the girl.

Birdie nodded.

I watched the two of them, kicking dirt around with their feet, trying to think of what to talk about. If Cynthia had been a dead beetle or a multicolored rock, Birdie would have had plenty to say.

"There's a wedding going on in there, isn't there?" Cynthia pointed.

"Yeah."

"How do you know the bride and groom?"

"The bride's my big sister."

"She's pregnant, isn't she?"

"Uh-huh."

This awareness startled me. I then realized the whole neighborhood must know about the Rayburn family black sheep.

Cynthia sat back down on the grass by the fence and fanned her dress around her.

Birdie watched her get in place, then sat down too.

"My Mom knows your Aunt Hazel from the Peaceful Palace Nursing Home. She's a nurse there. I flew here last night for the weekend to visit her."

Birdie looked puzzled. "How long are you staying here?"

"Three days. My father's coming through on business, then taking me back home day after tomorrow."

"Where do you really live?"

"In Florida with my Daddy."

"I know where Florida is," said Birdie. "My uncle, the one Hazel was married to, moved there."

"I know. With some other woman, right?" asked Cynthia.

Birdie nodded.

Again, I was ashamed of the widespread knowledge of our family's illicit approach to social norms.

"You're lucky," said Birdie. "It don't snow in Florida, does it?"

"No."

"You're lucky."

"I like snow," said Cynthia.

Birdie copied Cynthia's moves, crossing her arms, tapping her feet, scratching her legs.

"What about your Daddy?" asked Birdie.

"What about him?"

"I mean how come he don't live with you and your Momma here in Kentucky?"

"They're divorced so I can live in two places if I want."

Birdie picked up a stick and ran it back and forth along

the fence, considering this. "Do they both take you on vacations?"

"Yes, lots."

"You're lucky. Do you get to go to Disney World?"

"Every summer and Christmas and some birthdays."

"Did you ever see Snow White?" Birdie looked excited to hear about this. I knew how much she loved all that Disney magic stuff.

Cynthia hesitated. "I think so. Why?"

"Because she's so pretty, that's why. I seen her on TV in a commercial and once in a movie. She's just so pretty."

"Yeah, I saw her." Cynthia fiddled with the lace on her dress.

"You're so lucky," said Birdie.

Cynthia smiled.

Both girls were quiet for some time, and darkness was beginning to fall. I propped my feet up on the fountain edge, loosened my ankle straps, and tried making a boat out of my fork and paper plate. I put the rose Birdie had given me in my hair.

"Hey, you know what?" asked Birdie after quite a while.

"What?" asked Cynthia.

"You could be Cinderella. In that pretty dress, you look like a fairy princess." Birdie pulled at her own faded dress. "This is sort of new," she said.

"I used to have one just like it," said Cynthia. "It was exactly the same. I wore it in my first piano recital last year. But I outgrew it and my Mom gave it away with some of my other clothes to some poor people."

When I heard this, my heart sank. It just then dawned on me that Cynthia's mother must have been the night nurse who gave Hazel those little girl clothes down at the nursing home. My throat tightened. I hoped Birdie didn't make the connection; she knew the dress was a hand-me-down.

At that moment, I realized it was Birdie, more than Florabelle, more than anyone, who deserved a new dress, and I decided right then that when I got home that night, I would start making her one. Any color she wanted. Even peach.

Suddenly, a woman called from the house, and Cynthia ran, without saying another word.

Birdie stood and watched the blue silk disappear into the house. Finally, she came back over to where I was sitting. She climbed up on the rim of the fountain and stared down into the blue-green bubbling water. "I'm lucky," she said, after quite some time, to her own reflection. Then she pulled off her bow and sash and threw them in the water to watch them sink.

7. Just Married

When we got back inside the reception hall, folks were dancing. I looked around and found Florabelle, dress hoisted up, dancing in circles around Jason and some of his friends. She was laughing and hollering, doing the rocking chair step to the tune of "Cotton-eyed Joe."

I stood off to the side and watched her whirl, supposing she had got over the cake topper. And by the way she was bouncing around, you'd never think she was two months from having a baby.

Jason lifted her up over his head and kissed her belly, right smack on her navel. She smiled at him, reached down and held his face in the palms of her hands. This display of affection, which was for the most part uncommon for those two, seemed to excite the crowd, and everyone whistled. It was curious to me, the ready acceptance of it all. The feeling in the room was genuine happiness. Bliss without shame.

"Wanna dance?" I felt an elbow in my rib and looked into the all-too-familiar face of Dwayne Crabtree, Jason's brother, the best man. Dwayne came into Clem's station a lot for gas, and it seemed like it was always when I was working and he always needed something done like his windshield washed or his brake fluid checked. Something where he could stand off to the side and leer at me while I was busy. A couple months back, I had finally just flat refused to put air in his tires, told Clem that Dwayne just wanted to stare at my ass. So ever since Clem started checking Dwayne's air pressure, he quit asking us to do it.

"No thanks, Dwayne," I said, staring up at his large, awkward frame. "Where did you ever find a tuxedo big enough to fit you?"

Dwayne was six foot four and a half, two hundred and fifty some pounds, as strong and as smart as an ox, and just as mean as a bull. I once saw him pull a federal mailbox up out of a concrete sidewalk outside the post office in Stanton and heave it through the back car window of a guy who spit on his truck tire.

"We rented them out of a store in the Lexington mall." He stuck his thumbs through his suspenders, leaned back. "Don't I look sharp?" he asked and grinned his stupid grin.

I just looked at him.

"Come on, dance with me."

"I said no thanks." I turned my attention back towards the dance floor. Hazel had Birdie out there twirling her around, trying to teach her the steps. I started to leave, but Dwayne grabbed my arm.

"Lighten up," he said, and winked. "You need to relax. What, don't you like to dance?"

"I love to dance, but I just don't feel like it right now."

"All right, all right," he said, shifting his weight to his other foot. He reached in his back pocket and brought out a can of Skoal, and staring at his hands, he mumbled, "But you sure look pretty in that dress." He pinched out a small bit of dip and packed it in his lip. His next words were even more muffled. "And that eye shadow brings blue out in your eyes like the sky." He looked up and smiled, as if he thought he'd said something accidentally beautiful.

I excused myself and headed for the rest room. Once inside, I spit on a few sheets of toilet paper, and wiped at my eyes until all the makeup was gone. I hated wearing it anyways; I always felt smothered by it. When I had it all off, I stepped back and stared at myself in the mirror. I looked thin, and the way the dress was cut gave me a waist and almost suggested a bust the way the bodice gathered at the sleeves. I really didn't look half bad.

Just then, the door swung open with a crash against the wall, and the woman we had hired from Lexington to take photographs staggered in, twisted her ankle, and grabbed me to stop a fall. "Hell of a party, ain't it?"

I nodded.

Then she pulled down her panty hose, and hovered over the toilet, without closing the stall door. "I was married once," she said. "Ten years, then off he went." She fumbled with the paper dispenser.

I left the bathroom. I wanted the night to end; I wanted to go to bed. But I knew I'd have to stick around and clean up. That was the odd thing about weddings, and graduations, or anything that you work for, plan, and organize. It comes, it goes, then the ones who are celebrating take off with a wonderful memory all fixed in their minds forever, and everyone else has got nothing but the mess to remember it by.

The deejay was now trying to gather up all the single guys and girls for the garter belt and bouquet toss. I was surprised Florabelle had even bothered with a garter belt. But she was smiling and poking a leg out from under her dress, teasing Jason, so I figured she had. I also couldn't help but imagine that her poking her leg out like that from under a dress was probably what started this whole thing in the first place. An inch of attention went a mile for Florabelle.

I was standing near the cake, which was nearly gone, when Daddy walked over to me and picked up a piece.

"Why ain't you out there?" he asked.

"What, you in a hurry to marry me off?" I asked. "Who would mow your grass on Saturdays?"

He chewed a bite of cake, mouth open, and said, "I'll worry about my grass; you worry about your future."

I stared at him. He looked decent, for a change, in his navy suit and tie, closely shaven and hair combed. We were so used to seeing him in his work shirts or overalls, and it wasn't often that we even saw him after he had showered.

He really wasn't bad looking for his age. He was forty-six his last birthday. We had tried talking him into wearing a tuxedo for the wedding, but he didn't see the need for spending the money. His suit, though, looked nice.

"Daddy, ain't nobody around here I'd have."

He grinned. "Sassy as you've been lately, ain't nobody here who'd have you." He licked some icing off a Styrofoam plate. "But get on out there and have you some fun."

So, if for no other reason than to avoid Daddy's hounding, I walked out to the floor, and of course Florabelle spotted me, and aimed the bouquet right at me. Out of reflex, when something comes flying at your face without warning, you grab at it, and that's just what I did.

And that's what Dwayne Crabtree did, when Jason flung the garter right at him, just like a rubber band. He grabbed at it, waving it high above his head like he'd just intercepted a play.

So there we were. Out there in front of everyone, me sitting on a chair, legs crossed, men whistling, Dwayne kneeling in front of me, making every kind of suggestive comment or gesture he'd ever seen, heard, and memorized, and Hazel with her Polaroid.

The hardest thing in the world I've ever done was to sit there and be a good sport and pretend to be having a good time. Dwayne working the garter up over my knee, inching it up my thigh, all his brothers egging him on.

When he leaned in close enough, through my teeth with a smile I said, "One inch higher and I'll kick your nads so far up that folks will be shaking you for weeks to get them back down." I knew I shouldn't have come right out and said it, not being ladylike and all, but I'd had my limit.

Dwayne froze. He removed his hands, threw them up over his head again, fists clenched, and beamed. Touchdown. We received a pretty hearty applause; I bowed my head a little, relieved of my duty, and walked off the floor.

I guess all the excitement was beginning to work on Jason and Florabelle, because it was then they decided to leave, the traditional way. He swept her up, dress, veil, baby and all, and they trailed towards the front steps of the hall.

Hazel and Momma moved about, handing out little peach-colored netted bags of birdseed that Birdie had put together which we later discovered was fertilizer instead, and a lot of people complained of their eyes burning that night. The deejay played the Rolling Stones' "I Can't Get No Satisfaction," and as they stumbled giddily to Jason's truck, folks pelted them with the seeds.

I stood on the front porch steps and watched them spin off, stirring up dust down Highway 15. As they pulled away, I read the message on the back window. "Just married," it said. How true, I thought, just married, and nothing else. No morals, no savings, no plans, no regards to the new responsibilities whatsoever. Just married.

Away they went, Pabst Blue Ribbon cans and balloons tied to the bumper, soaped windows and shoe polished bumpers declaring their greenness, boasting their beginnings. From the radio antenna, a condom waved like a pennant.

8. Passing Through

"What the hell we got coming here?" asked Clem, pointing up the road. He had just come out of the cashier's office with a box of quart-size oil and transmission fluid cans for me to refill the dispensers out by the pumps. He stood, squinting, arms full, as what looked like a purple U.S. Mail jeep bounced up the road and pulled into the station. It wasn't often that out-of-towners would happen by the station; Clem did pretty well just serving the locals. But every so often, folks would get off of 402 to see Natural Bridge State Park in Powell County, that was advertised on a billboard, and they'd wind up getting lost trying to get back on the interstate.

I was hosing down the pavement, trying to dilute some coolant that had leaked out of a Volvo wagon that had just been in for a radiator patch. A fan blade had broken off and had cut through both the radiator and the hood, and Clem had to send the guy on to a dealership in Lexington since we didn't have the right size fan in stock. If the guy had been a local, Clem would have mentioned Jake's junkyard, which was just about three miles up the road, but it was a whole family traveling north from Atlanta, and years of experience had taught Clem that folks from the city, who drove foreign cars, didn't trust junkyards. And Jake, Clem knew, didn't trust American Express cards.

As the grape-colored vehicle pulled up to the pumps, I shut off the water hose, and walked over. "Regular?" I called out to the driver, from the front of the jeep. Through the glare off the front windshield, I could make out three people.

I walked past the open window on the driver's side to get to the gas tank, hesitated, glanced inside the jeep. The driver was a young guy, probably close to my age, with sandy blond hair, kind of wavy, and a suntanned face. I expect that aside from Jim Palmer, whose baseball card I had carried in my wallet for almost nine and a half years, this guy was the most handsome I'd seen. He was wearing baggy, khaki shorts, no shirt, and his brown, hair-free, muscular chest made me uncomfortable.

Beside him was a girl, blond too, and she was wearing one of those Indian cotton, strapless sundresses that showed off her tan. They both smiled at me as I walked past, their eyes shaded by dark sunglasses. Another girl sat in the backseat.

I felt my face flush. For the first time in the four years I'd been helping out at Clem's, I was conscious and ashamed of my navy coverall uniform. Suddenly, my tire gauge seemed to extend out of my breast pocket like an antenna, my bright red name patch seemed to glow like a neon lamp, broadcasting to the world my worth, my identity, as an assistant service station attendant.

"Hi, Fern," said the driver, reading my patch. "A full tank of regular would be fine."

"Do you have a map?" asked the girl hovering over his lap, breasts tight against her dress.

"We sell them inside," I said. "Dollar for Kentucky, dollar-fifty for U.S. and Canada."

"We're looking for Transylvania, it's a college in Lexington," said the girl.

"I know what it is," I said, pumping gas. "I've been to their library. You're not too far from there, about another forty-five minutes heading northwest. Stay on 11 until you get to 402."

"Say," said the girl, "is there anything around here to do?"

"Like what?" I asked.

"Well, like touristy stuff," she said, grinning. "We're from Orlando, Florida, and we have Disney and all; is there something like that here?"

I put the gas nozzle back in place and came around to the front of the jeep. She looked younger than him, pretty and comfortable with herself, a perfect fit for the little bucket seat she slid around in while she spoke.

"There's a sky-lift ride at the Natural Bridge, then there's the Daniel Boone National Forest up north of Stanton," I offered.

"What is there to see at Natural Bridge?" she asked.

"A bridge," I said.

The guy looked at her, then back at me.

"I know that. I guess what I meant is what does it look like? I mean, does it look like a real bridge?" she asked.

I thought of going inside the station to see if maybe we had a postcard of it that I could give her. Instead I closed my eyes and said, "It's a road that connects two mountains. Pretty up there at the top with the trees and all, and lots of blackberries growing. It looks like God punched a hole in the earth, then changed his mind and tried to fix it up and disguise the damage by using a lot of extra garnish."

I opened my eyes. The guy was still smiling; the girl stared at me. I turned around to see Clem walking out towards us.

"How are they paying?" he called.

"Cash," said the guy. "I don't think I carry a credit card for Clem's," he added.

I thought for a second he was being smart-aleck, but the look on his face was kind, not condescending.

"Cash," I yelled back.

Clem disappeared inside again.

"Is that your dad?" asked the girl.

"No," I said. "Why?"

"Oh, I just figured it was, you know how a lot of you country people help out with your fathers' business. My best friend back at home sometimes helps her father, with typing. He's a lawyer with a big firm."

"A big firm what?" I asked, wincing, regretting it seconds later, but she was annoying me.

She frowned.

"Is there a hotel nearby?" asked the girl from the backseat. She had a short haircut, cropped around her ears, the same color as the guy's hair. She smiled at me as I bent down through the car window to talk to her.

"There's tons of them in Lexington," I said. "You're almost there. Then there's a motel in Stanton which is closer, but it's probably not your style."

"What about around here?" asked the guy. "It might be nice to stay somewhere in the country like this. Get some fresh air, away from the city." He looked at the girl next to him. "I'll be starting school there soon enough, might be nice to relax, do some fishing."

"I'm not interested in fishing," said the girl next to him.

"Oh, come on, it'd be fun," said the girl in the back.

The guy turned back to me. "Any lakes or rivers around here?" He seemed genuinely interested.

"Sure, there's the Red River Gorge, and there's a lodge you can stay in up at the state park. But if you're planning to do some serious fishing, you ought to just find a pond or creek around here off the road somewhere."

"You fish?" he asked.

I nodded.

He smiled, lifted his sunglasses. His eyes were crystal blue, almost silvery like spring water. "You know a spot?" He handed me the gas money, and our hands brushed. I felt dizzy all of a sudden.

"We're not staying in this little town," the girl in the front said.

The guy looked uncomfortable with his companion. "Maybe just one day," he said to her, then looked back at me. "If we stay here, I'll come back through for some pointers. You can tell me what to use for bait."

Then he winked.

My chest burned; the back of my knees felt tight. I felt stupid, like I was back in a schoolyard, staring at the gym teacher. "Fine." I looked away. "Still want a map?"

"No, I'll just follow your advice. Stay on 11. Thanks," he said, "we'll see you, Fern."

The girl in the backseat waved.

I watched them drive off, went back inside the station, and sat down on one of the customer waiting chairs.

"Where were they heading?" asked Clem, his head down.

"Lexington," I said, "to Transylvania."

"College kids," said Clem, cracking open a roll of quarters on the cash tray.

"Yeah," I said, "just passing through."

9. Garden of Esther

And Ester said, "A foe and an enemy! The wicked Haman!" Then Haman was in terror before the king and the queen. And the king rose from the feast and went into the palace garden; but Haman stayed to beg his life from Queen Ester; for he saw that evil was determined against him..."

Ester 7:6-7

The sirens and the yelling had made Grandma nervous, and now she sat trembling on the edge of her bed. Birdie sat cross-legged on the desk by the window, unclogging a Dristan spray bottle with a bobbypin.

I had been closing the cash drawer and adding up the totals when I had got Birdie's call. Grandma Trapper

Feezer's house was just around the bend from Clem's, so it had only taken me a few minutes to run up there.

Daddy owned her little house, and she'd lived there ever since Elmer, her second husband, who none of us were ever allowed to call "Grandpa," died.

Daddy had been making a little extra income from the folks who were renting the house before Grandma'd moved in, but Momma had insisted on moving Grandma into it since it was closer by than where she had been living in Stanton, so we could keep an eye out for her. Grandma'd left the gas on on the stove in her old house more than once, practiced little to no caution with cutlery, and carelessly mixed cleaning products.

After several moments of silence, Grandma spoke. "Birdie, now I don't want you to be mad at your old grandma over this." She took a breath and faced away. "You neither, Fern. I had no way of knowing that freak out there was your Daddy."

Evidently, Daddy had been standing in her garden, masked and solvent protected, spraying herbicide at the fence. A poison ivy vine had rooted at the gate, flourished, climbed, and extended to a height of greatness on the door of the toolshed he'd built in back of her house. He had been meaning for quite some time to come down and take care of it. Grandma'd spied him and reported a trespasser wearing a disguise, killing her pole beans.

Birdie wouldn't look up at Grandma.

"Fern's here," said Grandma, "so when your Momma comes home from the grocery with the car, they can go down there and fix this mess up. Don't you worry."

"Here you go." Birdie handed the Dristan to Grandma, still not looking her in the eye. "Three squirts; tilt your head way back."

"I just couldn't make out, through the kitchen curtains, who he was." Grandma sniffed hard at the bottle. "He was shouting and carrying on something awful through the mask."

"He's got a temper, and you set him off," I said.

"Well, he had no business being out there. And I told you I was sorry."

"He owns this house," Birdie challenged.

"That don't give him the right to go killing my garden plants."

"Did he get your Burpees?" I asked.

"No, they got him in time. Just my beans."

A car door slammed out front and Birdie stood up on the desk to see out.

"Who's out there now?" asked Grandma. "They bring him on back?"

"No, it's Momma," said Birdie. "And she's carrying in a Crock-Pot."

"Then stop sassing me and bring me my slippers."

Birdie ran to open the door for Momma. As she lumbered up the front steps, heading towards the kitchen, the floor shook on its cinder blocks. The doctor had put her on a strict low-salt diet the first of the year, but she ignored it. As she passed by me, I smelled ham hocks.

"Grab the cord," Momma said, "I'm liable to trip. Hope the peas didn't stick. Aunt Hazel called in the middle of everything and I had to run out and help push-start that car again so she could get on to work. Your Daddy's told her time after time she should just fix up that old Dodge they keep parked down at Peaceful."

"Smells like cigarettes," said Birdie.

"What, the ham?"

"No, that Dodge."

"Well, it runs fine, and the staff told her she could drive it." Momma sat down, huffed. "Why is your Daddy's truck parked out front here?"

"He was spraying that poison ivy," said Birdie.

I plugged the cord to the pot in the wall over the sink and sat down with Momma at the table.

"He's been saying he's had to get to that. Dern thing is growing over the shed. Where's he now?"

"At the jail." Grandma, in spite of her vexing arthritis, had managed to shuffle to the kitchen, robed and slippered, in time to confess. "And," she added boldly, "you and Fern've got to get back in the car and get down there."

57

Momma, not even looking up from thumbnailing out a Maxwell House coupon for decaf from an old newspaper, said, "Mother, stop talking your nonsense and go wash your hands to eat."

"She's telling the truth," said Birdie. "She didn't know it was Daddy in his mask and expressed charges for trespassing and some other misty meaner."

"Assault," I said.

"What in the Sam Hill are you two talking about?" asked Momma.

"Police locked his hands together and took him," said Birdie, glaring at Grandma. "I was on the swing set."

It was another two and a half hours before we got Daddy home for supper. We left Birdie to eat with Grandma and called Hazel at work to tell her not to walk over to Arby's on her break but to stay near a phone. It had taken us twenty minutes to find the key to Daddy's file cabinet where he kept the house papers, almost an hour to get through the Lexington rush hour traffic, and then another ten minutes just to find parking at the jailhouse. The officer on duty spent five minutes looking over the deed, made two phone calls, ordered his secretary to bring us some coffee, decaf if there was any, and to type up a dismissal for Daddy.

"I'll give her a week," said Daddy, lifting his knife to cut some fat away from his slice of ham. "We can put her in that home where Hazel works. It's close enough Birdie could go by and visit after school."

Momma huffed. "Raymond, you can't go and evict a seventy-seven-year-old woman. She didn't realize what she was doing, you just had her scared you were some maniac. Pass me some more peas; I was worried they'd burnt and stuck."

I passed Momma the peas.

"I mean what I say." Daddy chewed, swallowed. "We'll call her down here in the morning to discuss it. Have Hazel come over after church. We'll all sit down and make the arrangements."

"Oh, now, Raymond, don't be so hardheaded. You're just mad, and you have a right to be, but she's sorry. Now forget about it," said Momma.

"No, she's going in that old-age home," said Daddy.

I felt my stomach tense up and didn't feel like eating. I looked at the empty seat next to me. If Florabelle'd been there, she would've spoke up and said something. She would have taken a stand for Grandma, not just for Grandma's sake, but to argue with Daddy and stir up some more trouble. She'd only been gone for two days, and already things seemed different. There was no one there to balance the good and the bad.

Momma sucked gristle from a tooth.

I looked at Birdie, who had also stopped eating and looked about ready to cry.

Daddy looked at all of us. He put his fork down too, cast his napkin down in a tight fold on the table, scuffed back his chair. "One week," he said. Then he looked at Birdie. "Why don't you go on upstairs and practice your math tables?"

Birdie took a breath, chasing off the sobs. "School don't start for three more weeks."

"Well, now you don't want to get behind the eight ball, do you?" asked Daddy.

Birdie, frowning down at her plate, rose to leave. "She said she was sorry. Said she prayed for you while you was in jail."

"That's enough," said Daddy. He scuffled his chair, threatening.

"Birdie," said Momma, "bring your math problems back down here to Fern when you're done with them."

As soon as Birdie left, I got up and started clearing the table. Momma went to the hall closet, got out the ironing board, and set it up in the living room. Whenever we were nervous, we'd start cleaning, it seemed. We worked in silence. Daddy went over to the couch, lay down, and spread open the newspaper, scanning the headlines.

When I finished cleaning the kitchen, I brought up a load of clean shirts from the basement for Momma, and sat down in the rocking chair to read. I was reading a mystery novel and was halfway through it, wasn't really liking it, but

I wanted to distract myself from the tension in the house.

Momma turned on the burst-of-steam button. We sat and listened to water bubbling in the iron. The hiss reminded me of the sound the demons make that Reverend Whitaker had on a cassette he once played for us in a revival. The sound annoyed me, but I kept on reading. Daddy snapped his paper.

Momma looked up. "They' re your work shirts," she said, folding two sleeves together.

Daddy peered over his paper. "I didn't say word one."

Moments later, Momma steamblasted a collar. "What do you plan on telling Hazel and the rest of my family?"

"I said we'll discuss it tomorrow," said Daddy, this time not looking up.

"She ain't going to like the idea of living up there one bit," said Momma.

"We'll drive her up there tomorrow, let her take a look at it, walk around the grounds, check it out herself. We'll ask about contracts, health plans, insurance. I'll see what kind of benefits there are down at the plant."

Whenever Daddy took this authoritative tone, Momma would lose her battle and sulk. I looked up at her. She looked tired, worn. Even though she didn't have a job, she worked twelve hours a day just keeping up the place. She liked taking care of us, even though she complained a lot, but she considered it her assignment. The way she looked at it, she was put here to make sacrifices to see we were happy. She, out of a sense of duty, took care of Grandma too. I knew she was worried now.

"I think I'll go up and help Birdie," I said, closing my own book.

Momma looked up at me from her ironing; she seemed helpless. "Try to talk to her," she said. "Let her call Grandma and check on her, but tell her not to say anything about all this."

I nodded.

"Tomorrow," said Daddy, looking at me. "Be down here."

I knew by his tone he was counting on me to convince everyone that his decision was the best, the only option. He always expected this of me, to back him in his authority, to lobby his position. His government, our family.

When I opened Birdie's bedroom door, I really did expect to see her going through her equation flashcards. But instead, she was sprawled out on the floor with Polaroids of Florabelle's wedding spread before her. Because that photographer from Lexington had got so drunk at the reception, she'd dropped the camera, causing the film to roll out on the dance floor, and it got trampled. All we were able to get in the way of wedding pictures were some Polaroid shots Aunt Hazel had taken, which for the most part were too dark and blurred. Nevertheless, Birdie had collected the few decent photos there were and was sorting through them.

"What are you doing?" I asked.

"Making Florabelle a wedding album for a going-away present."

The fact that a "going-away" gift was already two days late did not matter to Birdie. She worked intently.

"Do you want to call Grandma?" I asked. "Momma said we could. To check on her."

Birdie abandoned her project and followed me down the hall to the wall phone.

It was several rings before Grandma picked up. Birdie, standing on a footstool to reach the phone, drummed the wall with her little fingers as she waited for her to answer. I pressed my ear next to Birdie's to listen.

"You okay now?" she asked

"Uh-huh," said Grandma.

"Stopped that wheezing?" asked Birdie.

"I took another Advil."

"Any trouble getting the bottle open?"

"No, I managed." Grandma hesitated. "Is he still mad?"

I nudged Birdie, warning.

"Uh, no," said Birdie, "He's just tired."

"Well, if the good Lord forgives us all and teaches us to do the same, then your Daddy has to forget this whole thing."

"Right," said Birdie.

"Good night, Bird. Say your prayers."

"I'm going to do math problems," said Birdie and hung up the phone.

10. The Discussion

The next morning, we talked Hazel into attending the sermon with us, and we were all real quiet driving home. Hazel drove, and Momma waited until we were in the driveway to tell her to come in for a family matter.

We found Daddy on his second cup of coffee, watching Andy Griffith. He looked up, but only for a brief second. "Lookie, here, Birdie," he said, pointing at the TV set, "this is that episode you like where Helen Crump's niece gives Opie a black eye over a baseball game."

"Flip it off, Bird," Momma interrupted, "we're all here now."

"Hello, Raymond," said Hazel. "I hear Mother did a number on you over the garden ordeal." She stood in his view of the TV set, winked playfully at him. "The old broad got you this time, huh?" She laughed, sat down on the sofa across from Daddy, and kicked off her sandal pumps.

No one said anything. Momma bored her eyes through Hazel.

"Well, would you look at these serious faces. Tell me, now, if this is going to be another long discussion like we had over those mortgage papers, I'm going to get up now and take these hose off." Hazel waited.

"It's about yesterday," Momma hinted. She eyed Daddy to see if he wanted to start it, noticed his tight lips, then said, "Raymond wants to move her up there to Peaceful Pastures. Next week."

Hazel sat up and frowned at her brother-in-law. "You know damn well she won't go, and, Raymond, I'd have to quit my job. No way I could work with her being up there. There's enough senile ones in that place without adding her to the bunch. What are you so mad about anyway; they didn't

62

make you pay the fine did they? You were only locked up for what, an hour at the most?"

"That's not the point," said Raymond.

"Daddy's had enough," said Birdie. She'd turned down the sound on the TV, but the picture was on. Opie was sitting at the dinner table, wearing dark sunglasses to cover his bruise.

Momma looked at Birdie, then at me.

"He's fed up," I said.

"You've had enough, Raymond?" asked Hazel. "Mother's a block aways from us now, so now you want to put her in a place where we are going to have to *drive* to, to take care of her? That's going to be even more trouble. Peaceful Pastures is a good fifteen miles from here, and you got the traffic to deal with; I hit it every morning."

"Well, that's just it," said Daddy. "With you working there, someone in the family would be looking after her. Full-time."

"Oh no, you don't. Fern, can you believe this? Tell your father I'm not going to be stuck with her alone," Hazel said.

I kept watching the TV, not saying a word. I felt my neck tense up, and rubbed the knot as if I were only scratching.

"Sylvia and the girls and I have been waiting on her every whim for five or six years, while you were gallavanting back and forth to Florida," said Daddy. Then below his breath he mumbled, "It's time someone else took the burden for a change."

I looked over at Hazel. Now Daddy had done it. She lit a cigarette and dragged so much her cheeks caved in. Mentioning the Florida ordeal set off her nerves.

Jimmy bounded into the room, tail wagging, and crawled onto Birdie's lap. He licked her face, looked around the room, pleased to find everyone in his sight at once.

"Hazel," started Momma. "You know I'll continue to help all I can; we'll all do our fair share. We can clean her room, press her clothes, pick up her prescriptions . . ."

"That's right," I offered, feeling I ought to say something.

"Hazel." Momma was trying. "We know you've been doing for her; we're, I mean, Raymond's just too tired anymore." Momma looked apprehensively at Daddy.

Hazel sat silent a few moments longer, sucking smoke. I watched her concave cheeks as she smoked her cigarette down past the line. She finally spoke. "Did you try the Addison Home or that Care Center up on Hillcrest?"

"Called them this morning," said Momma, head lowered, "Addison's full, and the Center don't allow plants in the room. Even called that new Franklin Manor Retirement Home just south of Pilotview; too expensive. They wanted four hundred right up front for deposits."

"I hear that Center has a great nursing staff, always on their toes and they're real nice to the residents. I know we got a problem with that at Peaceful; the wheelchair ones complain a lot." Hazel shifted on the sofa.

"Grandma needs to have her plants in her room," said Birdie.

"Birdie, Honey, why don't you go to your room. Take Jimmy with you. Don't let him lick your face." Momma frowned at her and nodded towards the stairs.

"No," Daddy said, "you go on up and get your grandmother together. Walk her down here in an hour."

"What are you going to tell her, Raymond, that you're just kicking her out? Just like that?" Hazel reached deep into her purse, shuffled things, unloaded a broken powder compact, an emery board, a few hair rollers, and finally found another pack of Winston Lights. She lit one up, sat back, and exhaled a long stream of smoke towards the ceiling. Then she pulled off her panty hose and dropped them in a wad down by the sofa. "I got to see this one."

I looked over at Momma. I knew she didn't agree with this decision. She knew, as well as I did, how much Grandma's sanity depended upon managing her little house and garden. But Momma was powerless with Daddy. His will crippled hers. At that moment, her weakness seemed strange in contrast to her massive body. I hated the way she such effort—a heavy hoist and sigh. Always left over right, foot suspended way out there, unable to swing. Her hem crept up midthigh, clung to her hips, with slip exposed, pantyhose stretched so tightly I could make out the separate nylon threads. She must be suffocating, I thought.

Birdie finally stood up, turned off the TV, looked at me for a signal. "Where should I tell her we're going?"

Hazel leaned into the coffee table to ash. "Tell her to Hell, Birdie. Might as well, she's gonna put *us* through it."

"Hazel," scolded Momma. She frowned upon profanity.

"No," said Daddy. "Tell her we're going for a ride."

11. Sinners Come Forward

Birdie and I walked up the road to Grandma's house and found her eased back in the orange vinyl recliner in front of the TV set, watching Billy Graham. The choir was singing "Pearly White City" and she was humming along. Other than Florabelle's wedding, Grandma hadn't attended a church in the past thirteen years; it was a strain on her bowels to be too far away from a rest room. She didn't look up as we came in.

"Anybody saved today?" asked Birdie.

"Not yet, he's calling them down to the altar now," said Grandma. She was eating a peach; juice dripped from her lips when she spoke.

"Get cleaned up; Daddy's taking us all somewhere," said Birdie.

"Where? Right now?"

"What shoes do you want? I'll get them." Birdie headed towards the bedroom.

I sat down on the sofa.

"Get my white ones with the buckles," called Grandma, then to me she said, "Are we going back to that Western Sizzlin? I didn't like my sandwich when we was there last."

"Then we won't go there," I said. "Throw that pit away."

It was an effort for Grandma to wrap the peach pit up in a paper towel; her knuckles were swollen more than average this morning. Birdie put her shoes on while I picked her hair and slipped a blue cotton sweater over her shoulders, the one we'd given her last Christmas.

"Can't we see how many sinners come forward?" she asked, watching Billy revive souls.

"No, everybody is waiting," said Birdie. "God forgives everybody anyway; you already know how it ends. Come on, let Fern button your sweater."

It took nearly thirty minutes for Birdie and me to walk Grandma back down the hill to our house. The doctor had told us back in January to get her out and walk once a day, but she fussed every time. Birdie would always try to coordinate this, usually at five o'clock, just before dinner.

We took Hazel's Dodge to fit everyone, as Daddy's truck was only a single cab. On the way there, no one talked about anything except to point out cars in which they thought they recognized the passengers.

Hazel saw two cashiers from Mac's Market. Momma saw our church organist's husband in his new sports car, with some woman she didn't recognize. I kept my eyes peeled for a purple mail jeep.

"Wasn't that Gertrude Hampton from the craft store?" asked Grandma, leaning over me, pointing a crooked finger at an intersection.

"No, it couldn't have been, Mother, she's in Arkansas visiting her daughter," said Hazel.

It very well may have been Gertrude Hampton, but whenever Grandma thought she saw someone she knew, we more often than not ignored her because of her cataracts.

"I could have sworn it was her," said Grandma.

I wondered if I would see those three strangers again at Clem's this week, maybe looking for a bait store. I could mention the fresh minnows in the pond behind the post office or suggest a lure. Maybe I could ride along with them to point out the good spots along the gorge, the places where I had been lucky. As I listened to the hum of the car motor, daydreaming, we passed a sign that said "Peaceful Pastures Nursing Home, Exit 21." I realized that Momma was trying to ask me something. I was angry with myself for letting my mind wander to such nonsense rather than concentrating on the situation at hand. "What is it, Momma?"

"Do you want to talk to your Grandma?"

I put my arm around Grandma and gave her a little squeeze. I didn't understand, right at first, what Momma was asking.

Grandma patted my hand on her shoulder, smiled at me, then yelled to the front seat, "Raymond, you passed all the restaurants, where are you taking us?"

There was silence. Daddy was driving faster than usual, though cautiously. He had the air conditioning set on max. Most times, he was more conservative than this. He looked in the rearview mirror at Grandma, who was wedged between me and Hazel. Birdie was sitting on Hazel's lap. Hazel had the window cracked open a bit to smoke, but Birdie had her hand over her mouth and nose to ventilate.

"Hazel, the air's on, roll up your window," said Momma, from the front seat. She always felt the need to break silence.

"Fern, why don't you tell your Grandma what this is all about," said Daddy, all of a sudden. He was looking right at me through the rearview mirror.

I looked at Momma; it was then I knew. With some effort, Momma shifted in the seat, and looked back at me, desperately. I had to be the one. Always. I was trying to think of something, something gentle to say to Grandma that would explain what was going on, when Hazel jumped in with no warning.

"Mother," said Hazel, "Raymond's taking us up to Peaceful Pastures to have a look around."

We waited.

"Is that what this is all about? I've done seen where Hazel works," Grandma said, disappointed.

There was another pause.

"You've never walked around up there," said Hazel.

"They've got a nice chapel garden, and every resident is allowed one plant in the bedroom and one in the garden. You can water it yourself if you want or have Maintenance do it."

Daddy looked back at Grandma to see if she had yet caught on to what was happening. She was staring straight ahead. Birdie and I exchanged looks across Grandma's lap. Grandma sat motionless. The way she drooled every so often nauseated me. Her chin was damp now with saliva.

"Mother," started Momma, "we think you'd like living up there. They take real good care of everyone; good food, they got TV lounges, aerobics, prayer groups, a bowling club; they let you cook your own meals on Saturdays, have visitors anytime, and all kinds of special parties and outings."

"I can come see you after school every day but Tuesday because of softball," offered Birdie.

Grandma began, then, to sob, which made Birdie cry. This would be the hardest for her.

Momma, too, was red-eyed and looked exasperated. Sweat beaded on her face and neck. Hazel sat looking cool and expressionless, but her hand trembled as she patted Grandma's other shoulder.

Daddy was the only one who seemed unbothered by this mission. He even looked relieved. He wasn't, by any measure, feeling like the bad guy.

"Mother," said Momma, voice tight and desperate, "we don't really have a choice; we're just all too busy to wait on you hand and foot all day, and you do need help with things, you know you do. You'll have a lot less to worry about up there."

No one spoke another word, nor even really moved, until we reached the Manor. As we pulled into the parking lot, we were waved through by a security guard standing in a visitor shack.

When Daddy had parked the car and shut off the motor, Grandma finally spoke. "I guess I'm being punished," she choked, "put to pasture. Looks like the good Lord has made up his mind about me."

12. Settling In

We spent all day Monday and Tuesday moving Grandma's things up to Peaceful Pastures. The staff said she cried off and on both days, but she seemed okay healthwise. No fever, no rashes.

We brought all her clothing, some personal items, and toiletries over in two loads. Hazel hung all her clothes on new hangers and wrote "Esther" on every shirt label, with a permanent marker. I labeled all her undergarments and folding clothes, and Momma took care of her lotion bottles, lipsticks, medications, and Kleenex boxes.

Grandma's room was small, with two twin beds, a thin curtain drawn between them. Next to each bed was a nightstand. Facing the beds were two identical chests of drawers, positioned between two small closets. One window, by the bed on the far side, where Grandma was assigned, overlooked the parking lot. A door opened into a bathroom, in the corner of the room. The toilet was in the exact center of the bathroom to allow space for a wheelchair on either side or in front of it.

We had brought a chair from Grandma's house, and we shoehorned it in between the nightstand and the doorway to the bathroom. As we worked at the labeling, Grandma lay in her bed, silently; Momma sat on the edge of it, me at the foot, and Hazel in the chair. Birdie was wandering around, exploring the place.

"This one's run out of ink," said Hazel, shaking her pen. "Fern, give me yours when you're done."

"Now, Mother," said Momma, "don't be opening all these lotions or nasal sprays until you've used up a whole one of the others. Just keep one of each thing open at a time in this drawer and leave the rest of the supplies in the closet. You can't afford to be wasteful, and you don't really have the room."

"They probably make you label stuff because folks steal it," said Grandma.

"Now don't start," said Hazel. "No one's going to take your deodorant or anything else."

I labeled the last bra and handed the marker to Hazel. Grandma wore a size 44, Double E cup, and the bra looked too large for the little room. I was beginning to feel cramped up, and I wanted some fresh air. The room smelled medicinal and moldy. This room is a world, now, I thought. Grandma's whole world, stuffed into a tiny closet and three oak drawers.

Birdie entered the room, eating a Snickers bar.

"Who gave you that?" asked Momma.

"A lady who thought I was her daughter-in-law, Patty. She gave me the candy bar and told me not to trust the painters, said they only give off frozen batteries."

"Alzheimer's," said Hazel. "Mossie Greene. That's Mother's roommate. She's always thinking everyone's her daughter-in-law. Just ignore her."

"Does her daughter-in-law get down here to visit her much?" asked Momma.

"I don't know that she's ever come here. Her son doesn't either. The old woman's got a lot of money, and rumor has it, they're just waiting around for her to go."

"That's awful," said Momma, shaking her head.

"Fern," said Grandma, "don't let anyone in here who's just going to talk nonsense to me."

"She's your roommate, Mother," said Hazel. "Don't pay no attention to her; she's harmless."

"What's Alzheimer's?" asked Birdie.

"A memory disease," said Momma. "Old people get it."

"It's the devil's work," said Grandma.

"It's aging," I said.

"Just lying there complaining is what's going to age you," said Hazel, not looking up.

"Yeah, Mother, you can't just stay in bed. Go down to the lobby and walk around. I saw a bulletin board down there with activities posted. Read that and join something." Momma patted Grandma's arm, encouraging.

"Ain't nothing to do here but grow old and die," said Grandma.

"Now, Mother, if you're just going to lie there and wither up, that's your choice, but if I were you, I'd get out in the halls and meet people," said Momma.

Birdie started to cry. I pulled her over to me and hugged her. Here we were, three generations crammed into this little room, this little world, overcrowded with care. "It's okay, Bird," I said, soothing her, "Grandma's going to be all right." I looked at Momma, who had at last finished labeling things. "We should go," I said.

"Guess we better," said Momma. "We can come down tomorrow and stroll around. Get to know the staff some. Mother, you are going to be okay, aren't you?"

"She can have them call us if not," said Hazel, getting up, anxious to get outside and smoke.

"Kiss your Grandma good-bye, Birdie," said Momma. "We'll come back tomorrow."

I lifted Birdie up high enough to kiss Grandma on the cheek. This made Grandma start bawling again, so we left quietly.

As we passed through the lobby, Momma asked, "Hazel, did you get your matches? You didn't leave them in Mother's chair, did you?"

"Got them right here," Hazel said.

"Good. Fern, did you put the cap back on the pen?"

"Yes, Momma."

"It's in her drawer?"

"Yes, Momma."

Mossie Greene sat by the entrance in her wheelchair, chewing her tongue. Hazel said hello to her.

"Bye, Mossie," said Birdie.

"Bye, Patty," said Mossie.

"Come on, Bird." I wiped my eyes on my sleeve and took her hand. "We'll see them tomorrow."

13. More Sinners

Wednesday morning, I was relieved to get back down to the station. So much had been going on at home, with all the changes. Florabelle had been down at the house for breakfast, for her first visit back, and she was going with Momma and Birdie down to the nursing home. Jason had dropped her off at 6:00 a.m. on his way to work, and Birdie, anticipating their visit, had been up since 5:30, waiting to present their wedding photo album.

Florabelle had thumbed though the pictures, commented on the fact that the film made her look tan, cast it aside, and went right over to a plate of bacon and scrambled eggs. Jason didn't even glance at the album, just poured himself a cup of coffee and left. I could tell Birdie was upset. She had gone to the extent of writing their names and had drawn two bells with glue and silver glitter on the front cover. She had created a precious piece of art, and all Florabelle had done was eat a piece of bacon.

I was sweeping the garage floor when Clem got in. He always went to the bank first thing to make a deposit from the previous day's earnings. I always came straight in, cleaned up, checked the supplies, reviewed order requests, then opened the station at eight sharp.

"How's your Grandma?" Clem asked. He carried with him a twelve-pack of toilet paper and several rolls of paper towels.

"Settling in," I said, grabbing the paper. It was also my job to stock the rest rooms. "What's worse is how Momma's doing. Florabelle and Grandma moving out in one week's time. She's so used to taking care of everybody."

Clem eyed me. "Well, it takes a while."

"I know."

"Lord only knows when I get that old what my kids will

do with me." Clem laughed. "They may just have me put to sleep like an old hound."

"Oh, Clem, you're never going to get old. You'll live forever just to spite us all."

"Maybe so, maybe so." He was grinning and shaking his head, then he looked up at me again. "And what about you? You going to get old in this station working for me? I keep telling you, a young lady with your handy talents, you ought to get out there in the world and become something, join one of them Four H clubs and do something with them hands of yours. Design some pretty dresses and make us all famous."

"I use my hands plenty around here," I said, bending over the dustpan.

"Changing oil filters never made anybody famous."

"Neither did threading a needle."

"What about Betsy Ross? Wasn't she a seamstress?"

"Move your feet, Clem," I said, sweeping right where he was standing.

Clem grinned at me; he knew when to quit. He was always getting on to me about starting up a career of some sort.

Clem opened the register, counted the silver, slammed the door shut. "Some fella came by here yesterday, looking for you."

"Oh, yeah? One of the Crabtree brothers? Jason was over this morning to drop off Florabelle."

"No, I didn't recognize him. Tall, blond guy. About your age. Says you told him where he could fish?"

I stopped sweeping, gripped the broom handle. My knuckles turned red.

"You know him?" asked Clem.

"Uh, yes. What did he say . . . what did you tell him?"

"I told him you were off for a couple of days taking care of family matters, that you'd be back today."

"Today?"

"Yeah, today. What? Something wrong with him?"

"Oh, no. Today's fine. It's fine."

I saw Clem stare at me funny; I felt myself flush. "I'll

go do the bathrooms now," I said. I reached for my purse underneath the counter, took a roll of toilet paper from the package, and headed to the women's room. Once inside, I emptied out my purse and rummaged for makeup. All I had was a tube of lipstick so I dabbed a little on my cheeks and lips, puckered at the mirror, finger-combed my hair.

I wasn't wearing any earrings and searched my purse for some. All I found was a pair of lime green turtle clip-ons, a pair of Birdie's. Whenever we went anywhere, she could only stand to wear them for a few minutes, then she'd pull them off and give them to me to hold. I clipped them on my ears, tucked my hair behind them. They looked silly; I grinned at myself. At least it was some color, and from a distance, no one would be able to tell they were turtles.

I loaded the dispensers, wiped the counter and toilet seat, checked the level on the Thousand and One Flushes, and locked the door behind me. Then I opened up the men's room with the key, and the air that hit me was foul. I quickly checked the paper stock, closed the door.

When I walked back in the station, Clem was still looking at me funny. "What's that on your ears?" he asked.

"Jewelry. Where's the Lysol? The men's room smells."

"Sure is green, bold enough to blind you."

"Lysol?"

"No, them earrings. That fluorescent stuff is in now, ain't it? My granddaughter wears those neon colors all the time, gives us all headaches."

"We got to do something about that bathroom. Water gets in around the door, and mildew just musters in there."

"I'll remember to seal it. Get on out there, now, we got a customer."

It was Brother Brewer, a retired minister, who came in once a week to fill his convertible Mustang. I loved his car; it was a Sixty-six, straight-six cylinder, two hundred engine. It was the original color, honey gold, with a white top, and pony interior. Once, I had rebuilt the carburetor in it. Whenever I filled the tank, I was careful not to let the cap drop down and hit the chrome fender. I respected the car more than some folks respected its owner.

Brother Brewer, at eighty-eight years old, still enjoyed hot-rodding around with the top down, but he did take real good care of his car. He also had an old Hudson parked in his barn that didn't run, but he washed it every Saturday.

He was a funny old guy, always pretending to be so reverent, but everyone knew he was ornery. Florabelle and I, a few years back, got a notion to set him up with Grandma, but Momma and Hazel had a fit. Hazel, who always flirted with him, said he was an old playboy. I didn't believe that, but I could see the signs of mischief. In spite of his ways, though, he and I were pretty good pals.

"Good morning, Miss Fern," he called, waving out the top of his car.

"Morning, Brother Brewer. Fill her up?"

"You bet ya. She's thirsty again."

"Well, all that sporting around you do, takes a lot of petroleum." I winked at him.

"Well, a man of God has got to spread the Word in style." He winked back.

We had this same little conversation, or something very similar to it, every week.

"You look mighty sharp today, Fern, a little color in your cheeks. Those are some fancy earrings, too. How's the family? Is Florabelle a Momma yet?"

"No, she's got about another month or so. Want your fluids checked?" I always liked any opportunity to tinker with his car.

"Steering's okay, but go ahead and check the transmission fluid and the oil if you want," he yelled from behind the wheel.

Brewer never got out of his car. He would even hold up cars at intersections, chatting with pedestrians, from the driver's seat. He was always going or coming. Forever in transit. I don't remember ever seeing his legs. Birdie once asked me if he had any.

I checked the dip stick, peered in. "You're about a quart low. Now start your car up." I waited for him to turn the engine over and removed the dip stick for the transmission fluid. "You're okay. Just a minute, I'll get your oil fixed up."

I walked inside, and Clem asked, "Where's he headed today?"

"Didn't say. Is thirty weight okay for him? We're out of forty."

"Yeah, don't pour in the whole quart, though. Ask him where he's headed."

I positioned the funnel, opened the can, and as it was pouring, I said, "So, Brother Brewer, what's on your calendar for today?"

"Just around and about, Fern," Brewer stretched his arms way above his head, faked a yawn. "Got some errands to run this morning, then thought I'd visit an old friend in Stanton this afternoon."

"That'll be nice." I wiped my hands, lowered the hood. "You want this on your credit?"

"Better pay cash, today. I don't want that bill creeping up on me." He handed me the money.

"You drive safely," I said. I wasn't really sure whether or not he still had a valid driver's license. We all wondered. He could be a real menace on the road; he never signaled.

"Sure will," he said, starting his car. "Fern, I heard about Esther. You give her my best. Peaceful Pastures is a good home; they'll treat her nice."

"Thanks, Brother Brewer," I said. "She'll appreciate that."

He tooted his horn as he drove away. His silver hair, combed forward and sprayed into place, blew up and over his forehead in one matted section, clinging by the roots, to the back of his neck. In motion, he looked bald. He was so tall that I imagined he rode with the top down because he had no other choice. What a car, I thought. What a character.

As soon as Brewer was out of view, Clem stepped out. "So where did he say he was going?"

"Why are you so hell-bent on knowing where he's going?"

"What did he say?"

"He's going to see a friend in Stanton. Satisfied?" I smiled, shook my head at Clem.

"Just what I thought!" said Clem, slapping his leg, proclaiming victory.

"Thought what?"

"I knew it. He's got something going with Mrs. Prettyman's daughter, Patty. She teaches kindergarten in Pilotview."

"Clem, you're out of your gourd. Patty Prettyman graduated from high school with me; she's a quarter of his age. Where did you hear rubbish like that?"

"Lonnie goes to school there where Patty teaches. She sees Brewer there in his Mustang after school every day."

"So maybe he's there to see someone else."

"Lonnie said Patty gets in the car with him and they drive off together."

"You're going to listen to your eight-year-old granddaughter's account? Clem, come on." Lonnie sometimes played with Birdie, and I had heard some of her wild fibs. She was rather spoiled, taking a bus into Pilotview to go to a year-round school with the city kids, and she was always bragging or blowing smoke.

"I know, she tells stories, but not this time."

"Well, I don't know." I put Brewer's money in the drawer, banged it shut. "Even if, what's the big deal? To each his own." Patty Prettyman had a reputation at my high school, for being fast with the guys. She'd slept with a few of the teachers, too, we'd heard. I decided not to mention this to Clem.

Clem stared at me, wide-eyed. "You ought to hang your head in shame, Fern."

"What?"

"Well, Brewer's a minister."

"*Was* one. But, so what?"

"Well, he can't be running around like that, romancing a . . ."

"Clem, he's a minister, not a priest." I made a note to myself, just then, that Brewer must *indeed* have legs.

"Fern, Patty's a married woman. She's Patty Greene. She married Larry Greene, that singer over at the Outpost. He's got a rich old momma up at Peaceful Pastures where your Grandma is. Rumor is, Patty married him for the family money. But she runs with Brewer."

"Mossie Greene?" I asked.

"Yeah, poor old widow. She's been senile for a few years now. Alzheimer's."

"I know her," I said. "That's Grandma's roommate."

"Tragedy."

"What's that?"

"Mossie's husband. Shot himself. It made her crack."

"Clem, let's go fix the bathroom doors." I didn't want to talk about the old, the dying, the doomed, nor the done unto anymore. This whole town was due for some serious penance.

14. Sorting Screws

Clem left for lunch at eleven-thirty; when he came back, my shift would be over. Half-days were enough with everything else going on at home, and the money was good. He paid me six-fifty an hour, for four hours, five days a week.

I was sitting in the garage sorting screws when I heard a horn. I turned, expecting to see Clem, who always honked when he came and went, and saw a purple jeep. Cross-legged, I felt my knees lock. The door to the jeep opened, and the driver stepped out and walked towards the garage. The crick in my knees grew dull.

"Hello, Fern," he said, smiling down at me. "Do you remember me? I was in the other day for gas. I don't know if I told you my name though. John Culler." He extended his right hand for me to shake.

"I remember you." I offered my hand, noticed the grease on my fingers, drew back.

But he kept his hand out there. "My friends just call me Culler."

"Culler, then," I said. I held out my hand, left it out there this time. "You mind helping me up? My knees have buckled."

"Sure," he said. But instead of taking my hand, he walked behind me, grabbed under my arms, and lifted me up.

He did it so fast, just hoisted me straight up, that it startled me. I hoped he didn't notice I was sweating. My first few steps were awkward, due to my knee cramp. I leaped over my pile of screws, hobbled over to the workbench and got a shop rag. "Here," I said, offering it to him. "Wipe your hands; I'm all a mess."

"I'm okay. You shouldn't sit so long in one position like that."

I could have told him that I spent most of my life in one position, the wrong one, mostly. But I stayed quiet and wiped my own hands.

"Take a few deep knee-bends. It will loosen you up."

After three or four bends, I asked, "You need some gas?"

"No, actually, I came back to take you up on that offer to show me some good fishing spots. I'm all settled in my dorm now and have some extra time on my hands before school starts next week." He looked around the garage as he talked. "I wondered if you could give me some pointers."

The way his eyes shifted around the place made me nervous. I hoped he wasn't going to ask to use the men's room since I hadn't cleaned it up yet.

I pulled a pen out of my front pocket. "The gorge is good fishing, but there are some hidden ponds scattered here and there where the catfish are great. We, I mean Clem and I, Clem's the owner here, we always say those spots are exclusive. Members only." I smiled. "But, I'll draw you a map to some of them." I led him into the station.

"What was that bridge you were talking about?"

"The Natural Bridge? That's a state park. You can't fish in the park. Law prohibits it. But there are some good lakes the river feeds into, near Slade. Back on 15."

"How far's that?"

"About a half-hour back. Towards your direction."

"Can you show me?"

"Sure. Take a look at this map." I unfolded a state map from behind the counter and began drawing circles around areas, the exclusive ones I'd mentioned.

Culler studied the map a while, intent. Then he said, "I have an idea. Would you maybe want to ride along with me? Do some fishing? I'd never be able to find my way around here, and it would be nice to have the company."

"No, I can't." Where was Clem, I wondered; what was taking him so long? I folded up the map and starting fanning myself. It was so hot in the station.

"Is there any time this week you could go?" he asked.

His blue eyes were eager, tempting me like two spring-water ponds. Hook, line, and sinker. I was in deep, and I wanted to go with him. "I have to work," I said.

"All week? What about this weekend?"

"I have things to do at home."

"Oh." His face got serious again. "You're married?"

"No, it's not that, I mean family. Sisters." I knew that Momma, Birdie, and Florabelle would be at the nursing home all day, and Daddy would be working. But for some reason, I was always compelled to refuse any offers, as few and as far between as they came, other than work. Declining invitations was a habit, automatic. And I was afraid.

Culler looked hurt and sat down in one of the customer waiting chairs. "How about if we find some place close, just for a few hours?"

I stared at him sitting there, with his head bowed, arms folded. I expected his lower lip to protrude any minute. "I don't know you," I said, frowning.

Culler looked up. "So, I don't know *anyone* around here, yet. Give me a chance. I'm safe." He smiled.

There was a honk. It was Clem. He got out of his truck, drinking an Ale 8. He always stopped at the Ale 8 machine in front of the funeral home and bought himself a pop to bring back to work. When he came in the station, he nodded a hello at Culler, looked at me, hesitated a moment, took a swig of his pop, then said, "Get the hell out of here,

Fern. Go on; I'm through with you for the day." He waved me out of the station.

"I was just asking her to show me some good fishing holes," Culler told Clem. He looked nervous, not sensing Clem's teasing.

"She knows all the spots," said Clem. "Ought to see her bait her hook. Keener than any of us. Fern, why don't you take him to that pond behind the post office? My brother's been lucky over there past two days."

"I was sorting screws," I said.

Clem ignored me, spoke to Culler. "My brother caught a seventeen-inch bass up there just yesterday. Should have seen him, biggest one I've seen all summer." Clem gestured with his hands. "His wife took his picture, stuck it on the fridge, wrote underneath it, 'the big ass with the big bass!'" He threw his head back laughing, coughed on his drink.

Culler grinned, starting to see through Clem, probably. "Is that close by?"

"Pond's right up the road a bit," said Clem. "Take you ten minutes to get there. Now, get on out of here, Fern. Your shift's up and you're costing me overtime." He winked at Culler.

I was trapped now, had run out of outs. A line from some poem entered my head: who would a' fishing go. Or was it a song? Mr. Frog went a' courtin' and he did ride, uh-hum, uh-hum. Or was it a' fishing? There was an Old Man Who Lived In the Sea. Or was it Under the Sea? Did he even fish? My mind wandered off.

Clem broke my spell. "Fern, go on; take the boy fishing."

"I'll want to change," I said. "Out of these coveralls."

"That's fine," said Culler. "Where do you live? I'll follow you home, then we'll leave one car and go from there." He was excited, walked around in circles.

"I only live up the road. I walk."

"Then I'll drive you home."

"No," I said, too quickly.

Clem sensed my discomfort. "What's your name, buddy?" he asked Culler.

"Culler. John Culler."

"Clem Proffit," I said, "my boss." I nodded at Clem.

They shook hands.

"Culler, my suggestion to you would be to go on down the road and get some bait, then come back and meet Fern here. You know women; they take so long to get ready. Save you some time. A mile or two up the road on the right, you'll see a fish camp. Flynn's. Ask for Grover. Tell him Clem sent you; he'll give a good deal."

"Is that all right with you, Fern?" asked Culler.

"Fine."

"Hey, thanks a lot," Culler told Clem.

Clem nodded.

When he was out of sight, Clem said, "A little fun ain't going to hurt you."

"I just don't have the time, Clem."

"Now you know that ain't what you mean."

"Oh? What *do* I mean, Clem?" I was afraid of his answer; he knew me too well.

Clem nodded in the direction of Culler, who had just started up his jeep. "You tell me," he said.

I watched the purple jeep disappear in the dust, down the road. I had imagined this, fishing with Culler, only a few days ago, on the way to the Peaceful Pastures. Now I had the chance, a real chance to do something that deep down, I really wanted. "Finish up those screws," I said to Clem. "They're sorted by size."

15. Slow and Steady

Half an hour later, I was wearing jeans and a red bandanna print tank top, sitting in the bucket seat of the jeep, holding a large army-green tackle box as I would a purse, on my lap, hands folded over it. It was a bumpy ride; my stomach already ached from nerves. The jeep reeked of worms. "Is this an AMC?" I asked.

"Yeah," shouted Culler over the wind. "It's a converted mail truck. The government auctions them off every so often when they get new models. I got a great deal."

"It needs new shocks," I said.

"I think you're right. It was a rough ride up here from Orlando. All that weight."

"That's where you're from?"

"All my life. Not many people can say they were born in Florida. Did you know that?"

"I've heard that."

"My Dad lived in Kentucky growing up. He came down to work for NASA with the start of the Apollo system. Met my mom there, then my sister and I were born, so they just decided to settle there. Twenty-five years ago." Culler turned to me and smiled. "Too much wind?"

"No. Your dad, is he an astronaut?"

Culler chuckled. "He's an engineer."

"Is that why you're in college, then, to be an engineer?" I had to shout over the wind. The air whipping through the jeep was invigorating. This must be what it feels like riding in a convertible, I thought. This must be what rejuvenates Brother Brewer. The fresh air whisking across his face all day long must be what kept him vital.

"Yes, as a matter of fact, I am majoring in engineering. But not in Aeronautics." Culler shook his head. "I want to be an architect."

"Design houses?"

"Houses, yes, but mostly buildings, more industrial and corporate."

"Oh, corporate," I said, fiddling with my tackle box handle.

"What about you? Born here in Kentucky? Don't they call you guys briars?"

"No. Just moved here three years ago. Came from Ohio. Not many folks go from buckeyedom to briarhood. Did you know that?"

Culler laughed. "No, I guess I didn't."

"So you're at Transy?"

"No, U of K. I've been two years to the University of Central Florida, but they are more known for their computer science and electrical engineering programs. University of Kentucky is more reputable for architecture."

"I've heard that."

He looked over at me again. "So I transferred. It's worked out really well because my younger sister is just starting her first year at Transylvania, so we're both in Lexington. It's nice that we're both up here."

"That is nice," I said. "Was she with you the other day?"

"At the station, you mean?"

I nodded.

"Yes." Culler paused. "She was the one in the backseat. Her name's Connie."

"In the backseat," I said.

"Yes."

"Connie."

"That's right."

We rode in silence a few moments, then I said, "Turn right up here. Slow down, though, watch for potholes. Pavement ends."

Culler slowed the jeep. "Right here?"

"Yes, keep it steady. The pond's at the bottom of the road. This thing front-wheel drive?"

"I think so," said Culler, concentrating on the road.

"Go slow," I said.

"That's right," said Culler, leaning forward.

"Who was in the front?" I asked.

"Front of what?" Culler kept his eyes fixed ahead of him.

"The front seat. Was that your girlfriend in the front seat?"

"Leslie? Yeah, I guess she's my girlfriend. At home, anyway. I don't know what's going to happen with me being away, though." He shifted into first. "I can see the pond now. Where do I park?"

"Just stop anywhere; we'll walk down. Watch those tree roots, though. They'll rip your tires right up. Is she planning to come up here to school, too?"

"Who?" Culler drove a little farther down the ravine, parked, pulled up the emergency brake.

"Leslie."

"Oh, she talks about it, but I doubt she'll leave her friends and sorority and all that. Girls need that stuff." Culler got out the jeep and walked around to my side to offer me help getting out.

I didn't need help and didn't pretend to. I climbed out.

"That sure was a rough ride," said Culler, opening the back.

"From Florida?"

"No, down to this ravine. Those bumps probably did a number on my suspension, huh?"

"You need a four-wheeler most places around here."

"You seem to know a lot about cars."

"You seem to know a lot about girls."

Culler grinned. "Not all of them. You hungry?" He handed me a brown paper sack. "When I went for the bait, I picked up some sandwiches, too."

"You didn't buy sandwiches from Flynn's Fish Camp, did you?"

"No. He did have a deal on the Night Crawler and Swiss on rye, though." He laughed. "I got subs and potato salad from some little grocery nearby."

"Mac's." I trusted Mac's food.

We walked down a few yards to the bank of the pond. I watched as Culler spread a blanket over a grassy patch and began unpacking the sack. He'd remembered the condiments, napkins, plastic silverware. I tried not to let on that I was impressed. College must make all the difference in the world, I thought. If it were up to Jason to get Florabelle lunch, she *would* be eating night crawlers.

I sat down on the blanket and crossed my legs.

"You better not sit like that again, you'll get those spasms again like you did sitting there sorting your nails." He winked, cut a turkey sub in two.

I shifted, straighten out my legs and lay on my stomach. "Those were screws," I corrected, waited as he got lunch all set. The breeze off the pond felt good. Even so, the humidity was bad, and my hair was sticking to the back of my neck. I reached over the edge of the blanket and plucked a long weed, gathered up my hair in a knot, and weaved the grass through it to hold it up.

"Here," said Culler, handing me a plate. "We'll split this one, and if you're still hungry, there's another. I like your earrings. Those are turtles, aren't they?"

I felt my face go red. I had forgotten to switch earrings when I'd gone home to change clothes.

"You remember the story of the tortoise and the hare?" asked Culler, mouth full.

"I think so, didn't they race?" I reached for my ears, spun the earrings to make sure the turtles were upright.

"Yes, and the tortoise wins. Slow and Steady Wins the Race." Culler took a bite of his sandwich, lay down on the blanket next to me.

"We should catch something with that bait," I said. "Flynn's worms are the finest." We touched slightly at the knees. I could feel my whole body go warmer all of a sudden.

"So this fishing spot is for members only?" Culler grinned.

"Not really. It's public property. We just joke like that," I said, sitting up. I gathered my legs up underneath me. "This is Toad's Pond."

Culler leaned up on one side, balanced on his elbow. "You seem to know all the secrets here."

"I do," I said, fixing myself another scoop of the potato salad. "And I take delight in keeping them."

"You say you've lived up here three years?"

"That's long enough."

"Were you born in Ohio?"

"Franklin."

"Did you go to school there?"

"I graduated from Carlisle High."

"No college?"

"No college." I took the last bite of my sandwich, leaned up, wadded the wax paper into a ball, threw it through the open window of the jeep.

Culler looked at the jeep a moment, turned back to me. "You think you'll go to college? There's a lot of good ones here in Kentucky. Perhaps you could get in on a basketball scholarship with that kind of hook."

"Speaking of hook, are we going to fish?" I didn't want to talk about school and careers, things of no concern to me.

"Sure, we'll fish. You just seem pretty smart. I think you'd like school."

"Maybe so," I said, rising to my feet. "I just don't think college is the right thing for me. I have a pretty full schedule."

"Tell me," said Culler, squinting up at me.

"Tell you what?"

"What is it that you do? What takes up all your time?"

"Besides Clem's?"

"Besides Clem's."

"I work a lot at home."

"Doing what?"

"Taking care of things."

"Big family?"

"We're growing. My sister's expecting a baby real soon."

"Babies are fun."

"You have one?"

"No, relatives. They're fun to play with."

"We'll see." I sat down on a log near the water and begin to prepare my tackle. "You about ready?"

"Yes," said Culler, but still lying on his side, watching me.

"Why don't you get your rod ready," I suggested, not looking at him, but sensing his stare. He had rented two from Flynn. I had my own, a Shimono, but I decided not to bring it. Maybe next time.

Finally, he rolled over and climbed to his feet. As he passed by me, he patted the top of my head. He walked back up to the jeep and was there for quite some time. I fixed a couple of lures, as a backup in case the fish weren't going for the worms.

When Culler returned with his fishing rod, he sat down

beside me and handed me the worms. "Here," he said, "I hear you are the expert."

Hesitating at first, I prepared his tackle. Then we both cast.

For nearly ten minutes, we sat in silence, watching our lines, holding them steady, waiting. It felt odd to be sitting here with anyone other than Clem. Sometimes I would take Birdie fishing, but mostly just in the pond behind our house, for minnows or guppies. Never out here. I stole a look over at Culler. He seemed to be enjoying himself. I felt fairly comfortable with him, and he looked like he knew what he was doing. I was trying not to feel guilty for not being at the nursing home, visiting Grandma. We'd only be a few hours, I told myself.

Then I saw my cork go under and hold. I began reeling in furiously. When I had it up out of the water, Culler gave a loud cheer.

"Look at that, is that about a foot?"

"Not even," I said. "It's got to be over twelve to keep." I unhooked the bass, wiggling in my grip, tossed him back.

"Well, that's a start," said Culler, gently, as if he thought my feelings were hurt.

"We'll get some," I said, getting ready to cast again. A worm struggled between my fingers. "Just takes time."

"Slow and steady, " said Culler.

I had the worm on the hook and leaned to cast. My left arm back, I went to throw the rod forward, but in trying to follow through, I realized I had caught it on something. I heard a gasp and a cough.

Culler was holding the back of this neck, and blood trickled from where the hook had gone in. The line was wound tight around his neck, and he choked for air.

I had hooked him.

Culler's breathing was convulsive for the next few seconds while I sifted through my tackle box for a small enough knife to cut the line loose, but not his throat. Finally, I found a razor blade.

"Hold your breath," I said. "Be real still." I pressed against his neck with one finger, pulled the line as far from his skin as I could, and cut the line. Dark blood pooled in his cupped hand and dripped to the ground beneath him.

Culler heaved in air, then started panting, trying to catch his breath. I had barely nicked the skin below his ear, where blood slowly dribbled. But the place where the hook had entered the back of his neck was now bleeding profusely. The hook was still lodged.

"We're going to have to get this hook out," I said. "It's in deep." My hands were shaking from jangled nerves and humiliation.

"Shouldn't we go to the hospital?" Culler looked scared. His face had gone pale and his labored breathing continued.

"Closest one's in Lexington. There's a doctor in town, but he only makes house calls." I rummaged through my tackle box and pulled out a little first-aid packet that I always carried. "Here's some tonic," I said, unscrewing the cap. "Special remedy to clean the wound." I dabbed the concoction around both cuts.

Culler hissed, gritted his teeth, with the stinging. "What is that stuff?"

"Mostly iodine. A little soap and water."

"It burns."

"It disinfects."

"Drive me back into town and call that doctor," he said desperately.

I studied the gash where the hook rested. The skin was swelling. "When's the last time you had a tetanus shot?"

"Just had one. Required for entering school." Culler grimaced. He took my hand and squeezed it hard. "You got to get me to the doctor, Fern."

"I'll drive you back to the station. We'll call the doctor from there." I dabbed some more at the cut with a left-over napkin from lunch. The napkin absorbed a large amount of blood almost instantly. This guy may bleed to death out here, I thought, and it would be my fault.

I took a deep breath and tried to calm myself. "This hook has to come out soon." I handed Culler a roll of smelling salts. "Hold on to this. If you feel faint, sniff it.

We'd better hurry." I took off my shoes and gave him one of my socks to hold on his neck to stop the bleeding.

Then as fast as I could, I gathered up all our stuff, ran back down to the bank and helped Culler to the jeep. "You're going to have to sit up," I said, situating him in the front passenger seat. "If you lie down or sit back against the headrest, you're going to drive that hook in deeper."

"Drive slowly," he said softly.

"Slow and steady," I said and gave his shoulder a pat for reassurance.

16. More Needles

It was an effort to get the jeep up the ravine, back out onto the road. I put the seatbelt around Culler's waist but folded the shoulder strap down to keep it from rubbing his neck. Once on 15, I drove as fast as the roads would let me. I paid careful attention not to hit any bumps that might imbed the hook even further.

Pulling to a stop at the station, I squealed the brakes. Clem was standing up on a ladder, hosing down the front sign, and I missed hitting the ladder by only a foot or two. He dropped the hose and glared down at me. "What on heaven's earth are doing coming through here like a bat out of hell? Slow down, or you're gonna hurt somebody!" he shouted.

"I already have." I jumped out of the jeep and ran around to Culler's side. "I hooked him, Clem. Help me out here."

"You what?"

"There's a fishhook lodged in his neck. He's losing blood. Call Dr. Glenn and help me get him inside."

Clem climbed down from the ladder, ran, turned off the water hose. We walked Culler into the station and sat him down in a chair. I gathered some clean rags from the garage and hurried around back to the men's room and wet them down with warm water. When I returned to the station,

Clem said, "Dr. Glenn is delivering a baby in Bowen. His wife said she'd try calling Dr. Erikson."

"Clem, Dr. Erikson is a retired racehorse doctor."

"Well, Fern, that's all we got right close." He hung up the receiver, walked over to Culler, studied his condition.

"That hook can't be in there much longer," I said. "Or he's going to have one hell of an infection. Go sterilize your wire cutters for me, Clem."

"What are you going to do?" asked Clem.

"I'm going to get that hook out of there. Hurry up with those cutters."

Culler groaned a little, slouched forward.

"Fern, you don't know how to do this," Clem said.

"I've had to get a few fishhooks out of Birdie's hand before. Had to pull some metal chips out of Daddy's hands before, too." I took Clem's jacket from the doorhook and balled it up to support Culler's back in the chair.

"You never worked on nobody's neck, Fern." Clem shook his head, worrying.

"Clem, I got it in there, and I'm going to get the damn thing out," I shouted. "Stop wasting time." I removed my sock from Culler's neck, quickly pressed a warm rag against the cut. The skin around the hook was puffy, blue.

Clem bent over, looked at the wound. His eyes grew wide, panicked. "You did this?"

I nodded. I looked down at Culler, whose face was white. He was slumped down in the chair, barely conscious.

Clem disappeared into the garage for a few minutes, came back with his knife, some rubbing alcohol, a few more clean rags, and a bottle of Jack Daniels.

"What's that whiskey for?" I asked, taking the supplies.

"The pain. Make him take a few swigs."

"Culler," I said, "you're going to have to lie down flat here." I looked up at Clem. "There's an old station wagon mat in the garage, rolled up on the shelf, on top of the oil filters cabinet. Go get it."

Clem disappeared again. A horn blew out by the pumps. I raised up. It was some young kids, out cruising around after school. "Go on!" I shouted. "We're closed.

Go on up a couple miles; there's a Sohio up there."

"What's going on in there?" yelled one of the kids.

Clem came back with the mat. He rolled it out on the floor, threw a towel down over it.

The school kids honked again. The driver revved the engine of an old Ford Pinto. His added-on dual exhaust system clouded up our parking lot.

"You heard the girl!" shouted Clem. "Get on out of here!"

The car squealed out, burned rubber on Clem's clean driveway.

"Crimony Jesus," said Clem. "Never thought I'd see the day when I'd be sending away customers."

"Culler, can you hear me?" I brushed the hair out of his eyes.

He nodded, reached for my hand.

"I know it hurts," I said, softly. "I'm sorry." I could see tears welling in the corners of his eyes. "I'm going to have to ask you to lie down here and let me get that hook out of your neck. Can you lie down?"

"Here," said Clem, handing Culler the Jack Daniels. "Have yourself a snort of this. It'll kill the pain."

I held Culler's head back, supported him with both hands, let him swallow a few sips of the whiskey.

"It throbs," he said.

"I know." I rubbed the top of his head. "Now lie down, there."

Clem and I lifted him down carefully from the chair and stretched him out on his stomach. When we had him positioned as comfortable as possible, I wasted no time. Slowly, I pushed the hook through his skin until the barb emerged.

Culler winced.

"Hold his head still," I told Clem.

Clem bent down, cradled Culler's head with his big, greasy hands. He made a wry face at the blood, turned away.

I snipped the barb and eased the hook out of Culler's neck. I could feel him stiffen as I loosened it from the grasp of his swollen skin. His whole body went tense. It was good that I couldn't see his face.

I laid a cold towel over the wound, held it tight. "It's out," I said, gently patting Culler's back. "You're okay, now."

"Clem, go thread me some fishing line, clean it good. I'll stitch him up."

"Where am I going to find a needle?"

"My tackle box. In the jeep, behind the driver's side. Just bring the box in."

While Clem ran around, following my orders, I rubbed Culler's back, soothing the pain. Blood caked and matted his sun-bleached hair against the back of his head. My stomach ached. I've done this to him, I thought.

Finally, Clem came back in with a needle and thread. I looked into his face. Sweat beaded his forehead.

"Thanks," I said. "You've been a help." I found the iodine mixture and dabbed it over the open wound.

Culler shuddered again.

Clem wiped his own face with his sleeve. He stood over Culler, arms folded. "That didn't bother you none, Fern?" he whispered. "My stomach went weak on me."

"I'm okay. Culler's the one hurt."

"Should we drive him to the hospital?"

"No, the hook didn't get any major veins nor arteries and I was careful not to hit any, either. He'll be sore, but it's not bad."

"You hear that, son? The doc says you're going to live." Clem nodded, approving.

"That's right," I said. "But I got to close up this hole, then you can get up." I poured a little whiskey over the cut.

Culler flinched.

Clem frowned at me, wasting liquor.

When I was just about finished sewing up the wound, another car pulled up to the gas pump. It was Dr. Erikson, the retired veterinarian.

He hurried into the station, stopped short when he saw us. He stared down at Culler lying prone on the floor, me sewing up the back of his neck. "What in Jesus name?"

"The boy got a fishhook caught in him. Fern operated on him, fixed him up," said Clem.

Dr. Erikson bent down over me, studied my work. "Well, I'll be damn," he said. "That's a finer stitch job than I've done on some horse's asses in my day."

That's reassuring, I thought.

"Dr. Erikson, this here is Fern Rayburn. She's my assistant." Clem looked proud, introducing me.

"How do you do, Miss," The doctor tipped his hat.

"Hi," I said, not looking up.

He opened his medical bag, removed a bottle of betadine. "Looks like I'm too late for the crisis, but I'll leave you this. It'll disinfect the cut, stop any infection."

"I used iodine."

Dr. Erikson raised his hand to his chin. "Iodine," he said. "Who is this fella?"

"Name's Culler," said Clem.

"Is he local?"

"Lexington," I said. I lowered my face down to Culler's neck, bit the nylon thread and stood up. "There."

We all three stood in a circle, staring down at Culler, lying silent on the floor.

We were interrupted by a hoarse little voice in the doorway to the station. "Fern."

It was Birdie. She looked down at Culler, then at all the rest of us hovering over him. "Where have you been?" She frowned. "Momma's got supper going, Florabelle's staying. They sent me down here to find you."

"I'll be home in a minute, Bird."

Still frowning, she stared at me, suspicious. "Who's he?" She pointed at Culler.

I followed her eyes down. "You're all intact now, Culler," I said. "Roll over and meet folks."

Slowly, Culler rolled over and stared up at all of us. Some color had returned to his cheeks. He smiled faintly.

"Well, young man, this lady, Fern, here, has sewed you back together," said Dr. Erikson.

"You look better than you did when you first came in here this morning," said Clem.

"Try standing up," I said.

"Who is he?" Birdie demanded.

"A friend, Bird," I said.

"Why's he bleeding?" she asked.

"He had an accident, but he's okay now. Run on home and tell Momma I'll be right there."

She kept standing there, looking around, still not satisfied. "Is your friend going to be eating with us?" Birdie regarded Culler. "Momma'll have to know."

I looked at him, still lying there, but now smiling at me.

"Yeah, tell her to set an extra plate."

Clem and Dr. Erikson helped Culler stand up while Birdie stayed long enough to see him get to his feet.

"What's for dinner?" he asked her, much too brightly.

Birdie shrugged, looked at me. "You're wearing my earrings," she said and ran off.

"How do you feel?" I asked Culler.

"A little rough around the edges. My neck is so numb I can hardly feel whether my head's attached."

"It's up there all right," said Dr. Erikson, assuring him. "How'd this happen?"

I turned away.

"Long story," said Culler.

"Well, I'm useless here." The doctor took his bag, turned to leave. "But you could come see me in a couple of weeks about those stitches. Make sure your tetanus is up to date, too. Clem, you take care now. If you ever want to lend me your assistant, I could sure use her help, too."

"Sure, Doc," said Clem. "I'll let you know. Thanks for coming down."

"Bye, then," said Dr. Erikson. He looked at me, tipped his hat again. "Good work."

Clem started cleaning up the stuff on the floor where I'd operated.

"Hungry?" I asked Culler.

"A little."

"Since I split you open, least I could do is offer to fill you up. Come over for supper. Momma won't mind."

Culler reached out, took my hand. "Let's just forget this, okay? It wasn't your fault."

"Accidents happen," said Clem, listening in.

"It's going to be some time before it heals," I said.

"You can help me take care of it," said Culler.

"May leave a scar," I warned.

"It'll fade," said Culler.

"Who'll see it?" Clem pointed out.

I hoped, too, that the memory of this day would fade. At least the bad part.

17. Spilled Milk

When we pulled up to our house, Heidi came running round from the backyard to greet us. I tapped the horn lightly, warning her. She pranced back and forth across the gravel driveway, barking.

"She just isn't going to move, is she?" said Culler.

"Don't pull up yet," I said. "She doesn't see us; she's blind." I called out the window. "Heidi, come on now, move!"

Culler leaned out his side and whistled at her.

After a minute or two of this, we had conjured up together enough sweet noises to lure Heidi out of our way. Culler drove on up the driveway and parked behind Jason's truck.

Before we got out of the jeep, I took a deep breath and said, "My family. They're tensed up over my grandmother getting admitted to a nursing home. Don't mind them if they're edgy."

"I hope they won't mind me coming over," said Culler.

"Not at all," I said. But I was dreading this whole thing. It wasn't that they didn't take to strangers, or that we weren't used to company. Momma liked entertaining at any opportunity. It was just bad timing.

The screen door to the front porch banged shut. Birdie came out, looked at Culler, then at me. "I told Momma you were bringing somebody and she said there might not be enough roast."

"Well, I'm not that hungry, so Culler can eat my share," I said. "Birdie, you didn't meet Culler. Say hello."

Birdie looked at him, waved.

"Hi there, Birdie," said Culler.

"Jason's eating, too," she said.

"We'll have plenty," I said.

We walked up the front steps. Heidi, following our voices, found Birdie and nudged her hand. Birdie petted her, bent down to give her a big squeeze. Then she grabbed her by the collar and led her back around behind the garage.

The house smelled like onions and was alive with voices. Jason's, Daddy's, and a newscaster's in the family room; Momma's, Hazel's, and Florabelle's in the kitchen.

When we walked through the family room, Daddy and Jason stopped talking and stared at me. They'd been discussing the news; somewhere a plane had crashed.

"This is Culler," I said. "That's my father and Jason, my brother-in-law."

"Hello," said Daddy.

"Pleasure to meet you, sir," said Culler. He walked over to the sofa, shook Daddy's hand, then turned to Jason.

Jason nodded a hello, but didn't offer his hand. He stared at Culler, frowning. "Man, you look like you just been horned by a bull. Your head's a' bleeding."

Culler smiled faintly, looked at me. "We had an accident with a fishhook. It's quit bleeding, though. Fern, is there a place I could wash up?"

I pointed to the downstairs bathroom.

When Culler closed the bathroom door, Daddy asked, "Where have you been? Working late?"

"I went fishing for a little while, just over at Toad's Pond by the post office."

"You've been gone all afternoon." He pointed at the TV. "Look at that mess, wiped out the side of a motel. Your Momma needed your help earlier."

"Birdie told me."

"You clean your fish already?" he asked. "Take it on in there, have your Momma throw it on the stove."

"We didn't catch anything."

"What took so long, then?" Daddy half listened to me,

half to an anchorman talking about the fatalities of the jet crash.

"We had an accident with a fishing hook. Kept us late."

"A hook got him?" asked Jason. "That was the blood?"

I nodded.

Jason smirked, then under his breath said, "Hell of a fisherman."

"It was an accident," I said. I didn't want to own up to what had happened, figuring Daddy would start putting up defenses out of fear that Culler would press charges.

"Sixty some dead," said Daddy, frowning at the newscaster. "There's a lawsuit."

I started towards the kitchen.

"Fern?" called Daddy.

"Yeah?"

"Who is that cat in there?" he asked, pointing towards the bathroom.

"A friend I met at Clem's. Goes to a college in Lexington."

Jason snickered again, louder. "College boy," he whined.

"Jason, let up." I said and walked away.

The noise of the pressure cooker muffled the voices in the kitchen. Hazel and Florabelle were sitting at the table, smoking, folding napkins and peeling potatoes. The room was dense with smoke and steam.

"Hey, Florabelle," I said. "How are you feeling?" It was good to see her; it had been almost two weeks, and I hadn't had much of a chance to talk to her that morning when I had headed out to work.

"I'm as big as a sow." She stood up to show off her stomach, sat back down, smiled at me.

"You've got good color in your face," I said.

Momma was at the stove. She turned around when I walked in. "There you are, finally," she said.

"Come here and talk to me, Fern," said Florabelle. "Birdie tells us you got a man out there." She raised her eyebrows, pointed towards the family room. "Something happen since I moved out?"

"Where did you meet him?" asked Hazel.

"Clem's. He's a friend. I just met him last week. Momma, is there enough food?"

Momma wiped her hands on her apron, walked over to the table. "We'll have to stretch the roast. When I heard Jason was staying for supper, I tried to find you to go buy me a few more pounds of beef. Then I heard you was bringing home someone else, so I fried a chicken and threw in two more ears of corn." She took the bowl of potatoes from Hazel. "Where is he?"

"Washing up. He got a fishhook in his neck. He's sore."

"Lord almighty," said Momma, mashing potatoes.

"That must have smarted," said Hazel.

"You want me to set the table?" I asked.

"Florabelle was supposed to," said Momma.

"I can hardly get up and down; you do it, Fern." Florabelle handed me the napkins she'd folded.

"Make sure there's eight there," said Momma.

"I counted, Momma," snapped Florabelle.

"Just make sure."

I took the napkins, went to the drawer, counted out silverware. Momma hated to be short a fork at the table, or for someone to find a stained one. She washed everything twice. Even our clothes were bleached and pressed with starch. When it came to bed linens, Momma's sheets were always the whitest of the whole town. Tuesdays were wash day for most folks, and from time to time, Momma would make Hazel drive her around, looking at clotheslines, to compare her sheets with others' just to reassure herself that hers were the whitest. And if they weren't, she'd bleach them again.

"How was Grandma today?" I asked.

No one spoke for a moment, then Momma turned to me and said, "She's adjusting."

"Bull," said Hazel. "She's meaner than a ol' cuss. She won't let Mossie cross over to her side of the room to water the plants in the window sill, and yells at her for blocking the hallway with her wheelchair."

"It's going to take time for her to get used to sharing a

room with someone, that's all. She's had a house to herself for so long," said Momma.

"Well, that old Mossie woman is cuckoo," said Florabelle.

"Now, Florie, she can't help it," said Momma.

"Mossie Greene," I said. "I heard her son married Patty Prettyman."

"That slut," said Florabelle.

"Florabelle," scolded Mom.

The pressure cooker whirred.

"Who's this?" asked Hazel.

"This girl from our high school who screwed practically everyone in Carlisle. Look's like now she's moved her bumps and grinds across the state line."

Momma pulled a beater out of the mixer, walked over to Florabelle, thwacked her between the shoulder blades. "That's enough, Miss Foulmouth. She was at the wedding, Hazel," said Momma.

"And who invited her, I can't figure. I sure didn't ask her to come, and I don't even think Jason knows her," said Florabelle.

Birdie walked in through the garage door about that time, carrying Jimmy.

"Birdie, what have I told you about bringing him in the kitchen?" Momma said, shaking the beater at Birdie. Mashed potatoes dripped to the floor. "People eat in here."

"Is that guy still here?" Birdie asked me, struggling with Jimmy's weight.

"Yes. He'll be eating with us," I said. "Go out there and talk to him. Show him Jimmy. But put him down and let him walk; he's too big to be carried."

"No he ain't," said Birdie, relentless. Her face was pink from the strain.

"This boy," said Momma. "He works for Clem?"

"No, he bought gas there. Lives in Lexington. We were just trying to catch some bass up a ways here," I said.

"He's from Lexington?" asked Hazel.

"He's there for college. He's *from* Florida."

"Will he eat turnips?" asked Momma.

"Florida?" asked Hazel.

"College?" asked Florabelle. "You went fishing with a college man?"

Hazel looked at Florabelle, mused a moment, nodded in approval.

"They didn't catch any fish," said Birdie.

"How long will supper be, Momma?" I asked.

"'Bout another ten minutes. I just need to drain this corn. See what everybody wants to drink. Florabelle, Hazel, put out your cigarettes, clear them catalogs off the table. Birdie, put Jimmy in the garage."

When I went back through the swinging door, Culler was sitting on the other end of the sofa, watching TV. No one talked to him. A news team was at the scene of the crash, interviewing survivors.

"Supper's about ready," I said.

"What is it?" called Jason, feet propped up on the coffee table.

"Roast and potatoes. Wash up."

I smiled at Culler, motioned for him to come on. I quickly introduced him around the kitchen.

"Hope you like to eat," said Momma. "We got enough for a whole picking crew."

"*Sure* we do," said Hazel. She looked at Culler. "So you're from Florida," she said, accusingly. She associated everyone from Florida with her ex-husband's affair, since that was where he'd run off to.

"That's right," said Culler. "Orlando."

Florabelle waddled over to Culler to shake his hand. "Fern says you're going to college."

"That's right," said Culler.

Florabelle sneered at Jason, turned to Culler. "What are you studying at college?"

"Engineering."

"That must be interesting," said Florabelle. "You'll probably make lots of money." Again she frowned at Jason, scoffing.

"Florie, sit down," said Momma. "Birdie, pour your sister some milk. A full glass."

I sat down between Culler and Hazel.

As everyone got settled at the table, Culler fiddled with the salt and pepper shakers, trying to make small talk.

Birdie said grace, showing off.

Daddy usually did. He carved the meat.

"Is it too tough, Raymond?" asked Momma.

"No, Sylvia, it's fine."

Momma asked that same question every time we sat down to eat. Daddy would always tell her the meat was fine, even if it was charred or too rare.

"Pass the potatoes," said Jason.

"Wait for the company to get his first," said Florabelle.

"What company?" Jason scowled.

"Fern's friend." Florabelle smiled at Culler, set the bowl of potatoes down gently in front of him.

As the serving bowls were passed around the table, no one talked. Momma cleared her throat twice, breaking silence, and Jason belched once in his beer, breaking rules.

Except for the clinking plates and glasses, the room was quiet for five minutes maybe. I kept watching Culler for a sign, boredom, perhaps, or fear. I wondered how he must have felt, surrounded by us, realizing for the first time perhaps that at the end of some driveways are completely different worlds.

"Plane hit the control tower in Detroit, killed sixty folk, they think," Daddy said.

"God help 'em," said Momma, chewing fat.

"They don't make those airplanes safe enough to fly a mule," said Hazel.

"That ain't true," said Jason. "I flew up to Canada on an Eastern plane that had no trouble whatsoever."

"See, Hazel, them planes are fine for mules," said Florabelle, looking at Jason.

"Culler's dad works at the Space Center as an aeronautic engineer," I volunteered.

"Where in Canada did you fly?" Hazel asked Jason, ignoring what I said.

"Trenton," said Jason.

"That's on Lake Ontario, isn't it?" asked Culler.

"Sure is," said Florabelle. "Blew all his money on some dumb fishing trip."

"I brought you home some pretty good size trout, though, didn't I?" Jason swigged his beer, crushed the can, threw it at the trashcan by the garage door, missed.

"Go pick that up," said Momma.

"I could care less about fresh trout," said Florabelle. "If you hadn't blown your wad on that trip, we'd probably had a honeymoon."

"Well, we didn't need a honeymoon to get sparks a' flying, did we?" Jason leaned over, ribbed Culler and started heehawing like a mule.

"Cut that out," said Daddy. "We're at the table."

"Florabelle, you ain't touched your milk. Drink it up," said Momma. "Baby needs it."

"I'm so sick of folks telling me what this baby needs. What I'm saying *I* need is a honeymoon."

"Florabelle doesn't want her baby," Birdie told Culler.

"That's not so, Bird," said Momma, "she's just scared, it being her first."

"*I* want it," said Birdie.

"Birdie, a baby ain't no doll to play with," snapped Florabelle. "It's not like having a puppy either."

"When is the baby due?" asked Culler, being polite.

"Any damn day," said Florabelle.

Birdie looked at Culler. "Are you going to make Fern pregnant?"

"Birdie!" said Momma.

Culler smiled. "I only lured in the catch today."

Everyone looked at him.

I could feel my face flush.

"Speaking of fishing," said Momma, sensing my embarrassment, "Fern tells us you got hurt today."

"Yes, ma'am. I got a fishhook caught in my neck, but Fern got it out and put in stitches."

"*Fern* stitched you up?" asked Hazel.

"Why didn't you call Dr. Glenn?" asked Momma.

"We did. He was in Bowen," I said.

"You let *her* sew you up?" Jason used a fork with meat on the end of it to point at me.

"Sure did." Culler scooted his chair out a little for everyone to see his wound and admire my work.

"Get a load of that," said Florabelle.

Hazel got up to have a closer look. She leaned down over Culler's head and squinted. "Sylvia, come see this."

Momma and Hazel hovered over Culler, evaluating. He looked a bit self-conscious.

"Fern, did you use a closed cross-stitch or open-hole?"

"Open," I said.

"Birdie, go get your Aunt Hazel her glasses," said Hazel finally.

A few moments later, Birdie came back with Hazel's glasses. Hazel, Florabelle, Birdie, and Momma all gathered around him.

Looking through her bifocals, Hazel ran her finger lightly over Culler's stitches. "Did you double the thread, Fern?"

"No need to; it's nylon," I said.

"Tie off the knot?" she asked.

"No, not supposed to," I said.

Hazel stood there a few more minutes.

Culler kept his head bowed over his plate.

"I'll be damn. That's some needlework," said Hazel.

When they'd all sat back down, I looked across the table at Daddy. He was eating, not paying a bit of attention to any of us. "Culler's going to be an engineer," I said, signaling him to talk.

Daddy frowned when I kicked him under the table, and put down his fork. "Mechanical or electrical?" he asked.

Culler finished chewing a bit of food. "Architecture."

"Hmm," said Daddy. "I was just going to say there's some whippersnapper college kids down at the plant where I work in Service who think they're experts on everything. I never went to no college, and I know more about pump machinery and all their workings than any of them. You don't need college to know how to fix things."

"That's probably true," said Culler.

Jason reached across Culler for the salt. "If you're going to be fixing things, what you need is a hammer, not a college diploma. I always say there ain't nothing you can't fix with a hammer. If you can't repair it, then you can bust it up and throw it away." He reached again for the pepper.

"That's what he gave me for a wedding present," said Florabelle. "A goddamn hammer."

"Florabelle," scolded Momma.

"Well, that way if I ain't home and something breaks, you can fix it by yourself," argued Jason. "All it takes is a hammer and a steady hand to hold the nail head."

"I'm fixing to use that hammer on your head. Steady or not," said Florabelle. "And quit reaching over people. If you want something, then you ask somebody to pass it."

Jason stared at Culler. "Pass the turnips." Then he took another large helping and kept the serving spoon in his own plate. "What I'm saying is a hammer fixes everything." He turned to Florabelle and mumbled, "Everything but a broken record."

"Culler's planning to design and build," I said, "not fix."

"That'll be something," said Hazel. "Maybe you'll design homes for the movie stars. I once had a hair customer come through Dayton who claimed she'd decorated Lucille Ball's home in Beverly Hills."

"You can build houses?" Birdie asked Culler.

Culler smiled. "I'm learning how to."

"Jimmy needs a doghouse," she said.

Culler looked at me. "Maybe I'll survey the yard sometime and give you an estimate." He leaned forward and looked at Birdie, who was sitting on a phone book at the end of the table. "What do *you* want to be when you grow up, Birdie?" he asked.

"I am grown up," she said.

"What about when you're a big girl, like Fern? What do you want to do, then?" he asked again.

Birdie looked at me, hesitated. "I guess I'll do whatever I'm supposed to do."

"Birdie's going to surprise us all, I bet," said Hazel. "She'll go off and be a dress designer or a famous Hollywood cosmetologist."

Birdie frowned, still looking at me. "I don't have to go anywhere if I don't want to," she said.

"That's right," said Momma, "You can stay here and take care of your Grandma. That reminds me, Raymond, Mother needs more storage space. Her room is cramped. You reckon you could get down there sometime and put up a couple shelves? There's just no room for all her things."

Daddy looked at Momma, eyes narrowed. "I don't have the time."

"It wouldn't take you long, Raymond," said Hazel. "She just needs a couple small ones up over her bed."

"I said no," said Daddy.

"Daddy, Grandma needs shelves," said Birdie, defiantly.

"Don't sass me," said Daddy.

"Raymond," said Hazel, "you can't stay angry forever. It'll give you ulcers." She poked me under the table. "Talk to him, Fern."

I looked around the table; all eyes were on me. "Daddy," I started, "you're going to have to get over your mad. For everyone's sake. Grandma still needs our help."

"Oh, like the kind of help you were today?" he barked.

I took a deep breath. "It was just this once," I said. "And I wasn't gone long."

"All afternoon," he said.

"You know why I was late," I said, avoiding his eye.

"You didn't tell Momma where you were going," accused Birdie.

"Hush up!" I told her.

Everyone was still staring at me, except Culler, who was trying to concentrate on his food. Birdie started to sob.

"This is ridiculous," I said. "I go fishing for a few hours and you all act like I was gone a week."

"Raymond," said Hazel, "I agree with Fern, you can't carry this grudge towards Mother forever. All we're asking you to do is hang a shelf."

"Leave me out of this," said Daddy.

"Leave you out of it?" yelled Hazel. "If it weren't for you kicking her out of her house in the first place, we wouldn't be having all this trouble!"

"She had me arrested, for Christ's sake," yelled Daddy.

"She's sorry!" Birdie was bawling, now.

"I have an idea," said Florabelle. "Jason, since *you're* such a expert on *fixing* things, *you* do it. *You* have time. *You* go down there tomorrow after work and put Grandma up some shelves. I'll even let you borrow my hammer."

"She's no kin to me," said Jason.

Florabelle's face turned bright red. "SHE'S MY GRANDMOTHER AND YOU'RE MY HUSBAND!" she shouted.

"AND WHOSE IDEA WAS THAT?" yelled Jason. "You had to go and get yourself knocked up . . ."

"Pipe down, the both of you!" said Hazel.

Florabelle picked up her spoon and threw it across the table at Jason.

The spoon flew between Birdie and Jason and hit the refrigerator.

Birdie ducked, dodging the spoon, sat up and glared at Florabelle. "Pissant."

"Birdie, that's enough out of you, now," said Momma. "Drink the rest of your milk and go to your room. Hustle."

Birdie stood up, dumped the rest of her milk. It splattered to the floor.

"God help us," said Hazel.

"Hey!" yelled Daddy. His fists hit the table. "I've seen and heard enough!" His eyes were fierce. He looked at Birdie. "You quit your crying and clean that up!" He pointed a finger at Florabelle. "And you get up right now and pick up that spoon. And don't ever step foot in this house again if you're going to act like that."

Florabelle stood up, waddled over to the spoon, picked it up, hurled it in the sink. It clanked against the dishes and cracked a glass as it landed.

Momma gasped, looked at me.

I continued to eat, not flinching.

Culler, too, kept right on eating. He never looked up.

"That's it!" shouted Daddy. "Fern? You see what you stir up by going off horseplaying instead of being here where you supposed to be?" He scuffed his chair back, left the table.

Birdie was kneeling on the floor over the puddle of milk, her face streaked with tears, eyes red with anger. "See," she shouted. "If Fern can be grown up and stay here, so can I!"

Her reply hit me like a line drive in foul territory. I recognized for the second time just recently what my worth was as an individual. I had forfeited self. I was an assistant, everyone's helper. In the big game of life, I was second string.

I felt Culler's hand take mine under the table. He gave it a hard squeeze. I fought back tears.

"Jason, we better go," said Florabelle. "Thanks, Momma." As she passed by me, she touched my shoulder, lightly. "See ya, Fern."

Culler got up quickly to move his jeep.

When it was just me, Momma, and Hazel in the kitchen, Momma said, "Fern, you shouldn't have snapped at Birdie."

"She needs to grow up," I said.

"She's just little," said Momma.

"So was I once."

"Well, she don't understand what all's happening."

"Yes she does; that's just it." I rose from the table and went out through the garage to meet Culler.

He was still in his jeep, pulling it up closer to the house. "I guess I should go," he said.

I nodded. "I'm real sorry."

He reached out the window, laid his hand on my face, wiped away a tear. "It's not like you didn't warn me." Then he leaned out and kissed me lightly on the cheek. "I'm going to call you."

I looked up. "You sure you want to?"

He smiled, nodded, and this time leaned way out the open window, careful not to bend his neck, and kissed me hard on the mouth. "Remember," he said, "slow and steady."

18. Dollars and Scents

After the table had been cleared and all the dishes were put away, I went upstairs to find Daddy. I didn't think that everything that had happened at dinner was all my fault, and I wanted it settled.

Daddy had a room upstairs in the back of the house where he, alone, enjoyed a hobby. Daddy collected guns. He had revolvers and rifles, some bolt-action, and he would spend hours polishing the stocks. He would clean the barrels, align shells among other miscellaneous projectiles, and peer through the site at simulated danger around the room. Every gun had an appointed storage or display location, whether in the cabinet, vault, or drawers; and the workbench was draped with royal blue velvet for examining pieces of particular interest.

He had a favorite, a Smith and Wesson that he believed resembled a Colt Gold Inlaid of 1851, popular during the Civil War. This treasure, kept in a safe-lock leather case with a large gold embossed "R," brought Daddy supreme joy. Its chambers, he boasted, were grand enough to sip brandy through.

Daddy had collected guns for fifteen years now, and Momma still strongly objected to his fascination, forbade Birdie from coming into the room, argued that the room should instead accommodate sewing and embroidering activities, and feared for our lives. She was constantly leaving articles from *Ladies' Home Journal* on the back of the toilet, about guns going off accidentally and killing entire families.

Daddy had a .22 fully disassembled when I walked into the room.

"Cleaning the barrel?" I asked him.

"Just messing," he said, not looking up at me. "Kitchen cleared?"

"Yes."

"Birdie in bed?"

"Sound asleep."

I noted how carefully he turned the gun parts over in his hand, as if they were precious gems. I didn't know how to ask what I wanted so I just stood there a few moments, watching him.

"What is it?" he finally asked.

"I was just wondering why you were so angry with me at dinner."

"This house was in an uproar this afternoon."

"That's not my fault."

"If you'd been here, you could have kept everything from getting out of hand. Running off fishing was fool-hardy."

"That's not true. This all has to do with Grandma, not me. She's not liking it at the home. That's got Momma and Hazel upset. And Birdie misses her."

"Everybody's got to get used to it."

"Don't you even worry about her?" I asked.

"I got enough to worry about here."

"Well, it's going to be quite some time for everyone to get used to Grandma and Florabelle living somewhere else."

He finally looked up at me, laid down the gun. "There're other factors involved." He sighed.

I looked at him, waited.

"Things aren't so good down at the plant. Jobs aren't coming in. They're automating the manufacturing process so much, they won't need us all. First layoffs are hitting Tuesday."

"Aren't you union?"

"Yeah, but that only guarantees pay rates."

I looked at his face, his eyes lined with fatigue and worry. "Is *your* job in jeopardy?"

He sighed. "I've only got a little over three years in. There's some guys down there with thirty years."

"Why don't they retire those folks?"

"There's talk. They might put us on a rotating layoff. One week of the month, cut the hours back."

"Without pay?"

He nodded.

"You'll know Tuesday?"

He nodded again. "Hazel may need to pay me a little more for her share."

"Why don't you try selling that little house, now that Grandma has moved out of it?"

"No one is going buy a house up in these parts. I don't know why we made that investment in the first place. It needs a lot of work anyway. Needs all new shingles." He took a pipe out of the top drawer, packed it, put it back.

He'd quit smoking, but it had been a struggle for him.

"And it's costing us to keep your grandmother up there at Peaceful," he continued. "She ought to appreciate it." On the corner of his desk was an antiquated adding machine. He turned it on, punched in some numbers. "You may have to help more, too, Fern."

"I do more than my share here."

"I mean with the bills. Can you ask Clem for some more hours?"

"Maybe."

He tore a section of tape off the machine, jotted down some figures on a notepad. Then he looked at me, narrowed his eyes. "A few more dollars coming in from you would sure help."

"I'll see," I said, and turned to go. I wanted to be alone, do some thinking. I knew that he was concerned about the money, but it really bothered me that he could just ignore what was going on with Grandma. He seemed so heartless.

"Fern?"

"Yeah?"

"No need to mention any of this to your Momma until we know something."

I nodded.

"She don't need to be worrying."

"Okay."

"And Fern?"

"What?"

"Don't be getting any big ideas in your head about traipsing off to school."

I was already halfway out the door when he said this. I stopped, frowned. "What are you talking about?"

"Well, if you're going to be hanging around that boy, he might try and talk you into something."

"I just met him, and no one's said word one about me going to school."

"All I'm doing is warning you. We need the extra dollars around here, and besides that," he said, "you ain't right for it."

"Ain't right for what?" I asked, still annoyed.

"College."

"I said it's not even an issue. But why do you say it wouldn't it be right for me? I made mostly A's in high school."

"You just wouldn't fit in," he said. "Like you do here."

I shut the door and walked down the hall towards my bedroom. Jimmy was lying in front of Birdie's door, whining and pawing. I wondered why she had shut him out; she usually slept with him. I bent down, scooped up his wiggly body and carried him to my room.

It was too hot and sticky to put on a nightgown, so I slipped on a cotton camisole over my underwear. I slid under the covers and situated Jimmy at my feet. In spite of the heat, it felt good to have his warm little body snuggled up against me; it softened the emptiness. Grandma should have a dog, I thought, a constant companion to fill her new void.

I listened to the darkness. With Florabelle gone, the room seemed deserted. It even smelled empty. Every night before going to sleep, she would spread Chantilly moisturizing lotion all over herself, and climb in bed naked under the window. The breeze would blow across her, and the floral scent would fill the room.

I lay listening for the familiar scratch of the creeping Charlie on the window, but the wind was still and the air was silent. I reached down and rubbed Jimmy's belly. He raised his head, nestled it in the bend of my knees. "If I get to go fishing again, you can come," I told him.

Today had been adventurous, daring on my part to take a few hours for myself. But to everyone else, I was thoughtless and rash. I was ashamed of the scene at dinner, and I felt even more lonely, realizing that I'd probably never see Culler again because of it. Spoons had sailed, beer cans soared, milk spattered, and profanity hurled, but my short absence from home today had been deemed the most reckless behavior of all.

I'd got a chance to play, and I'd struck out. I was more valuable on the bench, keeping it warm, than out playing in the field. Scoring, in my case, would never mean running over home plate, but running away from it.

Something else had happened, had calmed the evening storm for one brief moment. Tonight, I had been kissed for the very first time. And my family's languishing effect had dampened the moment. My spirit, sparked for the first time, had almost instantly ceased to burn. Momma had yelled for me to come in to bathe Birdie, as Culler had been leaning towards my face a second time.

My thoughts were interrupted by a knock and Jimmy raised his head, alert.

"Come in," I called.

It was Birdie. When she opened my door, I could see her silhouette from the light in the hallway.

"What is it?" I asked.

"I can't sleep without Jimmy," she said. Her little voice was husky from crying.

"He's in here with me," I said. "You can take him."

"Is he asleep?" she asked, still from the doorway.

I looked down at Jimmy whose ears were perked. He was more than likely curious about this late-night activity.

"He's lying down but seems a little restless. Probably misses you," I said.

Birdie stepped into the dark room and closed the door. She never came over for Jimmy, but I heard Florabelle's mattress springs squeak, then Birdie's hand patting the mattress, for Jimmy to come.

He jumped down from my bed, and a few seconds later, I heard him hop up to Florabelle's and sigh. His oily odor was no match for Florabelle's Chantilly lotion, but the faint snoring from the two others was a welcoming sound.

19. Gauging Age

Tuesday came and went, and Daddy survived the layoff at work. But they had cut his overtime option out completely. Birdie started back to school the same day, and that was also the day I asked Clem for some extra hours. He said he could try giving me eight more a week, but that was all he could afford.

Clem's was a full-service station; he did basic repairs and engine maintenance. He had a good reputation in the area, did a lot of work on plows and tractors. It seemed, though, in the past year, that there just wasn't much of a demand for plain service stations anymore; everyone was going where they could buy gas, beer, and cigarettes all in one stop, and were taking their cars back to the dealerships for repair work.

I had been helping him out at the pumps for over three years now, and most of Clem's customers were regulars who had been coming to him for years and felt obligated to come back. The Redimarts and Circle Ks in the nearby towns were killing Clem's business. And that was killing Clem. He'd aged more in the past year than he had in ten, folks said.

In July, he had printed up some calendars and tried giving them out to customers as sort of a promotional thing, but it didn't seem to bring in any more business. I kept on him to try selling a few grocery items, but it was out of the question. He was running a gas station, not a supermarket.

He had given me the keys to his truck that morning and had sent me to Winchester to stock up on radial tires. I had the windows rolled all the way down and the radio turned up loud on a pop station when I heard a horn honk in the lane next to me. It was Brother Brewer, cruising along in his convertible. He waved as he whizzed by me and I wondered if there was anything to that rumor about him and Patty Prettyman Greene. Surely a twenty-year-old married woman wouldn't be after a crazy old guy like Brewer.

But then again, I thought, love *is* crazy, all by itself. From what I could ever see, love seemed to be a disguise for something else. In Momma and Daddy's case, love's mask was duty. For Jason and Florabelle, it was spite.

It had been almost a week since I'd heard from Culler. But I wasn't at all surprised. He had acted upon a whim, I supposed, to want to spend a day in the country with a local girl. Curiosity is an urge, like lust, that builds up to a break-ing point and busts. Culler'd met his urge. He'd lain in the tall grass of the foothills, tasted the earthiness of a real farmer's daughter, and had left lip prints to mark his tracks.

The sign ahead read: "Them That Belief Are Saved TIRES." I pulled into the store parking lot and went inside. Clem had an account there, and I waited as two young boys filled the back of the truck with tires. It didn't take long; I signed for them, tipped the boys, and drove away. Heading back through Pilotview, I stopped at a trailer that was parked on the side of the road, selling candy, and bought a Mars bar.

Not too far back along the road, I again saw Brewer's mustang zip through an intersection, and, sure enough, there was a young woman seated next to him. He was driving so fast that I couldn't make out who it was, but it was a female all right, long blond hair blowing everywhere from under-neath a scarf. I remembered seeing Patty Prettyman Greene at Florabelle's wedding, and she *did* have blond hair.

I looked down at the dashboard clock; it was not even noon. Since I was so close by, I decided to stop in at the nursing home and visit Grandma. It was lunchtime at Peaceful, and I found her sitting in the dining room, still in her bathrobe, at a table by herself. I went and sat down beside her, trying to sneak up from behind and surprise her.

"What are you doing here in the middle of the day?" she asked, putting down her fork. "Clem fire you?"

"No, Grandma," I said. "Why would I be wearing one of his uniforms if I wasn't working for him?" I gave her a little hug, poured myself a glass of iced tea from a pitcher sitting on the table. "Besides, you know Clem would never fire me. I'm worth too much to him."

She watched me raise the glass to my lips. "I wouldn't drink that if I were you."

I took a sip. "Why not?"

"Could be poison."

"Grandma, don't act silly. Why aren't you eating?"

"Food's no good here. They hardly use any salt. Everything tastes blah."

"Salt it yourself. You've got to eat." I passed her the salt shaker in the shape of rooster.

"I'd rather starve than to eat this garbage." She pushed a plate of a half-eaten grilled cheese sandwich and bowl of tomato soup towards the center of the table.

"Well, if you're not going to eat it, I will." I reached for the sandwich, took a bite, chewed it well, as if it tasted great, and I took another bite.

She watched me eat the rest of her sandwich, silent.

I made every mouthful seem delicious. Not until I had eaten the whole thing and had wiped the crumbs from my mouth did I ask her, "How come you're not sitting with anyone?"

White-haired people occupied tables of four and six. Idle chat, wheezing, and clanking dishes were the sounds that filled the room at a medium buzz.

"I don't care to talk to any of these people. Half of them can't talk right anyway," said Grandma.

"I hear conversations."

"They don't make sense."

"I'm sure some of them do."

"Not many. Everybody's just here to die." A tear slipped out of the corner of her eye. She let it fall, staring straight ahead.

I swallowed hard. I didn't want to look right at her, so I gazed around the room. It was depressing, all the hunched-over backs, drooling mouths, occasional efforts failing to lift food from plates.

I reached over and touched her hand. "You're really going to have to try to make do, Grandma. For your own sake, make some friends."

She nodded, her hand trembling.

"Come on," I said. "Cheer up; you'll do fine here. Give it a chance." I gave her hand a little squeeze.

"Just look at these old hands of mine," she sobbed, "they're so old."

I turned both of my palms up. Grease discolored them, two or three layers deep. "Look at mine, they're as wrinkled as yours, and I'm a quarter of your age. You can't measure age by what's in front of you, it's what's inside you. It's how you feel. You taught me that." I took her hand again, held it to my chest a few seconds, then did the same to her chest. "Feel that? Our hearts are ticking at the same rate. You're only as old as your heart tells you."

"I always told your Momma that age wrinkles the skin, but giving up wrinkles the soul," she said.

"That's right, you told us that too, me and Florabelle. You also used to say, 'You're as young as your confidence and as old as your doubt.'"

We sat there a while longer, comparing. When the servers had cleared most of the plates away and the wheelchair patients had been taken out, I saw her, out of the corner of my eye, slip her dinner knife into the pocket of her robe. She was quick about it. It made me curious, but I decided not to say anything to her.

I kissed her good-bye on the cheek, left her sitting there alone just as I had found her. I needed to get back to the station; Clem would be waiting for his truck so he could go home for lunch.

In the lobby, I passed Mossie Greene. She was parked at the front door, shredding a handful of tissues on her lap.

"Hello, there, Mossie," I said.

"Patty?"

"No, it's Fern, Esther's granddaughter. How are you?"

She gathered up a few pieces of the tissue, tried to hand them to me. "I'm still trying to get this scarf done for my son, Larry," she said. Suddenly, she starting whimpering.

I kneeled down next to her. "What scarf?" I asked.

She pointed to the pile of light-blue, shredded Kleenex. "This one," she sobbed. "Patty took my needles away from

She fondled the tissue, worked it hard between her fingers.

I reached in my pocket, pulled out my tire gauge and handed to Mossie. "Here," I said, "use this needle. It's already threaded. Now you can finish the scarf."

She took the gauge, gripped it, smiled. Then she began tapping it loudly, in rapid succession, on the arm of her wheelchair. As she tapped, she banged out the rhythm of her speech. "This will do it," she chanted, "I will finish."

I walked away after that, but she continued with her cadence. The other patients began to yell at her to quiet down, and one of the staff assistants came over to try to control her. But she kept her sequence flowing.

As I was leaving the building, I heard her shout and drum, "I AM NOT OLD."

20. The Pecan Tree

I was in the middle of measuring Birdie's chest when the phone rang. She had been giving me the silent treatment ever since the night Culler was over, so I had offered to make that dress for her, the one I had committed myself to at the wedding reception, thinking that might bring her back around. She needed clothes for school anyway, so I thought I'd start with the new dress. She wanted it to be green, and we had gone to Cloth World the night before and picked out the material.

"Hold still," I told her.

"I want to get the phone," she said. I had lassoed her with a tape measure, and she was trying to break free.

"Momma will pick it up," I said.

"It might be Grandma," said Birdie.

"She'll let you talk to her if it is. Put your arms up over your head."

She squirmed. Momma had picked up the phone in the kitchen, and Birdie leaned towards the door, trying to listen.

"You're going to stick yourself with a pin if you don't hold still," I warned her.

Suddenly, Momma burst into the living room. I had already pinned down most of the pattern for a second dress, with the fabric rolled out on the floor, and Momma ran right across it.

"Watch it," I said, biting a straight pin.

"Is it Grandma?" asked Birdie.

"It was Jason," said Momma, panting. "Florabelle's had a girl. She's at the hospital in Stanton."

Birdie jumped down off the ottoman, forgetting about the pins, and stabbed her underarm. "Ouch," she said, turning to frown at me. "Can we go see her?"

"We have to wait 'til tonight, Bird, when Daddy or Hazel get home with a car," said Momma.

"Is the baby okay?" I asked.

"Jason said she was in a fine fettle, but Florie was sickly. Something about inducing labor."

"Jason's there with her?" I asked.

"He was heading on back to work. Says they gave her a pill to knock her out for a while."

"What's the baby's name?" asked Birdie.

Momma looked puzzled. "You know, I don't rightly know. Jason didn't say. He seemed disappointed it wasn't a boy." She stood there a few more seconds, frowning. "Fern, did you ever hear Florabelle say what she was going to name it?"

I shook my head, started packing up my sewing box.

"Well, I didn't either," said Momma. "I hope she thought of something. Bird, why don't you give Hazel a ring at work and tell her about the baby. She can tell your Grandma."

Just then, we heard a loud commotion outside in the backyard. It sounded like several barking dogs. Birdie, wearing nothing but her underwear, ran out.

I ran to the window to look. A pack of strays was on Jimmy. He yelped defensively and disappeared in a whirl of hair and gnashing teeth. Heidi, sensing the danger of the situation, ran wildly about. One of the dogs lurched and pounced on her. Birdie was screaming at the top of her lungs and throwing rocks at the dogs.

"God Almighty," said Momma, standing next to me. She cranked open the window and yelled at Birdie to get back inside.

I ran upstairs to Daddy's room, and grabbed a sawed-off shotgun that stood behind the door. I checked the barrel; it was loaded. As fast as I could, I ran downstairs and out the garage door.

I pointed the gun straight into the air and fired. The wild dogs ran back down into the hollow. I looked down at the ground. Jimmy lay in a mangled heap, and Heidi, bleeding from a severe tear in her side, stood over him, sniffing, licking his disorganized little wounds.

It was obvious that nothing could be done for him, but poor Heidi, whining in her grief and pain, looked as though she might have a chance.

Birdie dropped to the ground in front of them, crying into the weeds. Momma had come out and knelt down beside her, stroking her back. She, too, was crying.

I wanted so badly to bury Jimmy, to get him out of Birdie's sight, but I knew I had to help Heidi before it was too late.

I sniffed hard. "Momma, take Bird inside. I'm going to run down to Clem's and get his truck. Heidi needs help fast."

When I told Clem what had happened, he locked up the station and put the "CLOSED" sign in the window. He drove me back up the hill to the house, and together we hoisted Heidi to the back of his truck.

I went back inside to check on Birdie. Momma had carried her into the house, had her lying on the sofa.

"Momma," I said, "go downstairs and get me an old blanket for Heidi." It was hard for me to think straight, I was still in shock.

Momma disappeared down the steps and in a few minutes came huffing back up with a quilt. I recognized it as the one the old woman had given me at the first garage sale we'd stopped at that day, looking for a wedding gown. I had meant to give it to Florabelle for the baby.

Momma and I wrapped up Heidi's wound as tightly as possible with some old scrap rags, then worked the quilt up under her in the truck. Neither one of us said a word.

Meanwhile, Clem had gone around back to dig a hole for Jimmy. When he returned, his eyes were red. "I got him buried, yonder behind Hazel's trailer," he said to Momma. "You may want to go back there and pack the dirt down harder." He dropped his head. "He's by that pecan tree." Clem took a handkerchief out of his pocket and wiped his forehead. "There'll be buzzards," he added.

Momma nodded, coughed.

"Momma, run in there and call Dr. Erikson. Tell him we're on our way."

I rode in the back of the truck with Heidi to keep her from sliding around. Her breathing was erratic, and she whimpered quietly. I supported her head in my lap, smoothing down the hair on her head. "Hang in there, old girl," I told her. "You hang in there." She rolled her big blank eyes up towards my voice; they were wide, fearful, searching. I soothed her the whole way there, praying softly.

When we got to Dr. Erikson's house, Heidi was barely breathing. Clem and the doctor got her inside, laid her on a folding table in the garage. Immediately, Dr. Erikson gave her a tranquilizer, and started to take care of the wound.

Clem and I sat down on two lawn chairs and waited in silence. I couldn't seem to get the image of poor little Jimmy out of my mind. I couldn't tell if the pain I felt was a stomach affliction or heartache. It just didn't seem fair, after what we had gone through to keep him. I remembered Birdie telling me, when we couldn't decide what to do about Heidi's pups, that God didn't put babies here just to die. I'd agreed, had called it bad luck. Now I was beginning to wonder.

"Good thing the old doc was home," Clem said finally.

I nodded, looked around me. All three walls of the garage were covered with faded-out photos and posters of racehorses. There was one picture of Dr. Erikson in a white lab coat, standing next to Willie Shoemaker and Swaps, his racehorse, winner of the 1955 Kentucky Derby. Dr. Erikson wore a medal around his neck, and was pointing to a stethoscope that was hanging around Swaps's neck. I realized, just then, we had no pictures of Jimmy. Heidi, either.

"Fern," called the doctor, breaking my trance. "Can you come here a minute?"

I rose from my chair, looked over at Clem who nodded for me to go on back. I walked over to the table where Dr. Erikson was working.

"She's going to make it," he said. "The tear wasn't as deep as it looked, no damage to any organs. She'll be sore a long time, and you'll need to keep her inside, but she'll heal eventually. Nasty bite, though. Has she been vaccinated against rabies lately?" The doctor worked at the last of the stitches.

"I think it was only a year ago," I said, "but check her anyway." I sighed, relieved, reached down and petted Heidi's head. She was sleeping, at peace. "She's a real fighter," I said.

"She's a strong one, all right," he said. "Nothing but muscle, this one." He looked at me, his brows crossed. "Brave, too, I guess."

I nodded, told him the story.

He seemed sincerely sorry. "How long has she been blind?"

"She was born that way." I said. "We had an old dog on our farm in Ohio who had a litter when she was real old. Two pups were stillborn, this one was blind. We felt sorry for her, so we kept her. Turned out to be a pretty good hunter too, in spite of us pitying her."

"Was her pup blind?"

"Jimmy? No." It still hurt to mention him. "He was the smartest of the litter." I remembered the day he'd climbed in the truck tire to hide from us. "He could see all right," I said and turned away.

Dr. Erikson waited a few minutes to continue his questioning. He worked quietly; we had been there almost an hour. I stood behind him, arms folded, watching him tie off the last stitches.

Clem rested his head on the back of the lawn chair, eyes

closed, legs stretched out in front of him.

"How old is she?" the doctor finally asked.

"About seven years."

"She shouldn't be having any more litters, you know," said Dr. Erikson.

"I know. It's a problem for us," I said.

"Tell you what," he said. "You leave the old girl with me about a week, I got a pen out back. I'll keep a close eye on her, then when she's up to it, I'll spay her. No charge."

I looked at him, flabbergasted. I didn't know how to react. "Are you sure you don't mind having to take care of her?"

He shook his head. "There's a catch to the deal, though," he said.

"What's that?" I asked.

"When she's ready for spaying, you're to come back here and help me, learn how to do it."

I looked at him, puzzled.

"You seem to have a knack for this kind of thing," he said, putting away his tools. "I watched you stitch that boy up that day down at the station. You know what you're doing. Wouldn't hurt you to learn a few more practical skills, especially if you're a quick start." He watched my face.

I looked at the sleeping Heidi, patted her ruffled hair.

"We got a deal?" he asked.

"I don't know if I can do that," I said.

"Sure you can," he said. "You got a good mind, steady hands. Do yourself a favor, go find a library and check out some basic books on biology. Read up on the reproductive system, try to get familiar with the terms. I'm going to help you." He had begun cleaning up where he had operated.

It seemed an odd offer, but one worth taking. Spaying Heidi would save us a lot of worry at home. Sewing was sewing, I supposed. The books would help. And he had a point, I had done an okay job on Culler. "I'll try it," I said. "When do I come back?"

"A week from today. Meantime, I'll take good care of her here."

I thanked him and went to rouse Clem.

"How much do we owe you?" I asked the doctor as we were leaving.

"We'll work it out next week," he said. He shook hands with Clem, said good-bye, winked at me. "You get to a library now."

I nodded.

On the way home, Clem never spoke. When we got to house, he said, "You want tomorrow off?"

"No, I'll be there. Thanks, Clem."

"Hey, don't mention it." He waved, shooing me out of his truck.

"Clem?"

"What now?" He looked tuckered out.

"Tell your wife Florabelle had a baby girl," I said, slammed the door, and went inside.

21. Across The Woods

All the books on uteri were on the top shelf. I looked around and found one of those little footstools the librarians stand on to shelve books. I pulled down a book called *Biology of the Uterus*, looked in the index under H for Hysterectomy, discovered over three hundred listings. Then I found a vacant sofa and sat down to read.

It was a Saturday afternoon, and I was in the Transylvania University Library, reading up on how to spay a bloodhound. I tucked my feet under me, tried to get comfortable, but the sofa was stiff and seemed new. I didn't remember all this furniture from before. I used to come here pretty often when we first moved to Leeco.

Back before I got hired on at Clem's and had more free time, I'd come in and just read mystery novels. Of course I wasn't allowed to check out books and take them home; you had to be a student. So I'd just catch an early bus to Lexington on Saturday mornings, come here and spend the day reading, then ride home. I think some of the library staff had caught on to what I was doing, but they had never said anything. Whenever I couldn't find something, they were always very helpful.

I turned to the table of contents and read all the chapter titles. I would never have guessed that anyone could write so much about fallopian tubes. It seemed odd this time to be here to study something, not to just read to pass the time. I felt like a real college student.

I looked around me. There was only a handful of students reading and searching through the narrow rows of books, but it was the weekend, and Transylvania was a small school to begin with. It was a four-year liberal arts college, but the average enrollment was only about a thousand. Back when I first started coming here, I used to pick up brochures at the check-out desk, pretending to look for enrollment information. It seemed silly, knowing full well we'd never have the money for me to go to college, but I used to have fun imagining.

The name Transylvania always fascinated me. Not because it made me think of Count Dracula, but because the word comes from a Latin phrase meaning, "across the woods." I looked it up once. It seemed to suit the name of a college perfectly, because from my experience, any place or opportunity out of reach, going to college to name one, always seemed to be across the woods. Just too far away.

Another neat thing about the school was that it was established by Daniel Boone in 1780, over two hundred years ago. I always believed him to be the most courageous of all pioneers. Secretly, he was my hero. I always admired his legendary frontier spirit and the way he outsmarted the Indians. He was a much better hunter than he was a student, history books say, and yet he founded this school, the first medical school west of the Allegheny Mountains. I liked that about him. I wished I'd known him.

I had got through almost two chapters when a girl in a red Transy T-shirt walked by carrying an armload of books. She looked vaguely familiar, but I didn't know anyone in Lexington. I read the spines of her books. Accounting and

Finance, mostly. Watching her struggle with the load, I wondered if she had to read them all today.

Suddenly her stack gave way. I don't know if she stumbled on the corner of the rug or what, but the top three or four books fell off her pile and crashed to the floor. The library ceilings were high, and the noise of the drop echoed off the tall shelves.

She looked embarrassed, tried to lower the rest of the books down to the floor and pick up the ones that had fallen.

I got up from the sofa. "Here," I said, picking up some, "where are you sitting? I'll carry them for you."

She smiled, thanked me, and pointed with her chin in the direction of her table.

I followed along. "You have to read all these?" I asked.

"No; I'm writing a case study." She panted. "This is research."

When we got back to her seat, she dumped the books onto the table. Again, the noise echoed. I quietly set down the ones I had carried.

"Thanks again," she said, poking out her lip and sending a large breath of air up to her bangs. Her face was splotched.

I was glad I didn't have to do whatever it was she had to. "Good luck," I said.

"I'm going to need it. I don't even understand any of this garbage." She wiped her forehead, sorted books. "Have you taken Basic Accounting with Milstead?"

I shook my head.

"You've heard of him, haven't you?"

"I think so," I said, and turned away.

"He's whacko. Just wait," she said. "I can't grasp anything from that space case. My brother's supposed to meet me here later and tutor me. Better hope you never get Milstead."

"Thanks for the warning," I said. "See you." I went back to my sofa and sat down. She still seemed familiar to me, but I couldn't place her face. She'd been pleasant, down-to-earth, not like some of the kids I'd run across on the campus, who were snobby to me, eyeing my clothes, hair, or whatever it was that didn't meet their approval.

I felt bad telling her a white lie, acting like I was in school, but I knew I'd never have to see her again. Although she probably could have made a nice friend.

That was something I really missed. In Ohio, I had had a lot of girlfriends my age, ones I'd gone to highschool with, girls I'd known from Four-H.

Now, I really had no friends, except Clem. And Brother Brewer, if a fellow car hound counted. I had felt especially lonely that night, when Clem had dropped me off after coming back from Dr. Erikson's. Momma and Hazel had gone to the hospital to see Florabelle and the baby. Birdie was asleep on the sofa; Momma had made her drink a remedy she'd concocted to get her to quit crying and get some rest. It consisted of lemon juice, warm milk, and whiskey, did about the same job as Nyquil would have, but Momma had no confidence in over-the-counter medications.

When Daddy came home, I told him about the stray dogs, broke the news about Jimmy and Heidi. He didn't say much, just wanted to know in which direction they'd run off. Momma called later that night and asked Daddy to bring some of her clothes to Florabelle and Jason's. She was going to go home and stay with them a few days, until Florabelle felt better.

So I was left all alone. I really wanted someone to talk to that night, but there wasn't anyone. That's when I really started wishing for a friend, some girl my age, besides Florabelle, to talk to. The house was dead quiet. Anyway, silence in the house, instead of calming, was disturbing. Our home, in such a short time, had gone from a sanitarium to a mortuary.

I turned to Chapter Three on reproductive organs, skimmed through the pictures. I was surprised to discover that a uterus looked like an upside-down pear. I guess I'd never given it much thought before. I turned the book upside down, studied the illustration.

"Fern," said someone, standing before me.

I looked over my book. My heart stopped. It was Culler.

He smiled at me. "What are you doing here?" he asked, tilting his head to read the title of my book.

I slammed the book closed, set it down beside me, face-down. "Reading," I said, shocked to see him. I took a deep breath, paused, waited to regain my composure. After a few moments of him just standing there, arms folded, looking down at me, I said, "I'm trying to get a little background information to perform an operation on an animal."

"Well," he said, reaching to rub his neck, "you've had experience on a human, so I'm sure you can handle an animal just fine."

"I'm sure I can, too," I said.

"It's all healed up, you know," he said, turning for me to see. "Just a little scar now."

"That's good," I said. Of course *my* scar was still there, I thought. I hadn't yet healed from being blown off by this guy.

"How's your family?" he asked.

I couldn't tell if he was being sarcastic or not. "Everyone's fine," I said. "How's school? I thought you told me you're going to U of K."

"I do."

"What are you doing here at Transy, then?" I asked.

"Helping my sister with some accounting homework. She's over there." He pointed.

I followed his finger. It was the girl with all the books. Then I realized where I'd seen her before. She had been in the jeep with him, in the backseat, when they'd come through for gas at Clem's that first time.

She was watching us. She waved when I looked.

I smiled faintly, nodded. "So," I turned back to Culler. "You miss your girlfriend?"

He rolled his eyes. "May I sit down?" he asked.

Reluctantly, I scooted over on the sofa, made room.

"Look, Fern, I know you're probably a little bitter at me for never calling you, when I said I would, but—"

"Who's bitter?" I said, perhaps too quickly. "All we did was go fishing."

"Yeah, but I did want to see you again." He looked

128

down, picked up my book, flipped aimlessly through the pages. He stopped on a page that showed an exploded view of a penis and testicles; the veins were labeled. "I thought you wanted to see me again, too," he said.

There was a guy sitting on the chair across from us. I could tell he was listening. I spoke softly. "Well, it's been a couple of weeks. You never called. Can't say I blame you, though." I looked back over towards his sister. She was leaning on one elbow, tapping her eraser on the table. "Your sister's waiting on you," I said.

"She'll be fine. She's supposed to be reading, anyway." He looked back at her, held up a finger to tell her just a minute. "Fern, what do you mean, you can't blame me for not calling you?"

"Well, the way my family is. It's easy to understand how you wouldn't want to get involved with our bunch."

"Fern, that's just it. I wanted to see you, and I've thought about you a lot, really. Last week, I even filled my gas tank just enough to get to your station so when I got there, I'd have to stop in and fill up again." He sighed. "Then, well, it was just I got the clear impression your family didn't want me, or anyone, hanging around. So I guess I didn't want to create any problems for you." He put his hand on my shoulder, drew me close to him.

I moved away, shot a look at the guy sitting across from us.

He looked back down at his magazine.

"I know how important your family is to you, Fern," said Culler. "I just didn't want to make any more waves." He leaned forward, looked at me, waited for a response. "Understand?"

I shrugged.

"Come on," he said, suddenly standing up, "meet my sister."

I hesitated.

"Come on." His eyes pleaded.

Against my better judgment, I picked up my book and followed Culler over to where the girl was sitting.

"Connie, this is that girl, Fern, I was telling you about. The fishing trip?"

Connie looked at Culler, eyes wide. "She's the one?"
She grinned. "You're the one who hooked my brother?"

I nodded.

"He told me about you stitching him back together in a
gas station. That's great." She started laughing out loud.

"Shhhh," said Culler, "this is a library." He put his hand
over Connie's mouth. "Here's an idea," he whispered.
"Let's all read for another hour or so, then I'll treat you both
to lunch."

"I can't get this paper done in an hour," said Connie,
still too loudly.

"I'll help you," said Culler.

"I have to finish this book today," I said.

"The whole thing?" Culler looked at me, frowned.

I looked down. "I don't have a library card here."

"Connie can check it out for you," said Culler. "Take it
home and read it, bring it back sometime."

"You mean *on* time," said Connie. She looked at me
and smiled. "Actually, I don't mind. If it's late, you pay the
fine."

"I'll have it back," I said. "Thanks."

An hour later, we were seated in a cozy booth at an
Italian restaurant in the Lexington Festival Market, sharing
a pitcher of beer.

"So who are you neutering?" asked Connie, leaning into
her straw. She sipped hard, paging through the illustrations
in my book.

"Our dog, Heidi," I said. "She's getting too old to have
another litter. A friend of ours is a veterinarian. He wants
to teach me how to do it. Can't say I'm thrilled about it, but
I guess it will be interesting." I glanced across the table at
Culler, who was busy twirling spaghetti noodles around a
large spoon. "Who knows, learning how to do this kind of
operation may serve a bigger purpose one day."

"Somebody told me once that country people neuter
their cows by tying a string around their balls so tight they
just drop off from no circulation," said Connie.

Culler put down his spoon and fork, looked up.

"That's true. In some parts." I grinned. *"Parts of the*

country, that is. My Daddy always neutered our bulls, but he used a more scientific method. Razor blades."

Connie reached for another breadstick. "He'd cut them right off, just like that?"

"Do we have to talk about this?" asked Culler.

Connie laughed, slurped some more beer.

I'd never met anyone who drank beer through a straw. I was starting to like her.

"So, Fern, when are you going to take us *all* fishing?" she asked.

I looked at Culler. "I don't know if Culler would risk it again with me."

Culler sipped beer, licked the corners of his mouth. "I'd go," he said. "As long as someone brings a first-aid kit."

"Let's go tomorrow. It's Sunday," said Connie. "I'll pack a lunch, and we could come pick you up at that station where you work. What time are you off?"

"I don't work Sundays. But we have church," I said.

"Well, after that," said Connie.

"What's that state park you were telling us about that time we stopped in for gas?" asked Culler. "Let's go there. If we don't catch fish, at least we could have a good time exploring."

"Natural Bridge," I said. "The one your girlfriend wanted to go to."

"Oh, that bitch," said Connie. She looked over at Culler, sneered.

He ignored her. "Will you go, Fern?"

"I really do want to, but my sister just had a baby, and my Momma's with her helping out. Someone has to take care of Birdie." I really did want to go, but I knew what was facing me at home.

"Who's Birdie?" asked Connie.

"Her little sister," said Culler. "She's a cutie. Fern, we could bring her with us."

I thought about that a second; that could work maybe. "I don't know if that would be such a good idea," I said.

"She'd have a great time," said Culler.

"How old is she?" asked Connie.

"Eight," I said.

"Well, then, that's okay. As long as we won't be having to change diapers all day," she said.

"No diapers," I assured her. "It's just that her puppy just died. She's real upset. It may be hard to keep her interested in anything."

"That little dog died?" asked Culler, frowning. "So that blind one is the mother?"

I nodded.

"The one you're fixing?" asked Connie.

"Yes, she got hurt, too. A pack of strays came through. Attacked them both."

"That's sad," said Connie, stirring her third beer. "Don't you have a fenced yard?"

I shook my head. "We're going to have to do something for Heidi, though, to protect her. I haven't figured that one out yet."

No one spoke for a while, we just listened to the radio over the speakers. I really liked them both, and for a reason I couldn't understand, I felt at ease with them. And I barely knew them; they were from completely different walks of life than mine. They were, in essence, from across the woods.

"We'll go Sunday," I said. "Meet us at Clem's."

22. Gone Fishing

Birdie sat cross-legged in the center of her bed with Waylon Jennings.

"Bird, come on," I said. "You love to fish."

"I don't like those people."

"You don't even know the girl. They're nice. They want you to go."

She shook her head. "Daddy said no."

"I'll talk to him again," I said. "He'll let us go. He's just mad at you over what happened in church."

Birdie had done nothing but pout all morning. I knew it

was going to take time for her to get over Jimmy; it was a horrible thing. We had made a plaque in his honor and posted it on the trunk of the pecan tree over the grave. Hazel brought some roses from the nursing home that someone sent to a patient who no longer lived there, which Birdie put on the grave, too. But nothing seemed to help. I didn't expect her to act this badly, though.

It had been just Birdie, me, and Daddy at church that morning since Momma was up at Florabelle's. And she had showed herself in front of a lot of people and Daddy was angry with her.

She had taken a prayer request card out of the holder on the back of the pew in front of us, jotted something down, and turned it in. Reverend Whitaker, believing it to be in regards to Florabelle's new unnamed baby, read aloud, "Dear Lord, please bless Jimmy, keep him safe, and forgive Daddy for trying to drown him."

This accusation, even though it was meant as a confession, of course took everyone by surprise, and the congregation turned to stare at us the rest of the service. Daddy was so angry that when we'd come home, he had gone straight upstairs to his room and slammed the door.

I sat down on the bed beside Birdie. "Bird, I know you miss Jimmy. I do too. It's going to take some time to get over him. But we still have Heidi, and she's going to be better than ever now. No more puppies to have to get rid of neither."

Birdie looked at me, perplexed.

"I'm going to fix her," I explained. "A doctor is teaching me how."

"What if I *want* her to have more?"

"Bird, you know what we went through with Jimmy Daddy will never let us keep them. Besides, she's too old to be having any more babies."

"How old's Florabelle?" she asked.

"She's only nineteen. She's young enough to have plenty more."

"When can I see her baby?"

"Soon, just as soon as she's up to the company. Maybe tomorrow."

"When's Heidi coming home?"

"Next week." I gave her a little shake. "Now come on, change your clothes and come out with us. We're going to Natural Bridge State Park. Remember, they have that train that takes you around the picnic area. You can ride it."

"Can I take Hazel's camera?"

"I suppose. Do you know where it is?"

She nodded.

"Well, get changed, then run out to her trailer and get it. Leave a note we have it." I stood up to leave. "Meet me in the garage, I'll be getting our stuff together."

I didn't feel like confronting Daddy after what had happened in church; he always needed some time alone to let off steam. I made a couple of sandwiches for Birdie and me, just in case Connie would forget to, made up two more for Daddy and left them with a note in the kitchen: "Gone Fishing, Fern & Bird, be back around four."

I had all the gear together and was looking for a few more things in the garage when Birdie came out. She was wearing overalls, with no shirt underneath. I stared at her. I had not noticed, really, even while sewing for her, how much she was growing up.

"Bird, go put on a T-shirt."

"I'll be too hot," she whined.

"I can see your boobs."

She glared at me, reluctant.

"You can borrow one of my shirts," I offered.

She turned to go back inside.

"Bird?"

"What?"

"Have you seen my Styrofoam cooler I use for fishing? I've searched this garage over."

She turned around to face me, but lowered her eyes. "Momma used it for Jimmy."

"What do you mean?"

A tear fell down her cheek. "The turkey buzzards started showing up, so she dug him back up to put him in something."

"She buried him in my cooler?"

Birdie nodded.

I let go a big sigh. "That's all right. Now go pick out a shirt and hurry back."

We sat on the base of Clem's "GAS" sign out front, waiting for Culler and Connie to pick us up. Dwayne Crabtree, Jason's brother, drove by, saw us, pulled his truck to a screeching halt.

"Shit," I said, under my breath, but Birdie heard me.

Dwayne was wearing dark glasses, tight jeans, and no shirt.

"He must not have gone to church today," whispered Birdie as he approached us.

"Guess not," I mumbled.

"Hey, ladies," Dwayne said. He blocked the sun where he stood in front of us. "Can I give you a lift somewhere?"

"No, thanks, Dwayne," I said. "Our ride's coming."

"Where are you off to? Fishing, it looks like."

"You're sharp," I said, and pointed the end of my pole at him.

"Why aren't you over at Jason's and Florabelle's with the baby?"

"Our Momma's there," said Birdie.

Dwayne shook his head slowly, side to side. "I don't know, but I just can't see Jason being a Daddy. I hear they ain't even named the kid yet," he added.

"They're still deciding," I said.

"The whole thing's weird," he said, "them two getting married. All's they do is fight."

I looked up at Dwayne, pushed hair out of my eyes. "Well, we can all make the best of it."

"I'm its aunt," said Birdie.

"That's right, you are, ain't you," said Dwayne. "World's youngest I bet."

"And sassiest," I added.

"Just like her sisters," said Dwayne.

"If you came for gas," I said, "we're closed."

"No, I got a full tank, I just happened to see two good-looking women along the roadside, thought I'd stop."

Just about that time, Culler's jeep pulled into the station. He honked. Connie waved.

"What do we have here?" asked Dwayne.

I stood up, gathered our gear. "That's our ride. Let's go, Bird. Good talking to you, Dwayne. Stay out of trouble. You're an uncle now, time to get responsible." I waved good-bye to him.

But he didn't leave. He followed us right over to the jeep. Culler got out and walked around to open the back hatch.

"What the hell kind of ride is this?" asked Dwayne.

I rolled my eyes at Culler. "Culler, this is Dwayne Crabtree, my sister's husband's brother. Dwayne, meet Culler."

Culler offered his hand; Dwayne ignored it.

"Did you buy this from a toy maker?" asked Dwayne, circling the jeep.

"No, U.S. government," said Culler.

"It was a mail truck," I said.

"I'll be shitting," said Dwayne.

Connie got out of the jeep and came around to meet Birdie. "Aren't you a cute little thing," she said. "You look like Fern." She looked at me and smiled. "Are you ready to catch some fish?"

We loaded our gear into the jeep, tried to get going. Connie kept talking to Birdie, asking her about her school and all sorts of things.

Dwayne wouldn't leave.

I was in the front seat; Birdie sat in the back with Connie. She seemed to have warmed up to her, a lot quicker than she had with Culler.

"He's not going with us, is he?" whispered Culler.

Dwayne was still walking around the jeep, knocking on it, mumbling to himself.

I rolled down my window. "Dwayne, move away. We need to go. Pull out," I told Culler.

"Got some mail to deliver?" Dwayne shouted as we left.

"So, what's his problem?" asked Culler, grinning. "Is he hot for you, or something?"

"He's a horse's ass," I said. I was embarrassed to have even been seen with him and figured Culler must have been equally impressed with my extended family as he was with the immediate folk.

We found a grassy spot under a tall oak. Connie spread out a blanket; Birdie helped her. Culler and I unloaded the jeep.

"Is she okay now?" asked Culler. "I mean about the dogs?"

"She's getting there. This outing will be good for her."

We were standing behind the jeep. Culler was handing me things. "I'm glad you decided to come," he said. Then he kissed me. Twice.

"Me too," I said.

We threw a baseball around for a little while, until we got sweaty and thirsty. Connie had made ham and Swiss cheese sandwiches, and there were chips and dip, apples, and soda. As we ate, the little train that circled the grounds passed us every ten minutes or so. Each time it went by, Birdie waved to the kids in the cars. She seemed relaxed, enjoying herself.

A cool breeze blew through the leaves above us, keeping the flies away, washing us over with the smell of charcoal. The park was fairly crowded; several families were grilling hamburgers.

I remembered the one and only time our family had been here, back when we first moved to Kentucky. We drove down one afternoon and walked around, then bought pecan rolls in the gift shop and went home. There was a skylift that would take you to the top of the mountain where the bridge is, but it was those bench-type seats with no safety belts, suspended in midair over the mountainside. At the top of the mountain, just before disembarking, they take your picture, and for ten bucks, you can have an eight-by-ten of yourself in this thing with the valley in the background. That afternoon, a lot of people had been riding it and buying the photographs, but Momma had flat refused to let us ride.

"Bird, get the camera out," I said. "I'll take your picture."

She scrounged through our bag, handed me the camera. "Let me swallow this bite," she said, then wiped her mouth with her sleeve.

I took her picture, then she took mine, then one of Connie.

"Take one of Culler, too," I told her.

She dillydallied with the camera and took another extraordinary bite of her sandwich, but finally lifted the camera to snap his picture.

As she did, Culler crossed his eyes and stuck out his tongue.

Birdie put down the camera and frowned at him. "You'll ruin the film," she said.

Connie laughed.

"He's just messing with you, Bird," I said.

She didn't like his joke. For quite some time, she sat eating, very seriously.

When we were finished, I gave Birdie a dollar to go ride the train, and we cleaned up our lunch mess. We remembered to wave at her whenever the train passed us. She was amused, I could tell, but she was pretending not to be. She would roll her eyes each time we waved, pretending to be too sophisticated for this adventure.

We had to drive up the river a few miles to fish, outside of the park, where it was legal. Culler helped Birdie rig up her cane pole, but she insisted on baiting her own worm. Culler pretended to eat one of the worms in front of her and she told him he was gross.

I think she was starting to like him.

We fished for nearly two hours, and the only thing biting were the mosquitoes. We slapped at out ankles and arms, trying to keep the bugs away, giggling at our foolishness.

But we had a good time. Even Birdie did, who kept faking us out like she had a fish on her line. She'd reel in frantically, and we'd pretend to be anxious. Then she'd flip her bobber out of the water, dangle her worm for us, and screech with delight for thinking she had us fooled. We took pictures of her with her worms, like she'd caught them.

Once, Culler dove in the river, clothes and all, and made like he was swimming after a fish who stole his bait. It put us all into hysterics for quite some time.

As we were about to leave, I mentioned the skylift. At first, no one seemed too interested, but when I described the bridge for them again, everyone wanted to go. We drove back to the park and got in line for the ride. While we waited, a young girl in a gingham vest and cowboy hat talked to us about the bridge. She explained that it was the result of water working its way slowly through loose soil and soft rock.

I liked my theory better, that it was a hole God punched in the earth.

I rode with Culler, Birdie with Connie. I was surprised she wasn't afraid. I had asked Connie to hang onto her, not to let her swing her legs too much.

Culler and I waited to get a seat behind them so we could make out. It was such a wild sensation to be way up above the ground, and then to be high inside, too. I really liked the way he kissed me. I wanted the ride to last forever.

At the top, they took our picture, and Culler bought four copies, one for each of us. The pictures came out well; Birdie was so proud of hers. She showed it to a few strangers that got off the ride after us.

When we got to the bridge and looked down, it was beautiful. Just like I remembered it. Trees grew into the sides of it and wild flowers blossomed around the perimeter. There was also a nature trail up there, and we took that, too. Blackberry bushes were abundant in the woods, and I let Birdie pick some and eat them. Connie and I once tried to hide and scare Culler, but he was on to us.

We didn't leave until five o'clock. I realized we would be late getting home, but I didn't care. I couldn't remember, ever, having so much fun.

Connie and Birdie slept on the way home, but not me. I watched the scenery along the road and took in the fresh air. As we came upon the familiar hollows of home, I wished the interior of this little purple jeep was my world, not the one I was reentering.

23. Fences Up, Guards Down

When Birdie and I came home that night from fishing, it was almost seven o'clock, and Daddy gave us a real tongue-lashing. Hazel had cooked his dinner and had tacked the note I left in the kitchen saying we'd be home at four on the wall clock, just to let us know how late we were.

But I didn't care. I had other things to think about. For the next three nights, I stayed up late reading my textbook, studying the female reproductive system. Even though the books were about humans, I figured that dogs couldn't be all that different.

Birdie had forgiven me for Culler's significance in my life, and we worked on her dress after school every day. The dress, like her, was beginning to take shape. It seemed she'd done more growing just that summer than she had all year.

Momma came home from Florabelle's on Tuesday while we were hemming the dress and brought word that the baby had a name finally. Daisy. She explained that when Florabelle had been in the hospital, Jason had brought her a bunch of dandelions but because she was so heavily dosed up, she had thought they were daisies and named the baby after them.

Momma thought it was fitting how the name had something to do with flowers, as that was what she had in mind when she'd named Florabelle. She was just thankful that Florabelle was indeed out of it when she'd come up with the name Daisy, because she wouldn't want to be calling no grandbaby of hers Dandy Lion.

"Momma," asked Birdie, "Fern was named after a sort of flower, too, how come I wasn't?"

"After the Lord brought forth vegetation, Bird," said Momma, "He said, 'let the birds fly above the earth.' That's where you come in."

Birdie seemed to grant Momma's answer. She smiled, lifted high the hem of her dress on both sides, two great wings, and soared in a circle.

"Put your dress down and be a lady. And what's this about you being out late Sunday night?" asked Momma. "Hazel called me up at Florabelle's, fit to be tied."

"I took her fishing," I said quickly.

"So did Culler and Connie," Birdie challenged.

"Who?" asked Momma.

"My friends," I said. "Momma, come hold the end of this tape measure."

Momma took the tape measure; we both bent over Birdie, who was standing up on the ottoman, prissing.

"Hold still," Momma scolded. "And don't get any big ideas to go running off fishing this Sunday. Your grandmother's in a beauty contest, and we're all supposed to be there."

"A what?" I asked, standing up.

"They got something going down there at the nursing home where every year they hold a pageant and crown a queen who gets to say something on the radio. Families come and there's refreshments and dancing. Me, Hazel, you two, Florabelle; we're all going. I want your father to come, but he still ain't speaking to Mother. I wonder sometimes, how he can carry a grudge like he does."

"Hurry up and finish my dress," said Birdie. "I can wear it to the beauty contest." She jumped down and strutted around the room, swinging her hips, singing "Here she Comes, Miss America."

"What in God's name has gotten into you?" Momma shook her head at Birdie. "Quit that flitting around."

"Fern, come on in the kitchen and help me with the snap beans. Your Daddy's told me he's missed my cooking."

Daddy was cutting away at his second pork chop, when suddenly he put down his knife and said, "What in Christ's name is that?" He was looking through the window at the backyard.

"Too much fat around the bone?" asked Momma.

"No, there's a feller carrying a roll of fencing through our yard." Daddy stood up, peering.

"Maybe it's someone from the plant who's come to put a fence around the pumps," suggested Momma. "That one pump handle did come down and kill Bud Fowler's cow that time."

"I don't believe it's anybody I know from the plant."

He got up from the table, went out the door into the garage. He was gone for almost ten minutes, so we assumed it was someone he knew from work after all.

Momma went ahead and served dessert.

When Daddy came back inside, he was looking at me. "It's that boy, Culler. Says he's building a dog pen."

I went to look out the window. Birdie jumped up and ran outside.

"You mind telling me what's going on?" asked Daddy.

"Well, the vet did say we'd have to start keeping Heidi penned up for protection from those strays. Especially while she's healing." I watched as Birdie dragged fence-posts along behind Culler. They were talking animatedly. I turned to Daddy. "I guess I told Culler that."

"Who's paying for it?" he asked.

"I guess he is. It's okay, isn't it?"

Daddy looked at me in silence for a few seconds, then went over to the counter and poured himself some coffee. He sat back down in front of his pie plate. "I told him he was going to run out of daylight," he said.

"I'll help him," I said. "Momma, I'll do the dishes later."

She turned to me, looked at Daddy to make sure he wasn't watching, then winked. "There ain't much here," she said. "I'll take care of the mess, you get on out there and build that cage."

I don't know where Culler got the money, but he bought eighty-four feet of fencing to build a twelve-by-thirty run-ner. He wanted Heidi to have a lot of room to run around and be safe. He had sketched out the dimensions in one of his architecture classes, then explained the draft to me and Birdie. His plan was to get the fencing in place that night before darkness fell, then come back early Saturday morn-ing and build a doghouse to go inside the pen, for shelter from rain. Eventually, he was going to roof the whole thing with chicken wire.

We worked hard. Birdie and I rolled out the fence and held it while Culler cut it. Momma brought Birdie and me each a pair of gloves to wear, as well as the rest of the lemon pie and some coffee.

Around eight, Daddy came outside with a posthole digger. "I told you, you was going to run out of light," was all he said, then he went right along behind where Culler marked the ground, and dug the postholes.

When we were through, Culler shook Daddy's hand, thanked him for his help. It was almost ten o'clock, and Daddy looked beat. I watched as he walked back into the house. He was getting old. It seemed that for the last ten years, he hadn't changed a bit, didn't look a day older. Just lately, though, he was aging. He was beginning to move slower, put on weight, lose hair, lose spirit.

When Momma called Birdie in to bathe, as it was a school night, she put up a fuss, but Culler promised he'd let her help build the doghouse when he came back.

I walked Culler out to his jeep and trailer. It was a full moon, and I wanted to suggest a walk. But it was late, we were both exhausted, and I knew he had a drive back to Lexington.

"Here," he said, reaching in the front seat, "I almost forgot. I got you this from the library. You can keep it for two weeks." He handed me a large book, bigger than our family Bible.

I read the title. *Hysterosalpingography.* "Thanks," I said. I could barely grip it, my hands were so sore.

"It ought to give you all the information you're going to need for Saturday." He rubbed my cheek with the back of his hand. His palms were raw. "Good luck," he said. "Remember, just go slow and steady."

24. Living and Breathing

I was funneling a bunch of half-full transmission fluid cans into a larger carton, and I kept spilling.

"If you don't quit that shaking," said Clem, "you're going to end up slashing that dog of yours wide open."

"I've got the jitters about today," I said.

"You'll do fine. Erikson ain't going to make you do it all by yourself anyway; he'll do most of it. You're there to learn."

"I don't think I can handle it. You know it's going to be a tad more complicated than rebuilding a carburetor." I held the can steady with two hands. "This time it's a living, breathing thing."

"A carburetor breathes," said Clem.

"You know what I mean."

"Relax," he said. "What did you do, drink a pot of coffee this morning?"

It was true, I did drink too much coffee in general, but that wasn't the problem this time. I had stayed up almost the whole night reading the book Culler had borrowed for me. We knew he would be at our house at seven o'clock that morning to build the doghouse, and Birdie and I got up to wait for him. I had made us all breakfast, but I'd only had one cup of coffee and a Three Musketeers bar. It was just that I was excited about seeing Culler.

I decided not to tell Clem about it; he'd tease me for sure. "I got up early," I said.

"How long do you think it's going to take you up there at Erikson's?" asked Clem.

"I don't know, maybe an hour? According to that book I read, it's a pretty simple procedure."

"Oh, so you did do your homework?" Clem grinned, raised his eyebrows.

"You bet."

"You're pretty serious about this, aren't you?" He quit

greasing engine mounts and turned to face me.

"I'm interested," I said. "That's all, just interested in learning something new."

A horn honked at the pumps. I put down the funnel, went out front.

"You come back here and keep doing what you're doing," shouted Clem. "You're acting too goosey to gas a tank. Besides," he leaned out to see who the customer was. "It's that Crabtree boy you don't like." Clem put down his rag, wiped his hands on his pantslegs. "I'll take care of him."

When Clem came back in the station, he looked distressed. "Dwayne tells me you were down here Sunday with Birdie." He looked at me, arms folded against his chest, waiting for a response.

"That's right," I said, going about my business. "We didn't come in the station, we were just sitting out front."

"Waiting on somebody, I gather," said Clem.

"That's right."

"Don't be abusing that key," he warned.

"I said we didn't go inside."

"Dwayne happened to mention you left in some jeep," said Clem, still fishing for more. "I don't suppose it was a purple jeep, was it?"

"Clem, lay off it," I said, turning towards him. "What did Dwayne say?"

Clem grinned like a baked possum. "Aw, he didn't say nothing."

"What did he say?" I hated when he played this game with me, kept me guessing at things.

"Oh, he just told me you went off fishing with the mailman." He kept laughing.

"That ass." I took the carton of transmission fluid into the station to label and date it.

Clem followed me. "I'm sorry," he said, trying to contain himself. "I know he's a nice boy, it's just that I still keep seeing you hunched over him that day, sewing him back together. It was quite a sight. I think it's admirable he took his chances and went and fished with you again."

"We had a good time," I said. "No casualties."

"Well, Dwayne was mighty jealous."

"Dwayne Crabtree struts around like a rooster in high mud."

"Well, he was sure ragging on that boy—"

"—Culler."

"—Culler, the way he was making fun of that jeep."

"That's a great jeep. There's a 232 cubic-inch engine under that hood."

"I know, I know, I'm just laughing at that yahoo, Dwayne. He talks so big."

"He built Heidi a pen," I said.

"Dwayne?"

"Culler. Wednesday night. He's at the house now working on a doghouse to go in it."

"I declare," said Clem, musing. "He's handy, too?"

"Very handy," I said. "You sure you don't mind loaning me your truck today? I should get going. I told Dr. Erikson I'd be there by two."

Clem tossed me his keys. "Put gas in it."

"I already did."

"Fern, why don't you try and save up the money you're earning here, and buy yourself some old jalopy?"

"Clem, I told you, Daddy's not doing as many hours at the plant, with the layoffs. Only way I'm going to get a car is if someone kicks off and wills me one." I took Clem's wrist, pretended to check his pulse. "How old are you anyway, Clem?" I asked.

"Get out of here," he said.

When I got there, Dr. Erikson seemed to have everything all set in the garage. He led me around back where he'd been keeping Heidi.

I called to her.

She got so excited at the sound of my voice, whined and wiggled about. We opened the cage door, let her out, and I made over her for a few minutes, talking sweet to her. Bless her heart, she looked weak, and I could still see the gash and stitches where her hair was shaved, but she acted fine.

"She'll be as good as ever," said Dr. Erikson, petting

Heidi's head. "I've been giving her some vitamins that I'll send home with you. They'll give her more zip."

We let Heidi romp around the yard a few minutes, to run her energy off, then we led her back in the garage. While hoisting her onto the table and getting her situated, Dr. Erikson explained what anesthetic he'd be administering.

I was still real nervous but listened carefully. I had even brought my textbooks along, and had them open to diagrams I could refer to. I got a little queasy during the incision, but after that, I regained control.

Throughout the operation, step by step, he explained what he was doing in detail. He would start a task, illustrate the proper maneuvers, then hand me his tools to try on my own.

I asked a lot of questions, and he was very patient with me. He was real careful with Heidi, too.

The cervix was a very delicate thing, and I had to be extra cautious working around it. It was constricted; I had a hard time imagining that it had once stretched open wide enough for Jimmy to squeeze through. The organs were so supple; I never knew.

When we were through, he had me sew her up without assistance. I took my time, kept the stitches nice and even. She was beginning to twitch, and I was afraid she was coming to.

I took notes and by the time I left, my brain was on overload. Dr. Erikson had told me so much, and I needed time to mill and sort everything. I wanted to absorb it all.

Driving back towards Clem's, with Heidi's drowsy head in my lap, her body stretched across the front seat of the cab, I felt so relieved and proud. I couldn't help but wonder, though, what Dr. Erikson would do with her ovaries.

I bet Birdie would like to have kept them.

25. Queen Esther

There were white cotton curtains and blue hang-
ings caught up with cords of fine linen ...Drinks were
served in golden goblets, goblets of different kinds,
and the royal wine was lavished according to the
bounty of the king.

Esther 1:6/7

By two o'clock, most of the decorations were already up
in the dining room; a committee had been arranged for this
responsibility, and the taller, more capable residents were
hanging gold spray-painted stars from the ceiling.

The pageant was scheduled to start at four and go until
seven, with the six o'clock news coverage by the radio station sponsoring the event in between. We arrived early
enough for Hazel to roll Grandma's hair.

Birdie, Florabelle, and I, already dressed, sat at a table
in the corner, watching the preparation of this grand affair.
Today would be Peaceful Pastures Nursing Home's Thirty-
third Annual Beauty Pageant. By tradition, the most
recently admitted female would be crowned queen, kissed
by all the aging gentlemen, served dessert first, and pho-
tographed for the composite of former celebrated winners
of years past.

Everyone knew, including Grandma, that she, having
only been checked in for a month and a half before the
much talked about ceremonial event, would be crowned.

Blue crepe paper draped from beam to beam, was
wrapped around the curtain rods, and hung in long streams
against the white curtains. Rows of gold paper cups filled
with punch lined one of the tables. A crew from the radio
station were installing a strobe globe. Woody's Bakery
came in with a three-tiered cake with a big silver crown on
top made out of aluminum and glitter.

"It still gets me about my wedding-cake topper, " said

Florabelle, anxious to go outside and smoke.

I remembered the plastic family with the black baby. "You never found out who did that?" I asked her.

"Never did. Probably Dwayne," she said.

"Probably so," said Birdie.

We both looked at her. She was mesmerized with all the colors and activity. She was wearing the new dress I had made; we had stayed up late the night before to finish it. She was very proud of it, said it made her feel grown up. I had twisted her hair up into a bun. Other than her arms being scratched from the fencing, she did look rather mature.

"I want to go back up and play with the baby," she said.

Momma had Daisy upstairs, watching Hazel get Grandma ready.

When we walked back in, Grandma, robed and slippered, moved slowly back and forth from the bathroom to her bureau. She held her hands out in front of her, careful not to smudge her red nail polish.

Momma sat on the bed, holding Daisy, with Grandma's dress laid out next to her.

"Come on, Mother," said Hazel. "We need to get your hair up in rollers before it dries." She moistened a comb in a jar of Dippity-Do labeled "Esther."

Grandma was stalling, pretending to look for an extra box of Kleenex in the back of her bottom dresser drawer.

"I hope you and Mossie got everything straightened out over those window plants," said Hazel.

Grandma, still stooped over her drawer with her back turned, said, "I see no need to let her cross over to my side of the room. I told her I'd water them."

"She told the staff that you *claim* to sprinkle them when you do yours, but they all have their suspicions that you're planning to let hers die."

Grandma stood up, quicker than usual. "The staff'll believe anything she tells them on me."

I glanced over at the row of potted plants sitting on the windowsill next to Grandma's bed. "They all look okay to me," I said. "Which ones are yours, Grandma?"

"The two violets on the end and the one marigold."

"Well, they look fine," I said, sitting down on the bed next to Momma. I played with Daisy's fingers, let her grip mine. She was so tiny, it amazed me.

"Forget about the plants for a minute," said Hazel, "and sit down here so we can curl your hair."

Grandma moved the chair a little more in front of the bed so she could see out into the hallway. "If you wouldn't give me those cheap perms you do, I wouldn't have to mess with rolling it all the time," she said.

"Well, you can't afford no forty-dollar perm and you ain't got much hair left to roll anyway," said Hazel.

A door slammed a few rooms down. Grandma craned to see who it was.

"Sit still," said Hazel. "Where's Mossie? Why isn't she in here getting all dolled up?"

"She says she ain't coming," said Grandma.

Hazel smiled. "I bet she's a little upset about giving up her title as queen. She won it last year, you know. No one likes to give up a throne." Hazel forced a pick through a stubborn curler. "But she'll be there, I know her, she can't miss a party. Folks say she was so wealthy growing up, her parents threw society shindigs every weekend. She was even one of those debutantes. Can you even imagine that?"

Grandma cussed her. "I don't want Mossie there anyway," she said, rubbing at her head.

"Is all you two's trouble just over them plants?" asked Momma. "Seems like you could just forget about it and try and be friends."

"Have you told Raymond that?" snapped Grandma.

Momma got real quiet.

Daddy still wasn't speaking to Grandma.

Grandma noticed the silence, knew she'd crossed the line. "Mossie is just jealous of me for looking so much younger."

Hazel rolled her eyes at us over Grandma's head. "There, that's the last one." She put the leftover rollers in the basket labeled "Esther," and stored them away.

"They said they was bringing a TV camera today," said

Grandma, looking in the mirror. She opened her top drawer, took out three pill bottles, counted out capsules.

From the bathroom, Hazel spoke through a comb in her mouth while she washed her hands. "A disc jockey from the local radio station is coming to do the music, and Channel Seven's doing their weather broadcast live at the party. Sylvia, see that she takes those pills; she's been flushing them again."

She had to take one for the arthritis, one for high blood pressure, the same one Momma took, and one was a digestive agent. All medications made her drowsy and nervous, so sometimes, she'd try and throw them out. But we always caught her.

"Gargle Listermint," said Florabelle, "somebody might interview you." She was lying on the floor, looking up at us.

"You'll be on the news, Grandma, you got to look pretty," said Birdie.

"Speaking of all this, Birdie," asked Hazel, "did you get my camera?"

"Yes, but there's only a few pictures left on it."

"Who used up all the film?"

"Fern did, when we went fishing that day."

Both Birdie and Hazel looked at me. Hazel took the pick out of her mouth, shook it at me. "You better see if you can go get some more. And hurry back. Keys are on the dresser there."

At three-thirty, they started the music, and the aides, who were double-staffed that day, began helping everyone down the stairs. Guests and family members interested in the activities of their deteriorating elders were admitted into the dining room.

Some of the staff stood outside the dining room, pinning corsages on the ladies and trying to coordinate escorts for them. They were trying to match up wheelchair patients with ones that could walk and push.

All the men wore suits, plaid or plain, mostly double-knit, and bow ties of every size.

The ladies wore long gowns of many colors and styles.

Some looked like newer dresses that might have been worn in grandchildren's weddings. Some dresses were more ancient and reeked of moth balls and cedar. One of the older, less alert residents, with her walker, limped in, wearing a wrinkled wedding gown and veil.

Grandma's dress was red. Scarlet taffeta, cut low at the neck, gathered into a budding flower of material at her waist. It fell in ruffled layers to the floor. Her shoes were patent leather, red also. Several men whistled as she paraded into the room. She winked at the disc jockey.

"Did you see that?" asked Florabelle.

We were standing near the back. Momma was sitting in a chair against the wall with Birdie, who was holding Daisy.

"I've never seen her act so saucy," I said, watching Grandma swing her hips.

The disc jockey took a cue and faded the processional he'd been playing into Prince's "Little Red Corvette." Appalled, one of the staff nurses ran over and made him change it back.

"Just look at the way she's a'struttin'," said Momma, disgusted.

I turned around. "Where did she get that dress?"

"It's one of Hazel's," said Momma, shaking her head. "Your grandma looks like a cheap floozy in it."

When Grandma finally chose a seat against the wall opposite us, Hazel walked up to her and tugged Grandma's dress back up to conceal her sagging cleavage.

I read her lips across the room. "Shame on you," she said, and marched over to where we were sitting. "Can you believe that woman?" she said, hands on hips. "After all these years of acting like such a prude, then going out there and prancing around like that?"

"She's making a fool of us," said Momma.

"She's just getting old," said Florabelle. "Let her have some fun."

Hazel wasn't convinced and kept a keen eye on Grandma for another ten minutes or so. "Well, I have to serve punch," she finally said. She looked at me. "You keep an eye on her, you hear?"

I nodded, grinning. I thought it was funny how

Grandma acted, so out of character for her. I admired her spunk. But I kept my promise and watched her.

She walked over to a group of old men, most of them in wheelchairs, and leaned against one of them. She said something that made them laugh, and I saw her take advantage of the moment and jerk her neckline back down. From where I sat, it appeared that Grandma was feeling sexy. I smiled to myself.

We never saw her mingle with any of the women; she must have figured they were all jealous of her.

Florabelle and I went over and nibbled at the hors d'oeuvres at the buffet table. I ate two brownies.

"I bet all this stuff is laced with prunes," said Florabelle.

I noticed that she had lost a lot of weight since the baby had been born. She looked good. And when she smiled, which was seldom, she was pretty.

"You look nice," I said.

She turned to me, surprised. "You think so?"

"Sure, you've lost the extra weight."

She stabbed an olive on her plate with a toothpick. "I wish Jason would notice."

"Are you two getting along better now?"

She shrugged. "He wanted a boy."

She picked nervously at her food.

I changed the subject to Grandma, watching her showing off.

A couple of folks were attempting to dance, even a few in wheelchairs were out on the floor, spinning and inching back and forth to the beat of the music. It surprised me that Birdie wasn't out there messing around; she liked to dance. But she was playing with Daisy, her new friend now that Jimmy was gone.

It was getting near six, and the photographers were setting up their tripods. Channel Seven cameramen were positioning lights and sound equipment. The crowning ceremony was about to begin.

"Holy shit, look who's here," said Florabelle, mouth full.

It was Patty Prettyman and her husband, Larry Greene. They were there to see Mossie.

"What's she going to do here with all these old folks?" asked Florabelle. "Tear up the rug?"

"From what I hear, she *likes* old men," I said and reminded Florabelle about the rumor of Patty and Brewer.

"Everyone knows she married Larry for his momma's money. She's as rich as possum gravy."

"Yeah," I said, "that's too bad. Larry seems like a nice man. Mossie's so kind, too."

"Well, that Patty's a witch," said Florabelle.

Patty had gone over to the cake and was staring at it, looking around. She kept fooling with her purse. I wondered if she was going to try and run her finger through the icing or something ornery like that.

"Ladies and Gentlemen," said the disc jockey into the microphone, "the moment we've all been waiting for." He had stopped the music and had a tape running of a drumroll. "The crowning of the Thirty-third Peaceful Pastures Queen. Our chosen raving beauty will represent this home in the Nursing Home Finals for the state of Kentucky in early February and win the chance of a cameo appearance on the *Golden Girls* TV show that premieres next season."

There were whistles and applause from the crowd; this was something new. The grand prize used to be an interview on the radio and a two-night cruise down the Ohio River to Cincinnati and back.

Hazel ran over to Birdie, took the baby from her, handed her the camera. "Go snap some of your Grandma. Get up there in front of everyone. They won't say nothing to you, you're little." Hazel ran back to her post at the punch bowl.

"But first of all," the disc jockey continued, "let's bring our former year's queen forward for the crowning of our new queen. A big welcome back for Mossie Green!"

The patients in the audience who could comprehend what was going on clapped and yelled mostly inaudible comments as Mossie walked to the front.

When she was under the light, she looked a little uneasy at the sight of the cameras, but not nearly as frightened as when she saw her daughter-in-law.

I wondered if Mossie was worried about Patty taking her sewing needles away from her again.

We watched as Patty made her way to the punch bowl. She picked up a plastic cup and napkin, looked around. Then she leaned towards Hazel, whispered something in her ear. It was an effort, no doubt, for Patty to talk over the party bluster loud enough for Hazel to hear. Hazel leaned way back, shook her head, confused, pointed towards the kitchen.

From this point, everything was a blur.

The lights went out in the dining room and there were several screams.

The Channel Seven cameraman got about a five second spot of someone lunging at Mossie, before the camera was knocked to the floor and the lenses shattered. She tumbled out of her wheelchair, and we heard her hipbone crack as it hit the floor.

Someone had robbed her. Everyone knew she carried a lot of cash in a purse strapped around her waist; she feared the staff would steal it so she kept it with her. Almost three thousand dollars worth of twenties.

When the lights came back on, someone noticed a tombstone made out of Styrofoam on top of the cake. The initials M.G. were printed on it, in red ink.

They finally got the party started back up again, but no one was in the mood, and most folks went home. Grandma received her crown, but all the majesty was over by then. She'd put it on, then hung her head and sobbed. We stayed late to help clean up and see Grandma off to bed.

When we got home, Daddy had terrible news for us. Brother Brewer had been electrocuted. Evidently, he had been driving in his car with the top down, lost control of the wheel, swerved into a cornfield, and hit a phone pole. The impact had caused a live wire to snap down into his car, strike him in the groin, and kill him almost instantly.

Patty Prettyman Greene had been in the car with him. She'd scratched her head on the dashboard when they'd crashed. The doctors had found three thousand dollars of cash on her when she went in for an x-ray.

Late that night, Birdie and I sat on her bed, looking through the Polaroid shots she had taken at the pageant. The ones of Grandma had turned out real well, and Birdie decided to try her hand again at making a photo album. She knew Grandma would appreciate it.

Birdie also had a shot of Mossie's accident and now we both could make out Patty Prettyman in the picture, struggling with Mossie out on the floor in her wheelchair.

26. Just Buried

When I got to work a few days later, Brother Brewer's mustang was sitting in the parking lot. The front end was caved in, but not too badly. The cornhusks he'd run through before hitting the pole had lessened the impact. I walked in the station and found Clem just sitting in the chair, hands folded over an envelope in his lap.

I was a little late getting in due to Brewer's funeral. It had been a small affair, no viewing, on account of how badly and where he'd been burned. He had no family left, at least none that anyone knew of, so the county officials had just wanted to cremate him since he'd had a fair start. But Reverend Whitaker had insisted on a small service and formal burial, out of due respect to his fellow clergyman. After the service, I had given him Birdie's photograph of Patty on Mossie.

I didn't really want to talk to Clem about the service, since he seemed a little more shook up about it than I'd expected, even leaving early, sneaking out during the prayer.

He looked pretty intent when I walked in. The ledger books were open on the counter by the register; the adding machine was still on, humming softly.

"What's up?" I asked.

"Not business," he said, staring at the floor.

"That bad?"

"Our expenses are ten percent over profit again this month."

Clem had finally broke down, had a Pepsi machine installed out front, and it hadn't even paid for itself yet.

"I thought we were pulling in a little more at the pumps," I said.

Clem shook his head. "My insurance premiums just went up, too. I'm considered high risk now, with no sprinkler system."

This was the gloomiest I'd seen Clem Proffit since I'd met him. He hung his head down, staring at the ground.

"Times are tough," I offered. "I hear Daddy talking about the drop in economy all the time now."

"Times aren't so tough for *everyone*," he mumbled. "There's an angel looking out for *some* of us. Those with great faith." He was quoting part of Reverend Whitaker's eulogy. He finally looked up, handed me the envelope.

"What's this?" I asked.

"Open it."

The letter was from the State of Kentucky Attorneys at Law, Will Executor. I read the letter twice, not trusting my eyes.

Brother Brewer had willed me his Mustang convertible.

27. When It Rains

For the next week, I worked on my car almost around the clock, repairing the damages of Brewer's accident. It rained so much, and the customers were few. I pounded out the dents, patched the radiator, and replaced the water pump. I picked up a Mustang parts catalogue from a Ford dealer in Lexington, and ordered new door panels and a rearview mirror. Eventually, I wanted to restore the whole car with factory parts, but that would take time and money.

Needless to say, Culler thought the car was super. Every night that week, I drove to Lexington, and we went somewhere in it with the top down. Sometimes we'd just go to the library so Culler could work on his school projects, and I would read.

One night, he took me to a college baseball game, and I really enjoyed that. I missed going to all the Reds games when we lived in Ohio. Culler was impressed with how much I knew about the game.

Connie thought the car was "totally cool," and came along with us sometimes. We would cruise down the streets of the Transy campus, and she'd wave out the open top to all the guys. This activity embarrassed Culler, but he let it pass. He said he was happy to be able to see me more often.

My whole family resented that I was gone every night, and they blamed it on the car. Even though Daddy could appreciate its classic value, he kept after me to sell it in a trade show and make some money off of it.

Momma, on the other hand, thought the car was snappy, and liked riding in it. But she still punished me for my frequent absence from home in more subtle ways like deliberately not saving me any leftovers for supper when I got home late, or making a point to wear the same housedress three days in a row, claiming that all the zippers needed fixing on her other ones.

Jason told me the car was a piece of junk, that Ford never did learn how to build a decent set of wheels, and too bad it wasn't a Chevy. Hazel saw it and cried, saying it reminded her of the car her ex-husband's girlfriend drove, even though that was a Mercury Cougar.

Birdie thought that I should save the car and give it to her when she was old enough to drive.

These were the accumulative reactions of my loving family when something good had finally happened my way. And inheriting a car was only the beginning. When it rains, it pours, even in Leeco, Kentucky.

Exactly one week after receiving the letter, another benefaction came to me.

I had taken all the chrome off the car and was in the garage polishing it when Clem yelled to me that I had a phone call. I wiped my hands on a rag, ran to the telephone, expecting it to be Culler.

Clem handed me the receiver, regarding me with suspicion. "It's for Fern Rayburn."

It was Dr. Erikson. He had another proposition for me. An offer more appealing than "neutering a bitch," was how he'd worded it. He had a friend at the Livestock Diagnostic Disease Center in Powell County who needed a full-time laboratory assistant. Dr. Erikson had recommended me for the job. He gave me the guy's number, told me to consider it long and hard, and call him with my answer tomorrow.

All Clem had heard on my end was "Thank you," and "I'll certainly weigh it over."

And when I hung up, he asked, "Was that Erikson?"

I nodded.

"What'd he want?"

I folded up the piece of paper on which I had written the number, put it in my pocket. "He was just asking after Heidi," I said.

"And how *is* Heidi?" asked Clem.

"Oh, she's doing real well. Hair's grown back over both scars. You can barely see them. Birdie lets her out to play every morning; she seems to be getting around better."

"So she's liking that fancy cage of hers?"

"Yeah, she does," I said, heeding Clem's attitude. I couldn't guess his stance. I wondered if he already knew something. "And that little house that Culler built keeps her nice and dry from all this rain we've been having."

"That's good," he said.

I headed towards the garage. "I'm just shining my chrome. Holler if you need me for anything."

I sat back down on the floor, dipped my rag in the paste, and started rubbing down the fender. I was glad to be doing something mindless because I was distracted by the phone call and couldn't focus on my task. I didn't know what to say about the job offer. It sounded like a great opportunity, a chance to do something worthwhile, something I'd become interested in. Something I really believed I could do.

But there was security for me here at Clem's. I didn't know how I would feel, abandoning him. And I felt bad for not being up front with him about the offer.

To complicate matters, clearly the business wasn't doing well. Clem could hardly pay the bills anymore. We'd cut way back on supplies, and he'd raised his gas price two cents on the gallon. I knew he depended on me; I understood him, and he knew I was dedicated. He was getting older, and he needed my help. There was no doubt about that.

But I had myself to think about, too. This may be my only chance, I realized, to break free of the rut that I'd worn for myself. Being in the companionship of Culler and Connie, people with aim, with the courage to blaze their own trail, had begun to work on me. I found it inspiring to watch them work so hard at a goal, to strive to achieve something that would be for them, and them only, to take all the glory. They weren't serving everyone else's needs, burdened with trying to please people.

I looked down at my watch. It was one o'clock. I still had an hour to work, but I wondered if Clem would consider letting me go early, without pay. I needed to talk to someone about this. Someone with wisdom and experience.

28. Crown of Glory

I found Grandma sitting in TV lounge B with some old man in a wheelchair watching *WWF Wrestling*. I recognized Hulk Hogan strutting around in the ring, in dark sunglasses, flexing for the fans.

Both Grandma and the man seemed heavily absorbed in the round. The man had his wheelchair parked right up against the vinyl sofa where she was sitting. It looked like they were holding hands, but I couldn't really tell. The only light in the room was the blue glow from the television set.

"Grandma," I said.

She looked startled to see me, nudged the man rather forcibly on the arm, then introduced him as Earl.

He smiled, turned up his hearing aid, which made it whistle sharply and Grandma yelled at him to turn it down.

Ever since she had been crowned queen, she seemed to be doing better in the home. She was getting along with the other residents, and participating more in group activities.

On Tuesday nights, just before *Moonlighting* came on, a group played Spoons in the TV lounge. This game was supposed to be therapeutic for the arthritic patients, as it challenged their reflexes and exercised their joint flexion. Grandma enjoyed the game, was getting quite good at it, and talked about it often whenever we came to visit.

The only trouble with her being selected as the queen, though, Hazel told us later, was that the crown was not hers to keep, it belonged to Peaceful Pastures to use as a prop each year, and Grandma wouldn't give it back. She had it hidden somewhere.

"Did anyone see you come in?" she asked, leaning to look behind me.

"No, why?" I asked.

"What about Mossie?"

"I didn't see her," I said, sitting down next to her on the sofa.

"She must be still out on the patio, then," she said.

"Where is she?" asked Earl.

"On the patio," shouted Grandma. "She's still looking for Orion."

"Who?" asked Earl.

"Orion," said Grandma, glaring at Earl. She was obviously annoyed with his questions. "Some star out there."

"From the movies?" he asked, starting to wheel towards the door.

"No!" said Grandma, exasperated. She grabbed his wheel to stop him and turn him towards her. "In the sky. Those people from that planetarium yesterday left a telescope."

"She's looking for a star in the middle of the afternoon?" I asked.

"She don't know the difference," said Grandma. "What did you come here for? Birdie tells me you have a beau feller."

"I do have a friend, Grandma." I looked at Earl. He was squinting to listen to us. "Do you mind if we go talk in your room a minute?" I asked her. "I need your advice on something." I signaled, with my eyes, towards Earl. "It's kind of private."

She hesitated, looked at Earl, back at me. Then she shouted, "My granddaughter needs to talk to me in private. We'll be right back, don't leave." She leaned in close to me, whispered, "He calls me 'His Royal Princess.'"

When we got to her room, she closed the door, and said, "You ain't pregnant now, too, are you?"

"No, Grandma, I'm not pregnant. It's actually more complicated than that."

"Well, that's a relief." She climbed up in her bed and lay down. "That little Daisy sure is a sweet thing, but Lord Almighty, she cries loud enough to put you into orbit. Reach down there and pull that afghan up over me. It's always freezing in here."

I covered her up. "Grandma, do you remember when we were little girls, Florabelle and I, and you'd tell us to wish for something big when we grew up?"

She hesitated a minute, thinking back. "Yes. I used to quote some verse. How did that go?"

"I can't remember the words, but it had something to do with failure not being a sin, but low aim is."

"It is not a sin to not reach the stars . . . but it is a sin to have no stars to reach for. Was that it?" She sat up, pleased with her memory success.

"That was it. Reaching for the stars."

She looked up at the ceiling, reciting. "Whether young or old, there is in every heart the love of wonder, the sweet amazement of the stars. The childlike appetite for what is next in store." She looked back at me. "You reckon that's what Mossie's doing out there, looking through that telescope?"

"Maybe. Maybe she hasn't lost hope in spite of all her troubles," I said.

Grandma mused. "She still don't know what happened to her that night. It's kind of pitiful. Fractured her hip and left a bruise." She sat quietly for a minute, then asked, "So what star are you after, then, Fern?"

"I have this opportunity, Grandma, to work for an animal clinic in Powell County, as a lab assistant."

Grandma looked at me, eyes narrowed. "You ain't

going to be one of those people shooting cancer into rats, are you?"

"No, I'd be helping farm animals."

"Well, what's hindering you from doing it?"

"I'd have to quit Clem's; times are bad for him now. I don't know if I should do it."

She nodded.

"I'd be working full-time so I wouldn't be home as much. Momma needs help, too."

Grandma was thinking.

I waited.

"Be true to thine own self."

"But what about Clem?"

"Miracles lie in friendships. Clem, he'll soon recover."

I had her going on the parables now; I knew I'd have to stop her. "Grandma, tell me in your own words, what I ought to do."

She sighed. "When I was only four, my Momma died. You knew that, didn't you?"

I nodded.

"Well, my Daddy split up me and Effie, my twin sister, and sent us to live with two different sisters of his. The aunt and uncle I'd been sent to live with were poor; they couldn't do much for me. As you know, I married off really young and had your Momma and Hazel. My job was to work the farm and raise children. Your grandpa did a lot, but he was off preaching, too. Now Effie, on the other hand, she went to live with a rich old aunt of ours who had a lot of land, and they sent her off to a school in Indiana."

"Did you two ever see each other?"

"We wrote letters now and then, but we lost touch. She's dead now, but she had gone out west to teach English at a college."

I sat quietly for a minute, taking in her story. "So, now do you look back and regret not doing something more with your life?"

She stared at me long and hard. Then she reached inside her dress and pulled out a chain around her neck, with a key on it. She took it off and handed it to me. "Open that top drawer of the bureau, there," she said.

On top of all her lotions and sundries was a rolled up red hand towel.

"Unroll that towel," she said.

It was the crown.

"Close my door and bring it over here."

I brought her the crown.

Carefully, she placed it on her head. "It is a peace of mind that crowns a busy life of work well done," she said. "I'm proud of my life. I accomplished a lot." She removed the crown and held it in her hands, turned it slowly towards the window; the rhinestones caught the sunlight. "Effie had other choices. Like you do. If I would've had them, I would've taken them." She handed me the crown. "Now put this away and don't tell a soul where it is."

29. A Bird Without Wings

It rained almost every day the whole week, and there was nothing to do around the house but sew and read. I was working full-time now, five days a week, with weekends off. I spent most of my evenings studying.

I was reading more and more, now that I had transportation and an in at the library. Connie kept checking books out for me. I'd go to the search terminals late Saturday afternoons, make a list, and she'd get me the books.

Ever since Brother Brewer had been electrocuted, I had become obsessed with neurology. Dr. Erikson had introduced it to me briefly that day we had spayed Heidi, but now, from observing the autopsies down at the lab, it was all beginning to make sense. It fascinated me how lightning could just fry the whole system in a quick flash. I was reading a lot about the brain, and I found the subject more engaging than the uterus.

Connie and I had become pretty good friends. She teased me that if I ever became a neuro-surgeon, I should give Culler a lobotomy.

Culler was busy all week with his midterms, so I didn't see him at all. But I was looking forward to the weekend.

Connie had invited us to a Halloween party at Transy. It was a traditional thing there; I'd read about it in the newspapers. Some of the fraternities on the campus decorated one of the assembly halls to look like Count Dracula's mansion in Transylvania, and all the students got dressed up and went there for a costume party. I was making our costumes. Culler was going to be Daniel Boone, and Connie and I were going as Shawnee Indians. I already had a fringed shirt for Culler to wear, and I was making his deerskin leggings. He was going to buy a tomahawk and a black felt hat. I was making our dresses out of some of Grandma's material scraps we'd kept in the basement in a cedar chest.

"Fern," said Birdie, walking in and closing my bedroom door quickly. "You'd better hide."

"Hide? Why?"

"Momma found them pictures."

I poked my needle into the bedspread. "What pictures? You mean the ones from Grandma's pageant?"

"No, the ones from the bridge that day. Of us on that skylift. She flared up like a green-eyed monster."

"Where did you have them?"

"Taped up under my bed. She was vacuuming."

Just then, my bedroom door flew wide open, hitting the wall.

"Just what did you have in mind letting Birdie dangle in the air like that, up over all them trees?" Momma shouted. She was holding up the eight-by-ten photograph of Birdie and Connie on the skylift.

I sat up in bed. "It was safe, Momma, people ride it all the time. No one's ever been hurt."

"Well, there's a first time for everything. Just what were you thinking? That if she fell she could just flap her wings and fly?"

Birdie had run in my closet; I could see her eyes blinking through the wood slats. "She's okay isn't she?" I said calmly.

"That's not the point." Momma followed my eyes, trying to see what I was looking at. "Who talked you into this? That Culler?"

"We all wanted to ride it," I said.

"That boy's been nothing but trouble. Ever since you started going with him, you've been doing all sorts of crazy things."

I frowned. "What sort of crazy things are you talking about?"

"Taking that job for one. You had a good job right down the road here, good hours, and Clem paid you good." Momma shook her head, judging. "Some way you paid him back, quitting on him like that." Her face was red.

There it was, the familiar journey of guilt. It was true Clem was sore at me, would barely wave whenever I drove by the station, but I was giving him time, as Grandma had suggested. It was really none of Momma's business, but she was huffed. Lately, she'd been a lot more uptight than usual.

I shifted on the mattress and the springs squeaked.

Birdie had to cough and tried to time it with the squeaks.

Momma looked around, suspicious.

"I made my own decision on that job, none of this has anything to do with Culler," I said. "Why are you so bent out of shape?"

Then Momma broke down. She started to cry and couldn't stop herself. "I could have lost her," she said.

"Who?"

"Bird," she sobbed. "She could've fallen out of that thing and died. Then I would've had nobody."

"Momma, come here," I said. "Sit down."

She came over to the bed, leaned on my shoulder. "Florabelle's gone, and now I'm losing you, too," she said softly. "And your Daddy's just so distant anymore, always worrying about work. Then there's the conflict between him and your Grandma. I wish he'd just forgive her and quit making it so hard on me."

I put my arm around her. "You're not losing me, or any of us. We all still need you, especially Florabelle now, with the baby. Daddy will let go of his grudge eventually."

"He just won't talk about it," she said, blowing her nose. "And you ain't here anymore to make him listen."

"You know he's stubborn" I said. "He does whatever it

is he thinks he has to. And *I'm* just doing what *I* have to. Don't you see, I want to learn how to do something special, something that will help more people in the world than just the ones here on this foothill. Can you understand that?"

"But we still need you here, Fern."

I could hear Birdie sniffling in the closet. "Come out of there," I said.

Momma looked up.

Birdie came out, sat down on the floor in front of Momma.

"Everything will be okay," I told them. And I hoped it would be.

30. He has Risen

Halloween night, I was ready to leave to take Birdie, who was dressed like Bat Woman, to a costume party at her school, when Hazel let out a bloodcurdling scream in her trailer. At first, we thought she was in the spirit of things, trying to spook us. It turned out, however, she had been in her bedroom, heard a noise outside, and something out there scared the living daylights out of her.

When we got to the pecan tree, several pieces of Styrofoam lay all over the yard. A small skeleton, with very little decay still rotting at the bones, was lying in the middle of the debris. The air was ripe.

Jimmy had risen.

It had been a scandalous attack. The only thing we could figure was that with all the rain we'd had that month, the ground was saturated, and the cooler that Momma had buried him in had just floated right up out of the ground. He'd been dead for over a month. Picked-over corpse littered the yard. Something wild had caught the scent and forcibly shredded the cooler to get to the source.

"Holy Mother of Christ," said Hazel. "That dog stinks to high Heaven." Her face was pallid.

Heidi howled from her pen, sensing the malice.

"Go back inside," I told Birdie.

She was standing there trembling in her bed sheet, pinching her nose, eyes wide open.

"Hazel, get me the shovel."

The ground was muddy; my feet sank as I worked. As I scooped the remains back into the deep hole, I prayed silently that Jimmy's little soul, at least, was free from toil.

When I dropped Birdie off at her school, she still hadn't overcome the shock. The whole ride there, I kept trying to explain that Jimmy was safe in Heaven, that those traces she'd seen really weren't part of him anymore. Souls rise, and only the bones return to the earth: from dust to dust, I reminded her.

She argued that when Jesus rose from the dead, he must have taken his bones with him because he was able to come back a few days later and walk the earth. He couldn't have done that without legs, she pointed out.

She was convinced that Jimmy was possessed by evil and he'd come back to haunt her on Halloween because she had let those jackals of Satan eat him up that day.

31. Hunter's Paradise

I had to stop and fill my tank at a Redimart in Clay City. Ever since I'd quit Clem's, I felt guilty buying gas from anyone else, but it was hard to face him. He took my leaving personally. I wondered how he was doing, if he had stayed open tonight, or if he'd closed up to trick-or-treat with his granddaughters. I missed him and wished he'd get over his mad so we could be friends again, go fishing or to a ball game, have lunch or something. Like old times.

Everything was different now. I spent less and less time at home, and when I was there, I read or studied mostly. Sometimes, especially when Florabelle was over with Daisy, it was hard to concentrate, and I'd get irritable and take it out on Birdie, then have to apologize later. She didn't understand my new objective. She called me selfish and took it personally, too. She resented both my job and Culler.

Daddy really hadn't said too much, as I was paying more on the bills. But I could tell Momma was alienating me. She and Hazel both laid on the guilt, almost daily, for me not going to see Grandma as much as I used to.

I had very little time for sewing anymore, either, but I hadn't lost my touch. I got plenty of needlework practice on sheep abdomens.

At first, the doctors at the lab had me cleaning beakers and measuring out samples, but when they realized how much practical knowledge I had, how much I had learned and memorized about physiology, they gave me more hands-on tasks with the livestock. I performed a lot of suturing and stitching, and was learning how to identify certain disease cells under the microscope.

They told me I had initiative. That made me feel good, hearing that said about me. I liked what I was doing, and was gaining more confidence. No longer was I conscientious about a uniform. Now, when I got to work and put on my lab coat, I wore it with the utmost pride.

Sometimes, I'd even wear it home, or leave it on when I went in the bank to make a deposit, or to the grocery store, just so everyone would see me and know what I was. Instead of a tire gauge, now, I had a pocket flashlight. I would do things to make people notice this, too, such as take it out and pretend to check the battery when I was in line at a soda counter.

There was one further step I had taken, and no one knew about it. I had applied for enrollment at Transylvania. I wanted to begin in the spring semester.

One night at the library with Culler, I had filled out the paperwork, without him realizing what I was doing. Then I had requested Carlisle High to send my transcripts, and one Saturday, I had pretended to have errands to run all morning, but really had taken a five-hour exam called the SAT.

I was waiting for a reply in the mail. Until I heard any news from the university, I wasn't going to tell anyone my plan.

I knew I could handle one or two night classes and keep working full-time, and still have money left over. Besides, I was in no hurry. I really didn't plan to try for a degree, but I wanted to take a few science classes to learn more about what I was doing at the lab. I wanted to start with Chemistry.

When I got to Connie's dormitory, I was late. It had taken me almost an hour to bury Jimmy and get cleaned up again. Culler's jeep was already there. I carried the bag with our costumes upstairs, and we had fun trying to get them on. Connie had bought some wine coolers, which we drank while we were getting ready.

"You look like the real thing," said Connie, tugging at Culler's bullet pouch.

"It was Daniel Boone's hunting skills that intrigued the Indians and saved his life," I shared.

"I heard that," said Connie. "His life story's all over this campus. Did you know the reason he left Kentucky and went back west was because he felt too cramped and wanted elbow room?"

"Yeah, but when he died, they shipped his bones back here to be buried. He called this place a hunter's paradise."

"*I* wouldn't exactly call it paradise," said Connie. "There's hardly any good-looking guys."

I had braided my hair and was trying to do the same to hers, but she kept jumping around the room, doing what she called a rain dance.

I told her we'd had enough rain lately, then told them what had happened to Jimmy.

Culler was deeply troubled by my story. He still wanted to get Birdie another puppy, but I wouldn't let him.

"That's pretty spooky," said Connie. "Maybe there's a full moon tonight."

I kept starting over with her hair. I had never been to a big party before, with people all my age, and I was stalling. Part of me was excited and curious, but then I felt strange, too, not really knowing how to act. College kids seemed to have a language, a walk, a style of living all their own. I felt safe in the company of my new friends, but I was still a little nervous.

The first thing we did when we got there was try the witch's brew. Connie explained later that this was orange Kool Aid and grain alcohol. To me, it tasted like just Kool Aid and we drank a lot of it while we were dancing.

Over three hundred students had come out for this event. Costumes ranged from everything such as Roy Orbison look-alikes to nuns in habits. One guy came as a penis, and kept tripping over large balloons tied around each of his ankles.

We stayed for almost two hours. Connie introduced us to a couple of people she knew. She finally hooked up with some guy in her Accounting class, who she'd had a thing for all semester.

Culler and I left around ten; the rain had stopped and he wanted to take a walk. He held my hand, and we walked around the campus, all the way down to the tennis courts. Here, we kissed for quite some time, then Culler got the idea to go riding in my car with the top down. It was pretty cool out, but the night seemed right for it.

There was something about Halloween that was always romantic to me, some element of mystery that made my spine tingle from excitement, not fear. My head felt funny, like it was floating about the car. It was hard for me to see the road in front of us; I was glad Culler wanted to drive.

We rode for several miles, not talking, just listening to a John Cougar Mellencamp tape we borrowed from Connie. We sang many of the lyrics into the wind and made up some of our own.

After a while, Culler shouted, "Let's go back towards your house. Spend some time alone in the country. It's so neat out here." He always teased me about being a country girl. Sometimes, I'd ask about his city girlfriend, the one in Orlando, but he never wanted to talk about her.

"And how am I supposed to get you all the way back to Lexington by midnight?" I asked, laughing at his suggestion.

"What, you still have curfew at your age?"

"Not an official one, but they wait up for me."

Culler looked at me, slipped his hand into my lap. "Well then, I'll let you go home, and I'll just sleep in the woods somewhere. You can drive me home tomorrow." He smiled.

My thighs grew hot where his hand rested. I tried to focus on the road, but my head was spinning. I wanted to lie down. I lay my head over the console, on Culler's lap. It was quiet now, down, out of the wind.

Culler turned the cassette tape over, brought his hand back to my head. Slowly, he worked my braid out with his fingers. When he was almost to the end of it, I reached to help him with the knot. As I did so, I brushed his lap, warm and stiff. My throat tightened.

He pulled over at Toad's Pond, the place I'd hooked him months back. It didn't seem like we'd been driving for an hour already. Culler walked around, opened my door.

The ground was cold, still damp from all the rain. I shivered against the moist grass. The stars hung low enough to touch. I reached up, Culler was pressed against me. He had taken off his vest, unbuttoned the front of my dress. His chest was heavy and warm.

He kissed me firmly for what seemed like forever, then inside me, something burned. I was a brave squaw. Daniel Boone was in control of me, and somewhere on a mountain pass, he was blazing a new trail. Captured, I surrendered to his flesh.

It began to rain.

Culler didn't stop, though, he kept us in motion, as the rain pelted off his back, splashed into my face.

Then I felt him splash inside me, and I winced.

He licked rain from my mouth and kissed me. "Are you okay?" he asked.

"I'm cold," I said, hugging him close to me.

"We'll go somewhere," he said. "But let me do something first." He reached into his costume belt lying next to him, pulled out the knife. Then, still inside me, he stretched above our heads, and carved into the tree.

My head spun, and the rain blurred my sight. I could barely make out the letters. J.C. loves F.R. Our trail was marked.

The rain was coming down in torrents now.

We ran back to my car, which was parked under a tree.

We got the convertible top back up, but the interior was drenched.

"I need to dry this out, " I said. "The carpet will mildew."

I was still naked and shivering. Culler eased across the seat towards me and started kissing me everywhere.

"Let's go," I said, moving his head away from me. "I know a place."

After standing there ten minutes, fishing for the key in my glove box, I unlocked the door to the station, walked through to lift one of the garage doors for Culler to pull the car in. I only turned on one overhead bulb, and it was hard to see what I was doing. The floor was slippery; twice, I nearly fell looking around for some dry towels.

Two pair of Clem's overalls were hanging on the closet door. Culler and I dried each other and put them on.

"Pull that door closed," I said. "If anyone drives by, they'll recognize my car."

I plugged in the blower to try it out, but I got so dizzy that Culler had to take over.

"Hurry," I said. "We can't get caught in here."

I found some change in the pocket of the overalls, eased myself out front, under the awning, to buy a Pepsi. I found Clem's kerosene lantern, one he kept in the garage for emergencies, lit it, and brought it into the station. I was afraid too much light would call attention to us.

My stomach was upset, and my legs were somewhat sore. I spread out another clean towel on the floor and lay down. The cold rain had sobered me a bit, and I knew it was wrong of me to be there, under the circumstances with Clem. I should have given him back the key in the first place, but he'd forgotten about it. So had I. Lying there, safe from the storm, I rationalized that it would just be a while, until the rain stopped. No one would know about it.

In a few minutes, Culler came into the station. "You feeling better?"

"Soda's helping some."

"Your car is going to be okay. I dried out the console, too." He moved the lantern from the counter to the floor next to us, and lay down beside me. "Seems like I've been here before," he said. "But you were working on me." He rolled over on me, kissed my neck, looked into my face. His eyes were glazed. "Now it's my turn to work on you."

He unzipped the front of my overalls, found my breasts, warming them with his hands. "I'm the doctor this time," he said. His hands were still rough from building Heidi's doghouse, and as he examined me, it prickled.

We lay there together, fondling and listening to the rain drum on the aluminum roof above us. Lightning flashed through the windows, and our cool, damp flesh glowed a pale blue.

He pressed into me again, and I stiffened.

"What is it?" he said.

"Did you mean it, on the tree, what you wrote?"

"Yes," he said. "I love you, Fern." He stopped, waited.

I didn't say anything then, just urged him deep inside me. I wanted to feel the same warm response I had felt under the tree at Toad's Pond. And we moved wildly until I did, more than once too.

I awoke to the sound of thunder. Culler lay across me, snoring evenly. I looked at the clock on the wall; it was 3:00 a.m. The rain still beat down and I felt a panic growing inside of me.

"Culler." I shook him.

He roused, rubbed my stomach as he stretched.

"We have to go; it's late."

Culler sat up, squinted at the clock. "Shit, " he said. "You have to get home."

We worked fast to get the place back in order. We were both groggy from the alcohol and staggered around in the dim light, then changed back into our wet costumes. I hung the overalls, folded all the towels, wiped up the puddles where we'd dripped. Culler backed the car out, I swept away the rain pool beneath it.

Before I pulled into my driveway, I turned off the head-lights. Heidi barked in her pen, but the storm muted her howling.

We tiptoed in.

The kitchen light was on, but it didn't sound like anyone was still up. The house was silent. I fixed Culler a bed of blankets on the basement floor, told him I would wake him early, before Daddy got up, and drive him home. He tried to coax me to sleep down there with him, but I knew Momma would be listening for me to come up the stairs.

I tucked a quilt around him, kissed him goodnight.

Upstairs, snug under my covers, I dreamed Culler and I were running through the warm rain of hunter's paradise, looking for elbow room.

32. More Sirens

It was the second time in two months the folks in Leeco heard sirens. The last time was when Grandma had Daddy arrested in the garden. This time, it was a fire engine out in front of Clem's. The station had burned down to the ground. The assumption was that lightning had struck; only the rain had kept the fire from reaching the pumps and spreading up the hill to the houses.

We stood out in our driveway, under umbrellas, watching the flames dance. At the bottom of the hill, the sky was ablaze. It was still sprinkling, the smoke hovered low, suffocating.

"Your Daddy's gone down there," said Momma, tears in her eyes. "He was still awake, waiting up for you, and heard the explosion."

"I heard it, too," said Hazel. "I thought for sure we'd been bombed."

I'd been home for two hours and had heard nothing. Momma had come in, shook me from a deep sleep, dragged me out of the house, worried the fire would spread. Standing in the cool, damp November air, I was still in a daze. It was hard to believe what was happening.

Birdie had run around to let Heidi out; she stood between us, shivering, knowing the danger. Birdie soothed her.

"Poor old Clem," said Hazel.

Momma looked at me. "He's had that place for almost twenty years. What a shame."

In silence, we listened to the crackling flames. We could see Daddy walking back up the hill in a yellow poncho.

"Anything left down there?" asked Hazel.

"Mighty nigh lost everything," he said, frowning. Daddy was drenched to the bone. "He had a lot of gallon jugs of gas in there, caught fire quick and spread. They'll look around, salvage what they can at daybreak."

"Nobody was hurt?" asked Momma.

"No one was even nearby." He looked at all our faces. "I was the first to report it. They figure it was lightning. One of the firemen said a bank was struck over in Campton. Nasty storm."

"Was Clem down there just now?" I asked. I felt a lump in my throat. The air was smothering.

Daddy looked at me, hesitated. "Yeah, they called him in. He's pretty shook up. Said he felt like he was watching his whole life blow up in smoke."

"I know he's insured," I said, looking down. My head was splitting.

Daddy nodded. "He wants me to help go over the policy with him tomorrow, check the fine print."

"Let's go inside," suggested Momma. "I'll put some coffee on."

"It's almost five o'clock, we'd be up in an hour's time anyway," said Hazel. "Let me go get some clothes on."

As we were walking into the house, Daddy grabbed my shoulder, pulled me back, waited for Momma to get inside. "Why were you out until two this morning?"

His grip throbbed and sobered me. I felt my heart stop. Right then, the whole night seemed such a blur, I couldn't recall the events. Suddenly, I remembered Culler was still in the basement.

Daddy was waiting for an answer.

"Car trouble," I lied. "Brakes are sticking. I didn't want to chance it with the roads slick." I hurried past him, stepped inside.

"You should have called," he said.

While Momma was making breakfast, I went in the bathroom and washed my face with cold water. I sat down on the toilet and tried to think of how to get Culler out of the house now that everyone was up. I hoped he was still asleep. I must have been in there too long, devising a plan, because someone knocked on the bathroom door.

"Who is it?" I asked.

"Me."

It was Birdie.

I opened the door.

"You look sick," she said.

"I'm okay. Is the coffee ready?"

"Yeah, but we're waiting on Daddy to eat. He's in the basement, drying off."

I stood up quickly, ran past Birdie, through the kitchen, downstairs.

Daddy was standing at the bottom of the steps, arms folded. He was waiting for me.

Culler was sitting up in the pile of laundry; his face as white as the sheets he used to cover himself. He looked a mess, afraid.

"Fern," said Daddy, voice shaky.

"Daddy, let me explain," I began. I was about to be sick.

"I'll listen to nothing," he said. Then he turned to Culler. "This is my house, and there are rules. You need to leave, son. Right now."

"Daddy, we were too tired to drive home. We were going to wait until—"

"—I said I don't want to hear it." He looked back at Culler one more time, glowered. Then started up the stairs. He passed me, looked right into my eyes. His were red. "You're a liar," he said and slammed the door into the kitchen.

33. The Smoldering

The stress in the house was so thick after Culler left that I made my decision fast. I went upstairs and began packing my things. Culler had insisted on walking to a pay phone and taking a cab home. I didn't even think a cab would come all the way out to Leeco, but he was hard set. He'd promised to call me later.

By the time I made my last trip, it was almost daybreak. I stood at the back door, gazed out into the dim light. The sky was overcast, ash gray. The air was still smoky from the fire, but the tension smoldering at home was worse. It was hard to take that first step, but I knew what I had to do.

I counted six stars shining through the clouds, and made five wishes. I would save one for later. Then I lifted my bags, stepped out into my freedom.

I had proposed to move into the little house Grandma had vacated and arranged to pay Daddy rent biweekly. It only took four trips to move my things up there, with the top down in my car. The house had three rooms: a living room, bedroom, and the kitchen. I took my Jenny Lind bed and dresser and some of Grandma's dishes and kitchen appliances we had stored in the basement.

Momma was bitter at me about the whole incident, but she was more hurt than angry. I had disappointed her. Everyone assumed I, not just Culler, had slept in the basement that night. What bothered Momma the most, though, was the fact that Daddy wouldn't speak to me, *nor* her. He blamed my lack of morals on her raising of me.

For the first three days, I had no contact with any of the family except Birdie. She would walk up the hill after school, help me clean and put things away. Momma, in spite of herself, sent Bird up with some extra pot holders and a juice pitcher.

The house felt strange, and looked different than it did when Grandma'd lived there. She had the place stuffed with things, most of which we'd pitched. When I hung some of my own pictures from home, they seemed almost offensive on the walls. The place issued forth a sense of grandmotherdom.

I hung the picture of me and Culler at Natural Bridge Park over my bed. It kept my guilt in check.

I knew I would have to add furniture slowly. It took a whole paycheck to turn on the water and power and buy some food staples. I would have to wait on a phone.

I didn't really have time to be depressed about what was happening as I was so busy scrubbing, painting, repairing, and organizing things. Birdie was good company and helped me ease into being alone. She stayed late one night when I made chili macs, and she ate with me.

The oddest thing I suppose about it all, the hardest part to understand, was that I couldn't remember anyone acting this mad at Florabelle when *she'd* disappointed them. There was no doubt at all about what *she'd* done; Daisy was blossoming proof.

Subconsciously, I think I was waiting for some sign. Either some surprise blessing that would let me know God understood and forgave me, or some lurking evil, bad news, and I'd know I was doomed.

Somehow, though, I didn't feel as guilty as I probably should have, as I'd always expected to. I believed that I loved Culler, and what we did seemed right to me. Luckily, I didn't have much time to dwell on it. I had to think about getting my house and life situated. Living alone was new territory. It would take some getting used to.

But in God's eyes, I guess the truth was known. Thou shall not fornicate out of wedlock. I didn't recollect where it actually said that in the Bible, but that was Grandma's and Reverend Whitaker's translation of committing adultery. Where once a tire gauge and then a pocket flashlight adorned my chest, I now imagined a scarlet *A*.

34. The Chair

The third day out, Hazel showed up at my door. She had a lazy boy chair she didn't think she really needed anymore, no one ever sat in it, and she wanted help unloading it into my living room.

Once inside, she sat down on it, the only chair in the room now, and I made coffee for us. I even had some cream and saccharin; she took both.

"So how long do you think your Daddy will stay mad?" she asked, engaging the footrest.

"I don't know. Seems he's always mad. He's angry with life these days." I poured cream into my mug. "Has he asked about me?"

Hazel shook her head. "Just told your Momma you better be good for your rent money."

I was sitting on the floor in front of her. I crossed my legs, blew across the top of my coffee mug. "Has anyone called there for me?"

"Not that I know of." Hazel reached into her hip pocket for her cigarettes. "Do you mind if I smoke in here?"

"Go ahead, but I don't have an ashtray."

"I'll watch it." She lit one, looked around the bare room. "I feel like I'm doing something wrong, you know your Grandma never allowed anyone to smoke in here. It must seem strange being here, without that old orange vinyl chair of hers, all them damn plants, Billy Graham a' blaring on the TV set."

"Yeah, it's sort of creepy. I feel like she's still here, though. At night, I think I hear her digging through the drawers for her Dristan."

Hazel blew smoke and chuckled. "I bet you do. She always had to have several bottles of it around, most of them empty. She still does that."

"Does she know I'm living here now?"

"No, I didn't want to tell her. For one thing, this whole

mess with your Dad would get her upset, and she still has high hopes of getting better and coming back here. Taking care of herself, living alone again."

"How is she doing?"

"Not too good. She's tired all the time, getting meaner, too. You know, she still won't return that crown."

I looked down, hid a smile.

"And get this. Some of the staff claim she's got a thing going with this old guy, Earl's his name. Crippled and hard of hearing."

I looked up, curious. "I met him. So is she?"

Hazel kicked the footrest back down, leaned forward, smirked. "Let me tell you this one on her. Growing up, we were Church of God. *Strict* Church of God. That meant no swearing, no dancing, no drinking. We weren't even allowed to have a deck of cards in the house. That was gambling. Well, when it came to sex, your grandma always used to be hushed about it. Then as we got older and started asking questions, she told us she just tolerated it with Grandpa, so she could have children. Tolerated it; *that* was her word. Now come to realize, in her old age, she's as horny as a toad."

"Well, I'll be." I smiled, thinking about my own predicament. "What did she do?"

"I'm getting to it." Hazel laughed. "Her and this fellow, Earl, they're always together. They watch the TV all day long sometimes. Well, one of the nurses, the one who gives us her daughter's clothes for Bird, she got this idea to build Esther's confidence, improve her attitude, by giving her some responsibilities. See, Earl has little to no bladder control, and sometimes he tries and anticipates the urge and warns someone so they can wheel him to a bathroom. And I'll tell you this, your Grandma moves as slow as a crippled turtle, always complaining she's so stiff, but I swear it, when Earl tells her he needs to go, she pushes him down that hallway faster than a scalded dog."

Hazel got up, walked to the door, opened it, ashed her cigarette, came back to the chair. "So this one night, she, the nurse, walks into the TV lounge, and there's Earl, lying on the couch with his pants down, his feeble little old legs spread wide open, and your grandma standing there tickling him."

"You're kidding me," I said, laughing.

"Even with her arthritis, she had the tape of his Depends ripped right off!" Then Hazel got the hysterics.

"What did the nurse say?"

"She was shocked! Just turned around and left them. She said Esther looked more guilty than a suck-egg dog."

"I just can't believe it," I said, shaking my head.

"I was just as doubtful, but now that I've been watching them two together, I'm starting to see it for myself. The whole idea was to give your Grandma some more get up and get. Well, I've seen with my own two eyes what she gets up and got."

"So, has Grandma told you, or anyone, about him? Does she say she likes him?"

Hazel threw her arms over her head. "Denies every-thing. Bad part about it is he's married. His wife's in one of the Carolinas, rich old lady, stepping in some high cotton and never comes to visit him."

"Whatever happened with that trouble with Mossie?"

"Oh, she's better now, still as crazy as a loon, but she's fine. That was sure something about that daughter-in-law of hers, robbing her like that. Creating that ruckus at the party."

"Yeah, that was cruel. And now we can be sure of who pulled that stunt with Florabelle's wedding cake, too."

"That's right, must be Patty's trademark, leaving a sign in the cake icing. That's just crazy."

"Is she in jail?"

"No, no one pressed any charges, but her husband left her."

"Can't say I blame him. Love's sure a strange thing." I stood up, stretching. "Want some more coffee?"

"Maybe one more cup, then I got to get going. I'm so tired, I'm dead on my feet."

When I brought Hazel her mug, she said. "So, Fern, speaking of love, tell me about this boy, Culler."

I jiggled a jar of nails on the floor. "What about him?"

"Are you in love?" She batted her eyes at me, like a toad in a hailstorm.

"I don't know, I guess. We get along."

"Is it true, what your Daddy says? He found him in your basement with his clothes shuck off?"

"He said that?"

Hazel nodded, winked.

"He probably was naked, but I wasn't down there with him. I was upstairs in my room."

"Well, Fern, times have changed. Like I said, when I was your age, all that stuff was forbidden. If I would've got caught up to mischief like that, I'd been sent away. But it's so different these days, people see things in a whole different way. They're more accepting."

"Momma sure ain't."

"That's true, your Momma is still pretty old-fashioned. She still goes by the old book. Probably always will." Hazel swallowed her last sip. "Hell, if your Grandma can do the hanky-panky, so can you." She laughed. "You do what's right in your book."

"That's just it. I don't know what I think, what's right or wrong when it comes to those things. It seems it's always some special circumstance. I'm waiting for some sign to tell me."

"Well, the sign's going to come from inside. Just search your heart, as they say. Can't afford to be superstitious about it." Hazel covered a yawn, shifted in the chair. "No sense in worrying about it, either. I made that mistake with your Uncle Ben. You said yourself that love is strange. Well, it sure is. When me and Ben first got married, I worried all the time, worked myself up over everything. Always fretted and wondering whether I did the right thing in marrying him, whether or not he'd always love me. But you never can be sure. You just have to give it a go and work at it. You decide and you do it. Well, I learned that too late. Worried him right out the door."

Hazel stared off a few moments, stood up, carried her mug to the sink. "I got to be getting back down the hill.

Got to work the breakfast tomorrow."

"I have to get up early, too."

"You like that new job?"

"A lot."

"Well, don't bring none of those diseased cows home, you hear? We've had enough bouts with animals around this place."

"Don't worry. Tell Grandma hi for me. Maybe I'll come up this weekend to see her." I walked Hazel to the door. "Thanks for the chair."

"You're welcome. I'll see if there's anything else to scrounge up I don't use." She walked back inside, checked around the chair to see if she'd dropped any ashes on the carpet. "Remember, love's first a feeling. It's a decision later. Take it slow. Right now, go with the feeling. You're young, and you ought to enjoy it while it lasts." She gave me a little hug. "Lock this door now."

I watched her walk down the hill until she disappeared, thinking about what she'd said. She was right: I should just go with my feelings. That's what Grandma was doing, anyway. And she would have sat here and given me the same advice.

Relaxed for the first time in three days, I sat down in my new chair, my only chair. My new seat of wisdom.

35. This Little Light of Mine

The weekend came, but I had too much to do to go to Lexington. I wanted to see Culler, but I needed to run errands and work around the house. The place was long in need of repair; it had been even while Grandma'd lived there. Daddy just never seemed to have the time to put into it, nor the money. Only thing he'd kept up was the shed out back.

I spent all day Saturday painting the outside of the house. I had decided on sunshine yellow with white trim. Birdie helped me by holding the ladder. I asked her if anyone had called for me, and she said no.

Sunday morning, I went to early church service and prayed for a light to be shed on my situation. I was still confused about what had happened between Culler and me. Not that I worried that *I* was pregnant, although the thought did enter my mind. But I could only wait and see on that.

I'd seen Momma and Birdie up front, but they didn't see me slip into a back pew. I missed Momma, wondered how she was doing, but didn't want to confront her until she was ready first.

It was hard driving down the hill each morning, passing the house I'd lived in for three years. But worse than seeing my own home where I was no longer welcome was having to look at Clem's lot, burned to the ground, nothing standing but a charred Pepsi machine. The county had razed what was left of the support walls. I worried about Clem, cried about him for two nights. I could only hope he'd made out all right with his insurance.

After church, I drove to Mac's and used a pay phone to call Culler. He wasn't there, so I left a message with his roommate. Then I tried calling Connie, who was also gone. I missed them both and decided to get a phone hooked up on Monday. I felt so out of touch with folks now. It was just me, my work, and my thoughts.

I went in the store for some food and household items and filled my cart with mostly soup and spaghetti. That was cheap, and it tasted good on a cold day. All the rain we'd had was turning to sleet now. Winter was coming.

When I got to the check-out line, Grover Flynn, the owner of the local fish camp, was in front of me buying beer.

"Fern," he said, tipping his dirty cap. "Where have you been hiding? You haven't been in to buy bait in a long time."

"I'm working full-time now, at an animal clinic up in Powell County. Not much time for fishing these days, unfortunately. How's business?"

"Well, you know it slows down when it gets this cold, no one wants to weather it. A few pike are running, but that's about it. What about your job, they paying you decent?"

"Pretty good," I said, unloading my cart onto the counter.

Grover looked at my items. "They must be paying you more than old Clem did, for you to afford all them vittles." He smiled.

I looked up. "Have you talked to him lately, since the fire I mean?"

"Yeah, he's been in a few times, looking for trouble. He wants to buy me out." Grover paid for his beer, stepped back to give me room at the counter. "Says when he gets his insurance settlement, he's going to buy the camp and turn it into some big year-round fishing resort." He snickered, shook his head. "That Clem, he's a crazy man."

"So he did get his money?"

"Well, not yet, but it should be coming to him soon. They're still tying up some loose ends. It's got to be positive it ain't arson, then it's all just a matter of getting the paperwork through."

"Well, nobody would've set fire to Clem. He doesn't have one enemy."

"That's for sure, the man ain't got no evil bone in his body."

"Then why don't they just pay him his money?" I asked, beginning to worry.

"The story goes that when they was cleaning up the place, the investigators found some lamp that had been burning. They don't know if it was the cause of anything, but they got to check it out. Clem don't deny the lamp was his, but claims he don't remember getting it out and using it. They think more likely, it was the lightning."

There was my sign. My body went numb.

The cashier was trying to get me to pay, but I was aghast. I swallowed hard. "What kind of lamp?" I asked Grover.

"One of them kerosene kind you use in a power out."

"They don't know if that was it yet?"

"No, like I said, it was probably lightning. That sure was a wicked storm. My antenna got hit, blew out my cable."

I quickly paid the cashier and left the store.

When I got to Peaceful Pastures, they were having a Bible class. I walked by the dining room, saw Grandma sitting there, thumbing through the pages of the New Testament. She was sitting next to Earl.

I passed through to the kitchen. Hazel was cleaning out the meat freezer.

"Hi, Fern," she said, stacking ground round. "Esther's in there studying Luke. It's her way of making up for all the trouble she causes around here."

"I actually came to ask you something."

"What is it you need?"

"Well, I've been wondering about Clem."

Hazel slammed the freezer door shut, threw her rag in a bin. "What about him?"

"Wasn't Daddy going to help him read his insurance policy?"

"Yeah, they read it. Doesn't seem to be any question about it though. Clem was over one night last week, believe it was Thursday."

"What's the deal, then?"

"Well, evidently, he still had a ten-year loan left on the station. As long as the cause of the fire turns out to be a natural act or accidental, the mortgage company gets their share, Clem gets his equity. Whenever the case is arson, and there's no suspicion of the owner, then the same applies. But if there's any doubt there was foul play on Clem's part, then the mortgage company gets what's coming to them, but Clem gets nothing."

"Well, what have they come up with so far?"

"There's two theories I'm hearing." Hazel craned her neck, looked towards the kitchen door.

Mossie had wheeled in.

"Mossie, it ain't time to eat, go on back out there and join the prayer meeting. I'll come get you for lunch," said Hazel. "They're always wheeling or strolling through back here, and they've been told it's off premises."

"What are the two theories?"

Hazel frowned at me. "One is that lightning struck

something, maybe the cash register, something near the front entrance. They've been able to detect evidence of that. The other is that some kerosene lamp was burning, tipped over next to some grease rags, some old towels."

"So what are they waiting on?" I asked, biting my lip. "To make the decision?"

"Problem is Clem claims he kept that lamp in the garage, don't know how it got over by the cash register where they found it. The investigators can't find no traces of breaking and entry, though."

"Then what's the holdup?" I could feel myself starting to sweat under my wool sweater.

"You know how those firemen are, especially in this little old town. They're so pokey, I don't know how they got down there fast enough to put out the fire in the first place." Hazel walked over to the dishwasher, loaded some coffee cups and saucers. "Why are you so hard-pressed about all this?"

"I'm just curious." I paced the tiled floor.

"You look like you're on pins and needles."

"I just want everything to work out for him, that's all."

"I'm sure it will. He's supposed to know something before the holiday." She started the coffeemaker. "We serve coffee and cookies after this prayer meeting breaks up."

"So he'll know by Thursday?"

"Supposed to. I'll tell you this, though." She lowered her voice to a whisper. "There's some who believe the old guy started it himself just to get the money. Of course that's a rumor, some folks would say anything just to stir up some trouble." She looked around. "It would make sense, though, you know, to do something like that."

The anger inside me was almost instant; my blood was starting to boil. "Clem would never, *absolutely never* do something like that. He is the most honest man I've ever known in my life."

"What is the matter with you? You came flying in here like you had some emergency." Hazel stacked cups on a tray, stood in front of me to stop my pacing. "Besides, I didn't say he did it, I'm just telling you what I heard. Calm down. It'll all work out for him. Shake it off."

I stared at the floor.

"Now, Fern, you coming down to the house for dinner Thursday?" she asked, passing through the swinging doors to the dining room.

For the brief moment she was gone, I took a deep breath to collect myself. "I don't know," I said when she came back. "Bird says Daddy's still mad, I'm pretty much fallen from grace. I doubt I'm welcome."

Hazel tisked. "Yeah, I wanted to bring your grandma home that day, too, but I know what would happen."

"You're right about that. Never can tell what's going to happen at the dinner table in that house," I said.

"Your daddy is sure a mess. He's so bitter, sulks all the time. He didn't used to be like that, you know. Back in West Carrollton, he was always on the go, much more pleasant to be around."

"It's been since he lost our farm."

"I guess that's it. But life goes on. He's got to let go of the past. Lord knows I try to. Things could be worse for him, you know. At least he's got his job, health, his family to be thankful for. This is the time of year to be remembering all that."

"Has he heard any more about layoffs?"

"No news." She filled another tray of coffee cups. "I've got to get out there. Do you want to have a snack with your grandma?"

"I'll stick my head in, say hello. But I have groceries in the car."

"I'll see if I can feel your folks out about you coming over for dinner. I'll let you know."

"Let me know how it goes with Clem, too."

"Bye now."

The whole way home, a lamplight kept flickering in my head. The light shone on my weakness, and I realized then, the weight of my sin. That night, I dreamed I burned up in flames.

36. Out of Line

Sunday evening I got my period and we got our first snowfall. I looked out the bathroom window and saw Birdie walking up the road with Heidi.

"Can you keep her?" she asked, shivering in my doorway.

"What do you mean?" I asked, buttoning my jeans.

"She's going to get cold out in the snow with her hair still not all grown back." Birdie pointed to Heidi's bald spot. "You can keep her in the house for company."

"Birdie, Heidi's never been a house dog, she won't like it being cooped up in here."

"I gave her a bubble bath in the basement. She's clean."

Heidi sniffed around the living room, found me, nudged my hand with her head. Her tail flapped, and her red coat shone like I'd never seen it.

"She misses you, too," said Birdie.

I sighed, sat down in the only chair. "I guess she couldn't hurt herself on anything in here, nothing for her to run into but this chair." I took Birdie's raincoat, hung it behind the door. "What did Daddy say about it, though? I don't want to stir up any more trouble than I already have."

"He don't care. He never hunts her no more anyway. She's mine now, he said."

"I guess it's all right." I went in the bedroom, came back with an old sheet to make Heidi a bed. "Here's a key to the house," I said. "Let her out to pee after school tomorrow. And don't lose it."

Birdie squeezed the key into the back pocket of her corduroys.

"Go put some water down for her," I said. "Are you hungry?"

"We just ate."

"Well, I need to eat. Come talk to me in the kitchen." I opened a can of tomato soup, heated it up on the stove.

Then I fixed a grilled cheese sandwich. "Would you like some ice cream? I have Rocky Road."

"Ice cream? It's freezing in here." She folded her arms, hugging herself.

"I have the heat turned down low to save money. You want hot chocolate instead, then? I have cocoa mix."

She nodded.

I found her a coloring book and crayons, and set her up on the kitchen floor with a book to use as a surface.

She complained that I didn't have a TV set for her to watch, but I argued that was too expensive. "I don't watch TV shows anyway," I said. In my opinion, she watched too much of it. It was warping her mind.

She colored as I boiled the water, then she got up, opened the refrigerator, browsed. "Can I have that Pepsi?"

"No, Birdie, that's the one Grandma saved that Elmer opened just before he died. I found it still in there when I moved in. I figured out it's four years old. That would taste awful, wouldn't it?" I laughed. "I guess that's how she holds on to the past."

"Hazel says to look only forward, not back," Birdie said, still holding the fridge door wide open.

"And she's right, now shut that. You're letting all the cold air out."

"You don't have much food in here."

"I don't need much."

"Thursday's Thanksgiving," she said.

The teapot whistled.

"I know," I said. "You get a couple of days off from school, don't you? That'll be nice." I mixed her hot chocolate and ate my sandwich, standing at the counter. I still didn't have a table.

"Are you coming over for turkey?"

"I don't know yet."

"Florabelle is, with Daisy."

"Isn't Jason coming with them?"

"He can't get off. Says he's got to work that day for overtime."

"He'll get time and a half, they probably do need the extra money," I said, mouth full.

"Are you working, too?"

"No, I'm off Thursday and Friday. Long weekend." I was hoping to spend it with Culler, but I didn't want to mention him to Birdie, not until everything blew over.

"Then why don't you come over for dinner?" she asked. "Momma already bought a twelve-pound turkey."

"She'll have to freeze a lot of it."

Birdie slurped cocoa, sulked.

"Did Daddy mention he wanted me to come?"

"He didn't say it, but you should."

"We'll see. I don't know if he or Momma want me to. They're both still pretty sore at me for acting out of line last week."

"Daddy thinks you do stuff on purpose just to aggravate him."

"You know that's not true, don't you?"

She nodded.

"How's Momma doing?"

Birdie sat quiet a moment, concentrated on the picture she was coloring. "She cries a lot."

"Has she been sick?"

"No, just depressed over Daddy. He hasn't talked to anybody but Clem for a whole week. He don't even turn grace over at the table anymore. Spends all his time in his gun room."

"How does he treat you?" I asked.

"Okay, I guess. Damn."

"Bird!" I said, having never heard her swear before.

"I went out of the lines." She ripped the page out of the book, crumpled it up, and started to cry.

I put my plate in the sink and sat down beside her. "I know it's hard to be around all that tension in the house. Unfortunately, though, part of growing up is having to try and understand it all. Realize why people act and react the way they do. I had to learn to understand it, I still have to try real hard sometimes, and I _am_ grown up."

"I wish I could live here with you," she said softly.

"So do I, but you still need Momma."

"Don't you need her no more?"

"Yes, I do. But as I was saying, sometimes things just

don't make sense. I wish I could talk to her, still be there with you all. I just have to try and understand how she feels and wait patiently until she's ready to forgive me."

"I don't like it there anymore. There's no one to talk to. I miss Grandma, too."

"When did you see her last?"

"At her pageant."

"I'll take you up to visit her soon. I promise. Now, here, color another picture. And don't worry about staying in the lines. It's okay to go outside them sometimes, can't always be perfect."

Birdie nodded, sniffled, started to color. "Daddy still hates Grandma," she said, choosing a crayon.

"No, he doesn't. It's just that some people don't know how to let go of their anger and forgive. That's something else you have to learn growing up."

"There's too much." She had the sobs. "I'll just stay little." A tear splashed on her picture.

I hugged her close. We sat huddled together, listening to the soft snow fall on the rooftop.

I looked at the stove clock; it was nine-thirty. "It's a school night," I said. "Let's get you home. Tell you what, if I can't make it Thanksgiving for some reason, you can come up later that night, after dinner, spend the night with me."

"The whole night?"

"The whole night, anytime you want."

This invitation seemed to satisfy her, so she stood up, put her picture on my refrigerator. It was two rabbits, hiding in a hollow from a bear. She'd colored the bear black, written "Daddy" beneath it.

37. Straying The Flock

Someone brought in a black sheep with anthrax, and I had to burn the carcass. When the farmer carried it in, the sheep was convulsing and burning up with fever. It only lived another fifteen minutes.

I knew humans could get the disease by exposure to infected animals, and I tried to stay away from it when the old guy brought him in. He suspected that the sheep had strayed the flock and eaten some contaminated grass somewhere. Our doctors advised him to bring the well ones in for vaccination.

Wearing gloves and a mask, I took the animal back to the crematory. This was the part of the job I hated, but just lately, I'd been getting used to it. Everything had to die, I told myself, and what we were doing at the clinic was trying to delay the inevitable.

But now the furnace, or any fire, made me think of Clem's dilemma. I was so bothered, wondering what the investigators would define as the cause of the fire. As the flames sizzled inside the oven, I could hear in my head the workbench, the supply shelves, the tool rack, all of it crackling in flames. I could smell the rubber burning from the tire pile. I could see Culler's bare chest, aglow in the lantern light.

I waited until the bones were few, crushed and sacked them. I would wait and see what the fire chief determined, then I would have to come forward. I owed it to Clem.

When I got home that evening, Birdie was sitting on my front stoop with the mail. She carried it up from the house every day. Heidi was running around the yard, leaving tracks in the snow. You could see her breath fog the cold air.

"Did the phone company show up?"

Birdie nodded. She was bundled up in a red wool coat that used to be mine.

We kicked the snow off our boots and went inside.

"Here," she said. "It's from Transylvania University."

With my coat still on, I opened the envelope. It was a letter of acceptance; I could begin taking classes in the spring.

"Bird," I said, beaming. "This is real good news."

"What is it?"

"It's a letter saying that I can attend their school. That means I can take a class that would help me learn more about what I do at the animal clinic."

"Will you have to move there?"

"I don't know." I hadn't really thought about that. Lexington was over an hour's drive. "I'll worry about that later. Do me a favor, though, don't tell anyone. I mean no one. I want to keep it a secret just for a little while, okay?"

She nodded.

"Good girl."

Birdie hadn't taken her coat off and turned to go. "I have homework," she said. "We have a spelling test tomorrow, then no more school until Monday."

"Do you want me to make flash cards?"

"I'll do them."

"Well, all right then, don't miss any of them."

"Bye, Heidi," she said, petting her. "Go lie in your bed."

Heidi obeyed her, made her way to her sheet, curled up and sighed.

"Fern?"

"What, Bird?"

"Don't come Thanksgiving. Daddy says no."

Her words stung, but I didn't want her to know. I looked at Heidi in the corner and spoke. "Then you just come up that night like we planned. Spend the night. Heidi would like that."

She nodded, closed the door.

My eyes watered as I changed into jeans and a sweat shirt. I had never spent a holiday away from my family before and wasn't ready to do so. I felt so estranged, so alone, but I didn't want to feel sorry for myself. I had made a mistake and would have to suffer the consequences.

Maybe I could cook my own Thanksgiving dinner, invite Culler and Connie over to celebrate. I would call and tell him the news. I had not talked to him and really needed to. I wanted the comfort and wanted to discuss some of the things I'd talked about with Hazel, about taking things slower. But I had made up my mind not to mention the lantern, not until everything was settled.

I picked up my new phone and dialed his number. His roommate answered, said he expected Culler any time now from class. I gave him my new number, told him to have him call me as soon as he got in. I knew he'd be happy about the acceptance letter. He'd be proud of me for trying, in the first place.

I made myself an omelet and tried to read a book to keep my mind off Clem, off the sheep, off fire, off Daddy, off everything.

The house was chilly, and I turned the heat up some, but the frosted air seeped in through the floors. Cinder blocks supported the house two feet off the ground. Although I was cold, I was almost thankful for no fireplace.

At ten o'clock, Culler still hadn't called, and I was getting tired. I wrapped the blanket I'd been lying on around me, walked outside with Heidi. Once out, she just stood there in the snow, with a blank look on her face. I tried to coax her to go, as long as I could stand the cold, then brought her back in. She ran straight to her bed and curled up, shivering.

It was only 10:04 when I came back inside, but I was afraid I might have missed Culler's call. Maybe I hadn't heard the phone ring over the howling wind. I tried him again.

"Hello?"

"Culler."

There was silence. "Oh, hi, Fern."

"How are you? It's been a while."

"Right. How are you?"

"Actually, I'm doing great. I got an acceptance letter today." My heart was beating fast in telling him. "At Transy. I can start class in January."

"You want to go to college?"

"Yes, I want to take some chemistry, biology, classes to help me out at work."

"I didn't know that."

His curtness and lack of enthusiasm hurt me a little. "I was keeping it a secret until I heard something. The letter came today. Isn't that great?"

"Yeah, that's great."

He sounded strange, as if he didn't know who I was, even. "Culler, is something wrong?"

"No, nothing." He paused. "I'm just so busy with school, that's all."

"You're not still upset about my Dad, are you? I figured you'd just blow that off. You know that's the way he is."

"What about you?"

"What do you mean, what about me?"

"Isn't he giving you a bad time?"

"I'm just not paying him any mind. But guess what? I have some *good* news. I don't live there anymore. I moved into Grandma's little house up the hill a ways."

"By yourself?"

"That's right. Carrying on my own. That reminds me of something I wanted to ask you."

"What's that?"

"I was wondering what you and Connie are doing for Thanksgiving dinner. You're not going home to Florida, are you?"

"No. Not until Christmas."

"Then, how about you two coming over here? We'll have sort of a housewarming, Thanksgiving, celebration dinner. I'll even cook. What do you say?"

Again, there was silence on the other end.

"What, are you scared of my cooking?"

"No, it's not that. But I'm afraid we can't. It sounds nice, though. Really. I'm sure you're a great cook."

I waited for him to explain why they couldn't come, but when he didn't, I asked, "What about this weekend, then, do you want to come over? Or me come there?"

"I don't think that's a good idea, either, Fern. I mean with what happened and all."

"What do you mean?" My stomach felt weak.

"I just don't think it's right to keep seeing each other, under the circumstances."

"What circumstances?"

"You there, me here."

"But it's worked so far. And, I'll be going to school *there*."

"But your family, they're against it, too."

"Who cares? They're against everything I do unless it's something for them. It's me this time. I'm thinking of me.

Besides," I said softly, "I thought last week, Halloween, I thought that meant something . . . You said it did."

"I know. It was nice, and it *did* mean something, at least then it did. I really thought so, up until that night. But I wasn't thinking clearly when . . . well, you know when. We both had a lot to drink. And I've been thinking about it a lot since then. It just could never work."

It was hard to believe what I was hearing. I couldn't think of anything else to say. Nothing I could say would change his mind about me, he sounded so matter-of-fact, hardhearted. His words, his whole attitude, were biting. I held the phone, holding back tears.

"Fern, congratulations, on the letter, I mean. That's really good. You'll do great in school. I know you will." His voice was shaky. "And I'm sorry. Bye now." He hung up.

The lump in my throat caused my ears to throb. I had not expected this at all. Things weren't happening as they were supposed to. I'd just wanted to take it slower, not end it. I picked up my letter, crumpled it, threw it at the wall. What good was the news without someone to share the excitement.

I didn't even brush my teeth, just took off all my clothes, climbed into bed. The sheets were cold, and I crawled way up under the covers and closed my eyes. I squinted hard to stop the tears. My throat still ached and my eyes stung.

The hurt felt very much the same as it did the night I'd moved out, only this was ten times worse. I really loved Culler. And he had me loving myself. I turned to face the pillow next to me, the one that I sometimes, real late at night, would pretend was Culler. The emptiness hurt.

Then I grabbed the pillow, stuffed it tightly under my raised knees. I lay in silence a while, listening for the soft snowfall. The cold wind sounded lonely, as if it was sharing my misery. I missed the creeping Charlie on my window back at home.

I moved the pillow to my stomach under the sheet, imagined being pregnant with Culler's baby. I wondered what Florabelle was doing right then; I missed her shortsighted fussing. I remembered her once telling me, before she found out she was pregnant, what I was missing by never going all the way with a guy. So this was it.

I moved the pillow behind me, propped myself up, tried to pray. But I felt like a fool, trying to say the words. I was angry with God. This was His way, I decided, of giving me a clear message, the sign I'd prayed for. I had justified my action with Culler by telling myself it was an expression of real love, not lust, and tonight I'd learned the hard truth; Culler didn't love me at all. It was all my own fantasy. What I'd done had been wrong. I had strayed, and I was being punished for it.

Then suddenly, everything welled up inside, all my sorrow overflowed, and I bawled relentlessly into the darkness. I cried not only for me, but for Momma, Daddy, Clem, Jimmy, the sheep, Culler, Brother Brewer, Grandma, even Mossie. For the first time yet, in my whole life, I released my pain.

Heidi, hearing me, came into the bedroom. Her nails clicked across the floor. She felt her way to the bed, nosed my hand. Sensing that I was upset, she grew nervous. Between my own sobs, I could hear her labored breathing. When I finally stopped crying, she, the brave bearer of greater pain, settled down, listening for my safety. Her company wasn't as comforting as Florabelle's had once been, but it lessened the grief. I realized, just then, how safe I felt in the company of a brave, blind bitch.

Until well after midnight, I lay with my arms crossed under my small breasts, staring at the flypaper hanging down from the ceiling. I couldn't and didn't want to sleep. I was afraid I'd dream about a black sheep, sizzling in the fire.

38. One Little Indian

When I got home from church, I made myself a cold-cut sandwich and put on a Christmas record. I had bought a turntable off of Dwayne, who'd bought one of those new stereo consoles that takes up a whole wall.

When I'd climbed up in the closet to get down my albums, I saw my Indian costume from the Halloween party and got depressed. Here it was Thanksgiving day, and I was a lonely pilgrim. I lay on the floor, cried to myself for about an hour.

Then I got the idea to go back to the church and try and catch Reverend Whitaker after the eleven o'clock service. Maybe confessing would help.

"What kind of sign?" asked Reverend Whitaker, counting the offerings.

"I can't really say," I told him, "but it was a sure one. I think it was because of a sin I may have committed."

"You may have or you did?"

"That's just it. At first I didn't think what I did was so bad, but now bad things are happening to other people because of it."

"What kind of bad things?" He was separating the quarters into stacks on his desktop.

I sat there silent for a minute. I didn't want to talk about Clem's situation until it was determined for certain what had happened that night, but I wanted to be right with the Lord in the meantime. Grandma always taught us to fear His wrath, and I was afraid He may make me turn around and set something else on fire, just as punishment.

"Well, for one, I've disgraced my family. They don't want me in the house anymore. I moved out."

The reverend leaned forward in his big vinyl desk chair, twisted his lips to think. He really wanted to help, I could tell. "Fern, you know how I feel about you and your family. I know your daddy has a lot of unrest buried in his soul, but as a good provider, I respect the man. Your momma, too. I think whatever it is you've done, they'll come around; they'll forgive you."

"Maybe. But there's other people involved besides them."

"Fern, if you're trying to tell me something, something you think *I'll* hold against you, you know better. I'd forgive you, too. And most important of all, the Lord promises us *all* forgiveness. If you've come to confess, well I suppose you've dropped enough hints that He's got the picture, but if you've come for advice, I need to know more specifics."

"I can't talk about it. Not yet anyway. Until I get an answer on something."

"An answer from God?"

"No, not really. From the county actually."

The reverend leaned back, folded his hands behind his head, stared across the desk at me. "Let's see if I've got this straight. You say you got this sign, some kind of message from God, but you're waiting on the final word from the government."

I nodded. "But I've been praying about it a lot, too."

He frowned, removed his glasses, rubbing his face. "Fern, I don't know what this sign of yours was, and I'm not the one to judge whether or not you've sinned. But I'll say this. You have to decide in your own heart what's right and wrong. No one else can tell you. I believe you may be confusing signs coming from the Holy Father with the ones your father in the flesh might be sending you." He stood up, walked around the desk, put his arm on my shoulder. "Fern," he continued, "you're going through some changes right now; you're taking on new responsibilities, adjusting to living on your own. That takes some getting used to."

"But you still don't even know what it is I've done."

"And I think you want to tell me but you're afraid. I don't have to know, though. I suggest you spend some time alone with the Lord. Times alone are times of growth. You have to quit trying to second-guess Him, though, looking for these signs. 'Wait on the Lord' it says in Psalms Twenty-seven. The *real* sign will come, and it will be clear as day to you." He walked me to the door. "Answers come not in urgent prayer, but as naturally as light comes from a lit candle. You go home, wait in silence on the Lord, he'll light your candle."

At around six-thirty, Birdie showed up at the door with a flashlight and a paper plate full of turkey scraps. She only stayed a little while because she had a head cold, and Momma wanted her to come straight home and get to bed.

I was disappointed she had to leave. I really could have used the company. Holidays are lonely, pointless, without family. And only one little Indian had come to share blessings. She was the last of my tribe.

39. Home Cooking

Around eight o'clock, I pulled back the tinfoil. It was the traditional Thanksgiving trimmings, baked turkey and dressing, mashed potatoes and gravy, green beans, cranberry Jell-o, and a roll. I sat down in my living room chair, said grace, and ate my dinner. I tried to do what Reverend Whitaker had suggested; I sat in silence, eating a turkey sandwich, waiting on the Lord.

When I'd eaten everything but the Jell-o, there was a knock at the door. I wrapped a blanket around me and went to the door. Heidi was whistling, nosing under the doorway where the freezing air seeped through.

"Who is it?" I asked, expecting Bird again.

"It's Clem."

My heart stopped. I didn't know what to say, but I opened the door.

"Can I come in?" Clem shivered in the wet snow, holding a pumpkin pie in his hand.

I stepped aside, motioned him to come in. "Sit down," I said, pointing to the chair.

He handed me the pie. "My wife sends you this. She heard you was living alone up here, figured you could use some home cooking."

"Thanks," I said. My pulse was going a mile a minute. "Can I serve you up a slice, some coffee maybe?"

"No, no thanks," he said, taking off his coat. "I'm stuffed to the gills. I just wanted to stop in for a minute, talk about few things."

I hung his coat in the kitchen. The jacket was cold, it smelled of him, a combination of Brut cologne and gasoline. I'd really missed him.

"How are you making out up here?" He looked around the little house. "I see you painted the outside of it. Looks real nice."

"Thanks," I said, leaning against the doorway to the kitchen.

Heidi had gone over to Clem; he scratched at her throat. "I see she's all healed up."

"Yeah, she's hanging in there. I'm keeping her in here, out of the cold, until all the hair grows back."

"So that job Erikson fixed you up with, taking care of them animals, it's working out all right?"

"Doing fine."

He sat quietly a minute, petting Heidi. Then he looked up at me and said, "I guess you know all about the fire."

I gulped, nodded.

"It hasn't been easy . . . folks I've knowed all my life suspecting me of starting it myself, thinking I could do something like that to get the money. That stung pretty hard." He looked back down at Heidi, patted her hip, sent her away.

I wanted to say something, say *everything*, but I couldn't think of how to begin.

"I came up here to ask you something," he said.

I let myself slide down the woodwork of the doorframe that I was leaning against, sat down in front of him. "What, Clem, what do you want to know?"

He let out a heavy sigh. "I came to ask you if you could ever forgive me. I mean for being so sore. When I first heard you took that new job, I was angry. Well, see, I was hurt. Business was slow, money was scarce as hen's teeth, and I needed your help."

"I know," I said, "I felt bad leaving, Clem."

"I couldn't look at what you were doing through your eyes," he continued. "I didn't see it as a good thing for you, I only looked at what your leaving would do to me. I lost sight of things." He looked up at me, eyes glassy. "Well, by acting like I have, ignoring you and all, what I gone and done was lose a friend."

I felt myself wanting to cry, but I knew he wasn't through with what he had to say. I only nodded, bit my lip.

"You see, I realized, during all this mess about the fire, how some folks stood behind me, my wife, Grover, your daddy, and a few others. Then there was some folks who I thought I could trust who turned on me, spread gossip. They thought maybe I was depressed, getting senile. Said I just couldn't handle failure and plotted to do something about it, so I burned the place down. That's pure hogwash, and that hurt." He rubbed his chin, looked away a minute. "Then I got to thinking who my real friends were, who I could really trust. And well, you see, that's when I got to missing you."

Heidi had her head in my lap, I was scratching her bald spot. "I've missed you to, Clem, but I just didn't know how to—"

"—I know, I didn't make it easy. But I've come to say I was sorry, and I hope we can pick up where things left off. I want to make things right between us again."

"So do I," I said, my throat tight. "I'm glad you came by. But there's something I have to tell you." Then I started crying.

"No, let's just put it all behind us. Let the sleeping dogs lie." He got up, came over to where I was sitting, patted my back.

This display of affection coming from Clem, who had never done more than wink at me, made it worse. I sobbed on.

"Don't you worry," he said. "It'll all work out."

"But I think I can help you," I said, hesitating, searching for the right words.

"No, ma'am," he said, shaking his head. "You've done enough already. It was your smarts and hard work that kept enough already. It was your smarts and hard work that kept the business above water as long as it was, and it turns out it was your smarts that's going to make me a rich man."

I frowned at him, startled. "What do you mean?"

"Let's just say, this Thanksgiving I had plenty to be thankful for, I mean *besides* my true friends."

"What, Clem?" I was anxious, a nervous wreck.

"See, they found my kerosene lantern, where it looked like it had been burning, but they couldn't really prove nothing. Remember that Pepsi machine you talked me into installing out front, the one that never did end up even paying for itself? Well, they finally detected lightning had hit it. It was a prime target. After searching the place over time after time for the cause, turned out to be that damn soda machine. The only thing left standing out there now. A goddamn lightning trap."

I was dumbfounded, speechless.

Clem was up again, pacing around the small room. The floor shook with his excitement. "So, now I got my money, more than I owed. I'm going to buy me a new truck and open a fish camp. Then I'm going to take the grandkids on a trip somewhere; they've been begging to go to Disneyland. May just go." He stepped over me, went in the kitchen to get his coat.

"I'm so relieved, Clem. I mean I'm happy for you. That it all worked out this way."

"So our trouble's water under the bridge, now?" He asked, "I'm forgiven?"

I stood up, slowly, though, shaky from the news. "Sure, Clem, as long as you forgive me."

"Like I said, I only got you to *thank*. If you hadn't talked me into buying the damn pop machine, I would've come out on the little end of the horn." He opened the door, stepped out. "Whoowee, it's as cold as a mother-in-law's heart out here. You take care of yourself up here, now, call us if you need something."

"Thanks, Clem," I said. "I'm glad you came."

"Get on in there, shut this door," he said, from way down the driveway. "And fix you a piece of that pie. It's

Thanksgiving, got to eat pie on Thanksgiving."

When I went to bed that night, it seemed a little less lonely. I gazed out the window at the wintry sky, and made a mental list of things I was thankful for. I fell asleep counting.

40. In Line

At least twenty more students stood in front of me, all wanting to sign up for the same course. The advisor from the Biology Department had warned me about this, told me to get in line early, as the class was only held twice in the spring. Registration had started at eight o'clock that morning, and about five hundred students were standing in one of several lines in the McAlister Auditorium at Transylvania University.

I'd asked permission to come in late at work so I could take care of this. They were all for it there, me going to school. When I had told the laboratory staff what I was doing, they complimented me on my initiative again. One of the head veterinarians had suggested an anatomy course.

It felt good to have Clem behind me, too. I was glad to have his support, especially since I didn't have my family backing me up. He and I'd tried ice-fishing together since we'd made up, and Birdie and I'd helped him Christmas shop for his grandkids.

I'd been in line under the "BIOLOGICAL SCIENCES" sign for almost a half-hour, my mind wondering. I began to worry that they'd close admission to the class that I wanted before I could get up there. I didn't know a soul in the whole crowd, and was a little scared just being there, in the middle of all the bustle. The sounds were so foreign to me.

I read the class catalogue and listened to conversations around me. The popular topic seemed to be what everyone did over the Thanksgiving holiday. It seemed to be a big sports-spectating weekend for most of them; I bet myself no one else had spent the day alone with an old blind blood-hound, waiting on the Lord.

The sound of noisy chatter and computer keyboard clicks filled the auditorium. I kept trying to see around the others standing in front of me, looking for the "CLOSED" sign to flash on the terminal behind the sign-up desk.

Then I saw Connie. She was just five people in front of me, waiting to get in the same class. I tensed up, opened my catalogue, and hid my face. I wanted to say hello, to talk to her, but I wouldn't know what to say if she mentioned Culler. I didn't want to talk about him, even think about him. I wanted to put the whole mess behind me. Seeing Connie brought him and his cold attitude to the forefront of my mind. Busy with work and getting ready for school, I hadn't realized how much his blowing me off still hurt.

Connie was at the desk. I could hear her familiar voice, making small talk with the administrators handling the registering. She wanted a Tuesday night class, which was the same one I wanted. When she turned around, she saw me and looked surprised.

I smiled faintly.

"Hi, Fern," she said. "Long time. Are you taking a class?" She shied away from me a little distance, looked behind her.

I nodded. "I applied back in October, I'm just taking one class, something to give me more of an advantage at work."

"So you're still working at that livestock center?"

"Yes, I like it pretty much." There was only one person left in front of me now. I paid close attention to the line.

"I'll wait over here." Connie pointed towards the printers, where class registrations rolled out continuously.

There were still three seats left in the class I wanted. I was relieved and felt important blackening in the little bubbles.

I joined Connie at the printers.

"So what class are you taking?" she asked, still acting kind of distant.

"Anatomy."

"Me too. What section?"

"Tuesday nights."

Her eyes widened. "Me too."

"That'll be nice," I said. "At least it's not another one of those accounting classes you had last term."

"That's the truth. I ended up with a C in there."

"That's okay."

"I'm only going to carry nine hours this semester, try and do better." Again, she looked around. "Want to go sit in the cafeteria? It's hard to talk in here, with all the noise."

I hesitated, knowing full well Culler would somehow creep into the conversation. But I had really missed Connie; it would be good to talk. I'd wanted to call her a few times but had lost my nerve. "Sure," I agreed finally. "I can't stay long; I'm going straight into work."

We both ordered hot chocolate and took a table by the window. Here I was, I thought, a real student in the cafeteria. About a dozen others were in there, comparing class schedules. Secretly, I was anxious to take my tray back up, put it on the belt that rode to the kitchen, just like a regular.

"How was your Thanksgiving?" she asked.

"Real quiet." Then, seeing no choice other than to reciprocate, I added, "Yours?"

She was silent a moment, blew at her hot chocolate. "Okay, I guess. I would like to have gone home."

"Did you watch football?"

"No. What about you? Did your family have a big dinner?"

"Every year," I said. I rubbed a circle clear in the window to look through. It was bitter cold out, the snow was almost a half foot deep. Students leaned into the wind, hurried to class. "It's freezing out there."

"So how are things? How have you been?"

"Real fine, just staying busy."

"I read in the newspaper about that fire, where you used to work. That was bad. Did they ever figure out what caused it?"

"Lightning. Struck a soda machine."

"That was really weird. I showed the article to Culler, he freaked out."

There it was. His name cut the air like a knife. I didn't say a word, only nodded.

Connie sensed my discomfort. "I'm sorry, Fern. It's hard for me, you know, you and I, we were friends, too. I wanted to call you, really, I must have picked up the phone a dozen times, but I felt awkward, like I was caught in the middle." She was jumpy.

"You don't have to apologize. You didn't do anything wrong. These things happen all the time. Win some, lose some."

"I know, but I still don't understand what happened. Culler won't talk about it. Not at all. He hates for me to even bring up your name. I just can't figure him out. The day after that Halloween party, all he could do was talk about you; I think he was crazy about you. He said he'd never met a girl like you before, such a live wire, or whatever he called it. But then the next day, when I showed him that article about Clem's place, he got real strange on me. Then after that, he wouldn't mention your name even."

I didn't know how to respond to what Connie was saying, but I couldn't help but wonder to myself if maybe Culler had remembered. Remembered everything about that night. If he knew, from the start, about the lantern.

"So now I feel bad," she continued. "That you and I can't talk. I knew he probably upset you, and I didn't know how to act. I guess I felt partly responsible, me being related to him."

"It's over now," I said. "Besides, you can't be responsible for someone else's actions. Let's just drop it. Maybe we can do things in the spring, when we're in class together. Just forget about everything else." I looked at her earnestly. "That is if you want to try."

"Sure. Sure I do, I've really missed you." She gave me a warm smile, slurped her cocoa through a straw. "I haven't met any neat girls like you around here. Most of them seem so stuffy, so preppy, like Leslie."

"Leslie?"

"Yeah, Culler's girl from back home. She was up Thanksgiving weekend. She drove us crazy. I don't know why he even invited her. They don't do anything but argue anyway. I can't stand her; she whines about everything. She's either too hot, or too cold, or too bored, or wants to go _do_ something. Drives me nuts."

Hearing about Leslie gave me a side stitch. I swallowed hard. "So they're going out again?"

"Not really, I think he was just lonely so he asked her to come up. I just don't get it. I thought he really cared for you; he told me so. Way back when we were coming home from that picnic. All I know is that he thought he caused you too much grief with your family, and that he got them mad at you for something. That's all he'd say."

"What's done is done."

"I know. I guess so." She picked up her spoon, stirred the chocolate mix that had settled, licked the spoon. "Remember that guy, the one from my class at the party?" The color had returned to her face at the mention of him. "His name's Jim."

"Yeah, what about him?"

"Well, we're kind of an item now. He turned out to be an okay guy. Pre-law major. I really like him."

"That's great. I'm happy for you."

"Me too. I just wish sometimes. . .oh, never mind."

"What?"

"Nothing. It's just that sometimes, I wish that we could have, well that we could have double-dated. You and Culler were such a great couple."

I could feel my eyes welling up.

Connie looked at me, understanding. "You still do care, don't you?"

I blinked. "Well, I'd be lying if I said I didn't." I wasn't too sure if I ought to open up to her, but I trusted her. "I still do care about him and think about him. But I'll get over it." I finished my hot chocolate, gathered up all my stuff. "I have to get to work, but you can call me sometime." I gave her my new phone number. "I live alone now."

"You have your own place?" She took the napkin with my number, put it in her bookbag.

"I'm renting."

"Wow, that's great." She stared at me, surprised. "Well, it was good seeing you, Fern. We'll get together soon. I really want to. See you in class, right?"

"I'll be there."

The snow crunched with every step as I headed back to my car. The ride home was a long, cold one. It was hard to keep any heat in a convertible. All the way, I thought about some things Connie had said about Culler. My hands and feet were numb. And I realized, driving along the icy road, it would be a long time before my heart thawed.

41. More Scents

After work, I was still depressed from hearing about Culler, so I stopped on the roadside in Stanton and bought a Christmas tree. I knew I could find enough fabric scraps and junk around the house to make some ornaments. Maybe if I decorated for the holiday, I'd feel better. I drove home with the top down, the tree sticking up out of my backseat.

Birdie was waiting to greet me with the mail on my front stoop. I didn't know how she could stand it, sitting there on the cold cement like that. She had her key, but would always go in, get Heidi, then wait outside.

"Anything for me?" I asked her from the driveway.

"Nope. But guess who came home?"

"Who? Grandma?" I opened the door. "Come help me get this tree in the house."

"You bought a Christmas tree?"

"Yeah, get over here. So Grandma's home?"

"No, Florabelle."

We dragged the tree in through the front door, and I brushed the snow off my boots. "Easy now," I said. "Let's lay it down by the window."

Birdie whistled for Heidi.

"Wipe her off," I said, opening the curtains. "A tree will look real nice here, don't you think?"

Birdie slammed the door and dried Heidi with a dishtowel. "Did you hear me? Florabelle's home."

"She was home last night, for supper, right? I think I saw the truck."

"Yes, she wrapped up some leftovers for Jason, went home and came back around midnight. Jason left her."

"What? What do you mean left her?"

"High and dry."

"He's gone for good?" I dropped the tree against the wall.

"She took a bus, brought Daisy and all her clothes with her. She's moved back in your old room."

"What happened?"

Birdie shrugged. "Nobody'll tell me. Florabelle's mad as a hornet one minute, crying the next. She won't talk to me, Daddy's mad, and Momma's trying to take care of Daisy. All's I know is that Jason took off to Tennessee with somebody. Maybe a girl."

"Poor Florabelle," I said. I sat down on the chair, slipped off my boots. "That Jason, I swear. He just never did care enough. Bird, why don't you tell her to come up here and talk to me, if she wants."

"She wants to see you. I told her I'd tell her when you got here. You want me to go in there and call her?"

"Yeah, but maybe you ought to leave us alone to talk."

Birdie folded her arms, pouted. "No one ever tells me what's going on," she complained.

"Sometimes you're better off not knowing everything."

"Are you guys going to hang ornaments?"

"I don't have any. But if we do decorate, I'll save the tree-topper for you. How's that?"

Birdie weighed the offer, nodded.

"Now go send Florabelle up. Tell her to bring me a strand of tree lights from the basement. There must be twelve strings of lights down there in a Mayflower box."

"Daddy hasn't got us a tree yet. Says he's not in the mood."

"Well you tell him you want one. Make Momma tell him."

"I don't want Christmas to come if you ain't coming home, anyway."

"Bird, maybe by then we'll have this mess all ironed out. Right now, Florabelle needs us the most. It would be a tough thing to have a little baby and have its father up and leave on you. Now go on, send her up, and tomorrow night we can all talk."

From the living room window, I watched Birdie dwindle into a little red speck down the hill. Bless her heart, I thought, all this feuding was really getting to her. It killed me to hear her say some of things she did. Deep down, I also hoped I'd be invited home for Christmas day. And Grandma, too. But it wasn't likely. Daddy was too stubborn.

I found an old paint can in the utility closet. Then I went back outside for some river rock and brought them in to weight down the can to support the tree. I worked with it a while by the window, trying to balance each side, snapping off the branches that stuck out farther than others.

Heidi, lying in her corner, sniffed at the fresh evergreen. I hoped she wouldn't get confused with a tree in the house. It looked like she was watching me; she was creepy that way. Even though she was blind, she always knew where to look, what was going on around her. Sometimes I would make a face at her, lunge at her quickly, do something just to test her. It always felt like she could see, or that one day she would just open her eyes and be able to.

I draped a white sheet around the paint can, fluffed it into a tree skirt. When I raised up, I saw Florabelle walking up the road with a bag.

I turned on the outside light and put on a Ray Conniff Christmas album. I thought maybe the music would cheer her up.

She charged through the door. "I got some tree lights in here. Took me forever to find them, though, that basement's a goddam pig sty." She threw down her bag, took off her coat. "Boy, this place sure looks different. I can't believe you can live here, don't it smell like old people?"

I opened her bag; buried under some clothes and other

overnight things was a strand of tree lights. "All I can smell is the tree."

"I smell moth balls."

"Help me string these lights," I said. "Tell me what happened."

"I'm tired of talking about it; I just told Hazel everything. The whole thing makes me want to puke." Florabelle flopped down in the chair.

Heidi, recognizing her voice, sidled up next to her.

"You let this damn dog in here? That's what stinks."

"It's been a bad winter so far. She's better off inside," I said, unraveling the lights.

"No shit, it's been a bad winter. You just ain't going to believe it when I tell you what happened." She let out a heavy sigh. "I've never come so close to killing two people in my life."

"So what happened?"

"First of all, I don't want to hear you saying 'I told you so.'"

"I wouldn't do that. You want something to drink, first?"

"You got any beer?"

"No, sorry, just pop and eggnog."

"Never mind." She picked up her bag, dug out a can of Pabst. "I stole one of Daddy's." She popped the lid, took a swig, sat back in the chair. "No, I don't want any lecturing. Daddy told me he had it figured all along, said I should've known Jason'd pull something like this. I swore at him, and Momma said 'don't be asking for no sympathy from her until I learn how to talk respectful.' Hazel just says it's just like a man to do this."

She had me curious, concerned. "So what is it? No lectures, I promise."

"You know yesterday," she began, "I was up at the house for dinner. Jason couldn't come, said he had to work on his brother's transmission. Well, I'd told him I was probably spending the night at the house on account I didn't want to drive home alone in the dark with the weather like it is. He said, fine, he'd ride to work with Dwayne today."

She sent Heidi away, irritated with her. "Anyway, Daddy was being such a butt rash that I got fed up and left right after dessert. Then I go home, right, and what do I find?"

I looked up at her; she was red as a beet. "Jason was home?"

"He was home all right. In our bed with Patty Prettyman Greene."

"What? No way! You've got to be kidding me."

"No, there she was, sprawled out across the bed, her fat legs draped over Jason, him lying there on his back, naked, hard as a pine knot. Well, let me tell you, I put Daisy down on the floor and screamed like a demon. Jason woke up real fast, covered himself, shouted at Patty to leave, who did, but not before telling me it hadn't even been worth the risk."

"God, that's terrible." I didn't know what else to say.

Florabelle fumed. "It makes me cringe remembering Patty taking her sweet merry time getting dressed ready to go. Standing there, showing off her big breasts and full fanny, strutting back and forth to the bathroom in a red half slip, and the whole time ranting about how Jason's pecker wouldn't even fill a thimble."

"That must have been a scene." I stood up, walked over to her, put my hands on her shoulders.

She shrugged them off. "I'm okay. I just can't believe him. I never thought he'd do something this bad. You know what kills me? What really tears me up? She's so fat."

I was surprised at how unaffected she seemed; it was more like she was angry, perhaps humiliated, but not that upset. "Patty's fat now?" I asked, still in shock.

"Plump's a better word for it." She shook her head. "Just doesn't make sense. Jason likes his women bony," she looked over at me. "More like you than me, actually. You know it was my legs that caught Jason's attention two years ago at a barn dance in Campton? I was two-stepping with some boy from church, I forget his name now, and Jason just walked right up, introduced himself to me. I remember him coming right out and saying 'them's a nice pair of legs you got there, couldn't help but notice while you was twirling around with that fella.'"

Loudly, Florabelle gulped beer. "Anyways, he offered to buy me a pop and I'd just been thinking right that very moment how an Ale 8 would cool me down. So that was the beginning."

I had the whole strand of lights untangled while she'd been talking, and plugged it in. Every bulb worked. I turned out the lamp. "There," I said, "isn't that pretty?"

"Are you even listening to me?"

"Yes, I'm sorry, I just wanted to get these working. I still can't get over you finding them like that."

Florabelle slouched down in the chair, released the footrest, stretched out her legs. "Look at these legs," she said, "They're still shapely." She wiggled her feet.

"They're nice legs," I said, draping the lights over the tree branches. In the dim moonlight with the treelights reflecting off them, her bare legs shone like silver batons.

"Grandpa Trapper used to tell me I ought to get them insured."

"He did, did he? Hey, if I make popcorn, will you help me string it?"

"Yeah, sure. I need something to distract me."

"Just look outside, how peaceful and clear it is. That helps me when I'm down on something."

"You down? What the hell could you be pining over? You got a job, your own place, and now you're the big college girl."

"I've still got my occasional woes," I said vaguely, not wanting to talk about my situation with Culler. That seemed trivial at this point. "When I look out at the quiet hillside, I can forget things, for a little while, anyway."

Florabelle tilted her head to see out the window, scoffed. "Doesn't help me any. See how them two tiny stars are close together like that?"

I saw them, nodded.

"Well they remind me of Patty's earrings. She had on them bright mirror kind that reflect back whatever color hits them. I swear I can see Patty's face in that moon, just sneering down at me." She was working herself up again.

"Don't be ridiculous. I know it's hard, but just try and forget about it. He was never real good for you anyway. You two were always fighting. It's going to take some time, but someday you'll see that you're better off without him. Momma, Hazel, we all can help you with Daisy."

Florabelle regarded this. "Bird's crazy about her."

"She's a sweet baby," I said.

"She is." Florabelle sighed. "Sad thing is that Jason wanted a new car more than he wanted a kid. And he really wanted a boy once he knew he had no chance on the car."

"Momma mentioned that."

"I really should've guessed something like this would happen; Momma's right."

"You can never know these things."

"Well, he never came home until late every night. Patty's a ticket-taker down at Lowe's Shows. Jason and the guys from the bedspring factory hung out down there after work. I don't know if something's been going on behind my back for quite some time now, or I caught them screwing on a wild whim."

I was in the kitchen and had to shout over the popping noise. "Well, now that we know she was at your wedding, what she did to your cake, makes you wonder."

"I thought of that, too. That bitch."

"So you think they're gone together?" I asked.

"I don't know where the hell he went, and I don't care. That house, or I should say that shack, it's in his name, so I don't give a rat's ass. I ain't going back."

"Did you get all your stuff out?"

"Everything I wanted. All my clothes and keepsakes. I did have this crystal ashtray I'd stolen from Opry Land when we'd gone there once. I threw it at him and Patty, though, broke it on the headboard of the bed."

I came back in the living room with the popcorn.

Heidi ate some out of the bowl while I threaded the needles.

"I hate thinking about it." Florabelle belched.

"Then don't. Come on, help me." I gave her one of the needles.

"I really should have known he'd do something this evil."

"You can't know, this kind of thing happens to the best of us, trust me." How well I knew.

"You know, though, I just can't help thinking about that pitiful thing we met in Stanton that day at that garage sale. Remember her? That girl whose husband left her and her kid had died?"

"I thought of her, too. That's what I mean. Bad things happen to everyone. For some, it's worse."

"I suppose so," said Florabelle. "But that day when we were sitting out there in the hot sun, listening to her tell us about her husband leaving, the baby dying, I just kept wondering to myself then, what if this happened to me."

"Well, you're luckier. You still have Daisy."

"Then why do I feel like that girl? I just don't have any friends."

"You've got me," I said.

Florabelle had tears in her eyes.

I couldn't remember ever seeing her cry. She was the hardest person I'd ever met in my life. "You're going to be okay," I said. "And remember, you're not alone. We're survivors, all of us. This family's tough as nails." Then I got up and changed the record.

For the next hour we strung popcorn, and then I broke down and told her my story.

It felt good to get it out, share my despair with someone who really cared. Talking about it somehow made it seem less miserable. I realized, compared to Florabelle's problem, mine seemed so small. But she listened, she understood my jealousy toward his old girlfriend, and she could see how much I cared for Culler. But most of all, she was sincerely proud of me for signing up for school. Growing up, she always told me I'd be famous one day, and she said it again that night. She decided I'd go on to become a prominent brain surgeon.

I had to pop four or five batches of popcorn because we kept eating it. After we got the strands dyed and hanging on the tree, I invited her to sleep over, thinking we could both use the company. She had already planned to, and had her flannel gown in her bag.

I let Heidi out, then locked up and climbed in bed first. As I lay there waiting for her, I prayed silently for both of us.

When she'd brushed her teeth, gargled, flossed, and put on all her creams, she climbed in bed next to me and folded her arms up under her head. "Did you know Jason never would even eat fresh vegetables?"

"No, I didn't ever know that." I said in the darkness.

I recognized the familiar scent of chantilly lotion, and for the first time in a long time, the bedroom smelled of sweet reassurance.

42. Voices

About a week later, I went into work one morning and received some good news. They decided to give me something like a scholarship, an offer to pay for my school, for any classes that related to the work I did there at the clinic.

I was in such a good mood for a change, on the way home, I celebrated and stopped at a Ben Franklin to buy a box of tree ornaments. Besides the popcorn and lights, my tree was bare.

I called Birdie and Florabelle to come down and help me hang ornaments, and kept my promise with Bird to place the topper. It was a silver star with angel hair. They brought little Daisy with them, and she lay on a bundle of blankets, staring up at the star for almost an hour.

Florabelle seemed to be in better spirits. She had it figured that Jason had taken off to Chattanooga, Tennessee, where another one of his brother's lived and ran a hardware store. She believed Patty was with him. She said she watched the news at night, and listened for the weather there in Chattanooga, hoping to hear news of Jason getting caught in a blizzard and freezing to death.

We decorated the tree and played with Daisy. Heidi didn't know what to think about her, never being around a little baby before, but she was gentle.

We talked about past Christmases and wrapped some little presents we'd bought for Grandma.

Florabelle told us that Grandma was allowed to come home and spend Christmas day, but she refused to unless she could bring Earl. Momma, though, was putting her foot down to the fact that he was a married man, and told Grandma she could just stay there at the nursing home for Christmas, if that's the way she wanted to be about it.

We all laughed at Grandma's stubborn old spirit. Then Florabelle took all my leftover vegetables out of the freezer and made us some soup. They stayed until late that evening, then I drove them back down the hill. It had been nice, hearing voices in the house. For such a long time, it seemed only the sounds of my own crying had occupied the space.

When I got back from taking them home, my phone was ringing.

It was Culler.

At first, I was silent on my end. Stunned.

"Hi, Fern. I talked to Connie. She said she saw you."

"We had a nice visit."

"So I hear. Fern, I've been doing a lot of thinking. I'd like to talk about something, I mean, if that's okay with you."

"I don't think there's much left to say," I said.

However, he went on about how he really did care for me, but felt so strongly that any relationship we may have would really put a strain on me with my family. He thought that after that last episode on Halloween, I'd never want to see him again. He was feeling guilty for what had happened and blamed himself.

"I'm on my own now, you know that," I said flatly. "I don't answer to them. I make my own decisions now."

"See, that's exactly what I've been thinking about. The fact that you've moved out, you're starting school, working full-time, carrying your own weight, well, it made me realize that."

"So, what's your point?"

"I guess what I'm trying to say is that I've been wrong about you," he admitted. "You're more independent, more strong-minded than I realized. I guess I figured you'd always stay at home and let your family run your life."

It upset me, hearing his opinion of me. It seemed in his mind, all this time, I was lacking will. "Well, now that you've told me that you think I'm a big baby, why are you calling me? What, does it make you feel better to get it out in the open? It's not helping me any." I was about to hang up when he dropped the big one.

"Fern, there's something else. I knew about the fire at Clem's. I remembered the lantern, and suspected the morning I left your house, how those flames may have started."

"That's history now. I have to go."

"Fern, wait a minute. After listening to Connie, I got the impression that maybe you still care for me. Am I right?"

I didn't answer. I didn't know right then, if I did or not.

"If I am, I'd like us to try again. Start over."

Then I hung up.

I sat in the chair, staring at my tree until all the little colored lights blurred together into one dim glow. The wind whipped through the trees, and my little house shook, creaked at the seams. I wondered how Grandma never got frightened, living alone up here, at the top of the hill. She always used to say she could hear voices, that these voices kept her company. We used to think that she was crazy, but sitting there that night, I realized that all the voices she'd claimed to hear were the howling of the wind. Just as I thought I heard one whisper to me, I fell fast asleep.

43. More Rattles

A nurse had given Birdie some coloring books in the waiting area outside Grandma's room. Florabelle was sitting on the sofa beside her, rocking Daisy, smoking a cigarette.

When I walked in, Birdie ran to my arms and burst into tears. "She's going to die," she cried, "Hazel's heard the death rattles."

We were in the Emergency Ward at Winchester Regional Medical Center. I shushed Birdie, looked at Florabelle. "How is she?" I asked.

Florabelle put out her cigarette, lay Daisy down next to her, blew her nose. "They say the heart attack was mild, but she's weak and critical." She eyed Birdie, lowered her voice. "They don't expect her to make it. Stress-induced, is what this cardiologist tells us. Asked us if she'd recently undergone any extreme domestic changes or suffered any severe emotional experiences." Florabelle tried not to blink. "Momma's blaming herself, of course."

"Where's Momma now?" I asked.

"In there with Grandma," said Birdie. "Hazel went to get coffee."

Birdie had quit crying, but was fighting uncontrollable gasps. "Momma said it probably was Grandma's depression of having to move out of her own house that brought it on. It's Daddy's fault." She broke into another outburst.

I hugged her close, and her tears soaked my lab coat. "It's no one's fault," I said. "Grandma's old. It just might be her time." My voice cracked.

"She knows you're living in her house," said Florabelle. I winced.

Hazel came back with a Styrofoam cup of coffee and a KitKat for Birdie. "Here, honey," she said, "eat this and cheer up." Then she saw me, acted surprised. "Fern, I thought for a second you was one of the doctors. I saw that white coat."

"When did this all happen?" I asked her.

"After lunch, I went in to give her her pills and found her crumpled up on her side, on the floor next to a box of old photographs. I screamed, the staff came in, called an ambulance. I left and drove straight home, got everybody, and rushed us here."

Birdie had been the one who had remembered the name of the place where I worked and called me to get there as fast as I could.

She opened her candy bar, sat down, and in between sobs, ate the whole thing.

"Did anyone call Daddy?" I asked.

"I tried," said Hazel. "Couldn't get a hold of him, I left a message at the plant."

"Can we see her?" I asked.

"Yeah, I was just in there," said Hazel.

"I don't want to go in there with the baby," said Florabelle. "I'm staying out here with Bird."

"I want to see her," said Birdie.

"Bird, the doctors don't want you in there right now," explained Florabelle. "It'll just upset you, seeing Grandma hooked up to all them machines."

When I walked in the room, Momma was sitting in a chair next to the bed. She looked up when I came in, her eyes were red.

I walked over and put my hand on her shoulder.

She stood up, and we hugged and cried. It had been almost two months since we'd seen each other.

Two hours went by. Momma and I sat together in Grandma's room, waiting. Hazel came in and out, bringing me and Momma Pepsis and chewing gum. It made her too nervous, though, to stay in the room for too long. There was a no-smoking sign on the back of the door.

Nurses came and went, taking measurements, recording and adjusting things, offering us kind words. Once they brought Birdie in, but she turned so pale they had to take her back out.

Grandma looked so pitiful, lying there with tubes up her nose. She was so peaked, and each breath was an effort.

Her breathing was raspy; she struggled to hang on.

I had never heard the death rattles before that afternoon, and thought they were the saddest thing I'd ever hear. The sounds of what could be Grandma's last breaths were more mournful than the whimpering of a frightened, wounded dog, a crying widowed woman, a family arguing, or the howling wind at night. Even a lonelier sound than silence.

It was close to ten-thirty when a thin, dark-complected nurse came in, nudged us awake, and said, "She has taken a turn for the better. It is most miraculous." Her accent was strong Spanish. "She is gaining consciousness and strength; the doctor is coming. And Mrs Rayburn, your husband wants you to call home."

We looked at Grandma. Her troubled breathing was beginning to ease and a little color had returned to her face.

"Praise the Lord," whispered Momma, taking hold of Grandma's hand.

I walked back out into the waiting room. The nurse had already given the others the same news. Birdie looked like she had just woke up, and was smiling at me faintly. Some male intern was sitting next to Florabelle, on his break, drinking a cola. He was giving her advice on child rearing.

Hazel looked totally wiped out. "You don't know how relieved I am," she said. "Mom's as mean as an old yard snake, but I don't think I was ready to let her go yet."

Momma finally came out to the nurse's station and dialed Daddy.

"You finally got a hold of Daddy?" I asked Hazel.

"Yeah, I reached him at home just a while ago. He was worried when nobody was home."

"Is he coming up?" I asked.

"I don't know. Sylvia was just supposed to call him."

Momma joined us in the waiting room, and Hazel gave her a hug.

"I told Raymond to come take Bird home. I want her back in her own bed now that everything seems to be all right." Exhausted, Momma went into Grandma's room.

Birdie had been able to sleep on the sofa, but she kept waking up with nightmares about worms crawling up her nose.

When Daddy got there, Birdie ran up to him and said, "Daddy, go in there and do something. Don't let Grandma die, she needs me."

We reassured her that Grandma was going to be all right.

Daddy led her into Grandma's room.

I followed them in, and sat down in the seat over by the window, away from the bed.

Daddy walked over to Momma.

She took his hand, squeezed it, let go. "She may make it," she said. Her voice was tired.

I looked at Daddy's face. He had not yet acknowledged me, or any of the rest of us, just Momma and Birdie. His face was strained, tight. I imagined that he probably realized what losing Grandma might do to his family. Birdie seemed to be the most important thing in the world to him, and here he saw how she was suffering. He had to know, deep down, he was part to blame.

He looked at Grandma, whose eyes were open, not focused, but alert. With all the tubing connected to her nose and mouth, it was hard to read her expression, but she was looking at him. Daddy didn't say anything; he nodded at her, as if to only acknowledge her survival, not necessarily give praise for it.

He turned to Momma. "I'll take Birdie on home, now. Anything else you need?"

She shook her head. "I believe I want to stay here tonight. Just in case."

Daddy hesitated, bent down, kissed her cheek quickly, then turned to go.

Not once did he turn to face me, nor did he look back again at Grandma. But I was almost certain, as he was walking out, that Grandma's eyes were boring through him.

44. The Couch

Grandma's recovery was slow, but steady. She seemed to have gotten over the hump. Her condition had stabilized, and she hadn't experienced a relapse, but they wanted to keep her in the hospital to monitor her progress.

I was off the whole week before Christmas, and Birdie, Florabelle, and I spent a lot of time up at my place baking cookies. Florabelle seemed to have adjusted pretty quickly to Jason being gone. He still hadn't called, but he'd mailed her an envelope with one hundred dollars in it to the house. She guessed that one day he would call, just to see how Daisy was doing, if for no other reason.

Culler had called for me again at work, one day before my vacation started, but I wouldn't talk to him. I didn't tell Florabelle. I wanted to concentrate on her dilemma, not my own silly affair.

I was beginning to understand Florabelle, to see a side of her I'd never known until lately. She was growing kinder, and I was starting to like her more than I ever had. Although I always knew she had a good heart under all that malice and resentment, she seemed to let a softness show a little more often these days. The bitterness and anger had somehow subsided. I supposed it was having Daisy, finding a constant in her life who needed her that brought on the change.

She had gone in with Momma and Hazel, and ordered me a couch from Sears for Christmas. I knew she must have used some of the money Jason had sent her to pay for it.

It was delivered Christmas Eve morning, and they were all there waiting for the truck to come, so they could see the surprised look on my face. Florabelle, Bird, Hazel, and Momma had walked up to my house around nine o'clock that morning. I was glad to see them all, but I was a little curious about their coming so early. It was nice to have

Momma there; she hadn't yet seen how I'd fixed up the place. It was when she and Hazel started moving my living room chair and bookcase, that I started to get a little suspicious. They were making a spot for the couch.

It was colonial style, with yellow and brown floral print fabric and a high back. It fit real nicely against one wall; I was certainly surprised. We all took turns sitting on it, getting up and down, and rubbing it. The print was bold and really brightened up the room. I could just imagine what the drivers thought of us, making over a piece of furniture like it was some rare treasure.

I thanked all of them, and gave Momma a kiss. She was determined I was going to come up the next day, and spend Christmas with the family. No matter what Daddy said. It felt good to be included. I was starting to feel whole again.

When they'd all left, I went in my room and looked for my letter from Transylvania. I found it, still crumpled up from when I'd thrown it, stuffed in the back of my underwear drawer. I unfolded it, carried it out to the living room couch, and sat down to read it again.

I had registered, received some financial support, and I still really wanted to go, but just in the past few days, a little bit of guilt was beginning to creep up on me. I knew that now that things were patched up between me and Momma again, she could use my help with Grandma sick and Florabelle back home with the baby. I was feeling the pull back to my post of duty.

Pressing the letter on my couch, I flattened out the edges. I thought of my own life, how for a while it would be smooth and wrinkle free, then the next minute could crumble. I lay back on the firm new cushions and fell asleep in the bright yellow flowers.

45. Guns and Roses

Christmas morning, I loaded up the back of my car with presents and drove down the hill to the house for the first time since the fire. While I was rushing out the phone rang twice, but when I picked up, no one said anything.

At the house, everyone was already up, and Momma had made a big breakfast of apple pancakes, biscuits and gravy, and grits. Hazel was there, and she volunteered, for the first time ever, to say the blessing.

Florabelle had told me that since Grandma's heart attack, Daddy had been a little bit nicer, treated Momma more decent, had finally put up a Christmas tree, but still wouldn't turn grace. She said he didn't have a whole lot to say and stayed up in his gun room or the garage more than ever.

He sat down at the table that morning, poured cream in his coffee, looked up and nodded at me.

"Good morning," I said, my throat tight. I took an extra sip of milk to wash down my grits.

"Merry Christmas, Daddy," said Florabelle.

Daddy mumbled. "Merry Christmas." He looked at Birdie. "Did Santie bring you anything?"

"I haven't looked yet," she said. "Momma wanted to wait on Fern." She looked at me, spoon in hand, smiled.

It was good to be home.

Suddenly, Daddy got up, scuffed his chair back and went outside in the garage. When he came back in, he was carrying a high chair, one I recognized that he'd designed and carved when Birdie was born.

"I smoothed the nicks out of it, refinished it." He brought it over to where Florabelle was sitting, sat it down next to her. "Thought you could use it for your baby."

Florabelle, who was balancing Daisy on her knee with one hand, trying to eat with the other, started crying.

This got Momma crying too, and Daddy got uncomfortable.

"It's the least I could do," he said, sitting back down at the head of the table. "After all the grief I've caused all of you this past year." He hung his head, stared at his pancakes, forked at them absently. "I can't ask you all to forgive me. The damage, as I see it, is done."

Birdie got up and took Daisy out of Florabelle's arms and tried to stuff her into the highchair.

"Be careful, " I said. "Her back isn't that strong yet. She'll grow into it."

Momma was still in tears.

Hazel looked around the table, trying to think of a way to free the tension. "Oh, Raymond," she said, way too loud to sound sincere, "don't go getting all sad on us, it's Christmas. Everything'll work out. Now let's all eat up and go open gifts."

"No," said Daddy, "you all go ahead. I've been doing a lot of thinking." His eyes were puffy, bloodshot. "You folks don't deserve for me to come in there and spoil everything." He looked at Momma. "I don't deserve your patience anymore either." Then he left the table.

We heard his footsteps on the stairs, headed for his room.

No one at the table wanted to move, but Hazel made us get up and go out to the living room and sit around the tree. She wanted this to be a nice Christmas, no matter what, because everyone was finally all back together. For all four of us, she had bought our favorite perfumes. She looked so proud as we unwrapped the small pretty boxes.

Mine was White Shoulders, she had bought Momma Chanel Number Five, Birdie's was Avon Soft Musk, and Florabelle's of course was Chantilly. She had bought Daisy a stuffed dog that looked a lot like Jimmy and made Birdie sob.

I gave everyone sweaters, and my gift from them had been the couch.

Momma and Hazel gave Florabelle a basinette, and Birdie got school clothes and a bead necklace. Santa had brought her a new Cabbage Patch doll, female, to keep Waylon Jennings company.

Birdie gave us all photographs of ourselves, pasted on construction paper, with poems she had written underneath them. Mine read, "Roses are red, Ferns are green, this sister's nice, but the other one's mean." I folded it up and put it aside.

We left Daddy's presents for him, still wrapped in a little pile under the tree. Maybe he'd come down later, we figured, when he got over his blues. It concerned Momma to see him like that, feeling so down on himself.

We watched the Christmas parade at Madison Circle in Indianapolis, then we watched Charles Dickens's *The Christmas Carol.* I'd seen it maybe ten times in my life already, but I always liked to watch it over the holidays.

Besides, it was so bitter cold out, that staying snuggled up together on the couch inside, seemed the best way to spend Christmas.

Momma got up and down checking dinner. She had a big ham in the oven, and brought us warmed up biscuits with honey from breakfast, to tide us over.

Around noon, we called the hospital to talk to Grandma. Her spirits were low, having to spend her Christmas there, but she was doing a lot better and the doctors told her she could go home soon.

Some roses had been delivered to her from the house, and she said that made her day. They made her think of springtime and gave her hope.

Birdie got on the phone to talk to her a while, and we told her to say that if the snowstorm let up, we'd try to come down and visit later tonight.

It didn't look too promising, the wind was blowing, and the snow fell in large flakes against the living room window. You could barely see out. The roads would be bad.

"Who sent the roses?" asked Hazel, hanging up the phone.

Florabelle and I shrugged.

"I didn't," said Momma. "Now, ain't that strange."

Right about the part in the movie where the Ghost from the Christmas Future comes to see Ebaneezer, we heard a gunshot upstairs.

Birdie screamed.

My heart stopped.

"Good God in heaven, what was that?" said Hazel, jumping to her feet.

Daisy woke up and started crying. Florabelle tried to quiet her, a look of panic in her eyes.

Momma ran in from the kitchen, white as a ghost. "Fern," she said. "Run up there, check on your father. Hurry!"

My body was frozen stiff.

"You reckon he's gone and shot himself?" said Hazel, shaking like a leaf. She turned the sound down on the TV set. Ebeneezer was off in the distance, looking on at his own gravestone.

"Hurry, Fern!" shouted Birdie.

Daisy still wailed, kicked and fussed at Florabelle who hadn't said a word, scared to death to move.

I looked over at her; she nodded towards the staircase.

As I climbed the stairs, my heart raced ahead of me. My legs felt like rubber, they were so wobbly. With each step, I had to hold onto the banister. I was almost numb, worrying about what I might find.

When I got to Daddy's room, I listened at the door. It was silent. I grabbed the doorknob and turned it slowly. Peering in, I saw Daddy sitting at his desk, staring at the wall.

"Daddy?"

I startled him. He turned around, looked at me. "I don't know if I hit that stud or not," he said, pointing at the wall.

All his guns were off the wall rack, the casings were empty. The desk was surrounded with boxes.

"What happened?" I asked, feeling my blood start to circulate again.

"Oh, I was taking these guns down off the wall here and throwing them in the box. One of them fired off. Didn't know they were all loaded." He picked at the wall, measuring the damage.

"We heard the shot," I said. "They're worried down there."

He looked around the room, threw up his hands, brought them down, slapping his knees. "I don't know where I'm going to put all this stuff," he said, exasperated.

"What are you doing?"

"I'm cleaning the room out, storing the guns. Making some room."

His desk was empty, all the things in the drawers were piled on top. A cloud of dust and gunpowder hovered above the boxes.

Daddy seldom had paperwork other than the bills and few pieces of junk mail to sort, but inside his desk, he kept his personal items like old letters from Army buddies, key chains from different places he'd been, and in the double drawer, a few childhood remnants like photographs and newspaper clippings.

"Come here," he said. He opened a cigar box, still strong with tobacco scent, shuffled through it, and took out an old photograph. It was a picture of his mother. In this particular setting, she was holding an infant, and four other small children stood around her chair. She looked about twenty-nine or thirty. The baby in her arms was him.

Daddy held the picture, studied it a while, handed it to me. His mother's expression was stern, lips tight. Her posture looked unnaturally erect, her knees touched, toes pointed in. Though it was not a face of kindness, or even beauty, there was a look of complacence, enduring strength, wisdom.

It was not the face of a woman who would have ever needed, or even accepted, nursing care, had she lived. She had died when Florabelle and I were babies.

"She was quite a woman," said Daddy. "Strong and clever." He shook his head. "Did you ever know that my momma and Esther were neighbors?"

"No, I don't think I did."

"Yes, when they were in about their midtwenties. We lived on adjacent farms and they competed for the earliest canning. It was always that way, one trying to outdo the other. But my Daddy and your Momma's Daddy, they got along. Then my Daddy died when I was about seventeen. And Adam Trapper, Esther's first husband, your Grandpa, was the minister of the town."

"Right," I said.

"Well, I met your Momma at his church. We were always forced to play together at the Sunday school picnics, and one year we played Mary and Joseph in a junior-high Christmas play, and afterwards, I asked her to go with me."

"You were in a play?" Somehow, I couldn't picture this since Daddy had always been shy, from what I could remember.

He leaned back, his chair creaked. "You know, there was a time when I had great respect for your Grandma Esther. In her life with your Grandpa Trapper, she was different. Much more strong-willed, very religious, subservient to your Grandpa, and dedicated to raising their two daughters in a stable home. I can still remember that house, everything being so clean and orderly."

Daddy got up from his desk, started packing more stuff away as he talked. "That Esther, boy let me tell you she was strict. I remember being a bit afraid of her. If she got mad at the girls, she'd sure give them a piece of her mind. Piece of a tree branch across the bottom, too. But I'll say this for her, she was brave. When your Grandpa died, she tended that farm alone for many years. And she remained very influential in the congregation." He laughed, tossed a pistol in a box.

Everytime he did this, I jumped a little, worrying another one might fire off.

"I'll share a secret with you, Fern. At one time it was Hazel I thought I loved, not your Momma. Sylvia was always more talented in the kitchen and better at sports, but it was Hazel who had the long lean legs."

I smiled.

"That's right. But it was Esther who made it clear to me which one of her daughters I was to like and pursue, and eventually marry. She just laid it on the line one day when I walked them both home from school. Told me, flat out, which one I could court."

"That's funny," I said. "I can just hear her, but why did she pick Momma?"

"Well, your Grandma always did take a liking to me. She never wanted me to know that, but she had a lot of respect for my whole family. She knew what I would grow up and want in a wife, and she also knew it would be Sylvia who would fit the mold. And she was right."

"That's a great story, Daddy; but I guess you could never tell Momma, huh?"

"I suspect she knows. She's a lot like Esther that way, always knows what people are thinking." He taped up a box, labeled it "HANDGUNS." "Years have gone by, though, loss, change, they've all had an affect on your Grandma, but I suppose deep down, that old spitfire's smoldering. I reckon she could still tell me which one of her daughters, or her granddaughters, is doing right by her book."

"Probably so," I said, watching him work. "Where are you going to put all this?" I asked.

"Attic, garage, basement. Anywhere it'll all go."

"Well, I'm going to tell everybody you're okay. You must have scared ten years of growth off Daisy. Come on down and open your presents."

"Fern?"

"Yes, Daddy?"

"Merry Christmas." He handed me a book off his desk. It was still in cellophane. The title was *One Hundred Uncommon Cattle Diseases and Common Cures.*

46. More Signs

"Do you want this in a bag, sir?" asked the checkout girl in Krogers.

"No thanks, I'll carry it like this. Just wrap up these hooks."

The girl yawned. "You taking that thing to a funeral home or something?"

Daddy tucked the frame under his arm, the portrait facing out. "No, by then it's too late."

There was no traffic this early in the morning, the sun was out, and the roads were clear.

It was New Year's Eve, and the three of us had gone out to get Grandma's welcome-home present.

Hazel and Momma had gone to bring her home.

I sat in the back holding the picture. The frame was gold spray-painted plastic. It was a portrait of Jesus. He had those eyes that followed yours, no matter from which angle you looked at it. It made me uncomfortable so I looked straight ahead.

On the way home, we passed Grover Flynn's fish camp. Next to the bait hut, a new building was going up. The cement foundation was poured, and lumber lay off to one side by the road. Out front, they were putting up a new sign. It read "CLEM'S TACKLE AND BAIT SHOP. COMING SOON: A FISHING RESORT."

He had done it. Clem had followed through on his plan. He was doing what he wanted to do, making his dream come true. And for that, he could always be proud. He always did hold a lot of stake in perseverance, stubborn old mule that he was. Clem had taught me a lot over the years: stuff about fixing cars, managing money, the economy; he'd even taught me how to drive. He had a lot of skills and could offer good advice on almost anything. But most of all, Clem set a fine example for friendship. From him, I learned to trust and forgive.

I glanced back down at the portrait and tried to imagine Clem Proffit with a beard and long hair, walking across Kentucky with a cane, guiding sheep. I propped the picture up next to me, facing forward, watched those piercing blue eyes. Come to think of it, Clem did sort of favor the Lord a bit. Same forehead, anyway.

Seeing those walls go up at Clem's fish camp had the opposite effect of seeing the ones at the station come down. The guilt of destroying something was gone, replaced with the hope of starting over. Clem's new sign brought back the vision of my own goals. I could do it, too. I'd go to school, and make myself proud. Maybe I'd make everyone proud and get them to understand. Sitting there in the backseat next to the Lord our Shepherd, I made up my mind to call Culler back, too. I had nothing to lose now.

When we got home from the store, Grandma was

already there, sitting on the edge of her bed. Momma was putting socks on her feet, and Hazel was sitting in a chair by the window, smoking a cigarette.

Daddy didn't speak, just walked in, right up to Grandma's bed with a hammer and the picture.

Grandma looked startled and frowned at Daddy.

He centered the frame directly over the bed, covering a hole in the wall, reached in his pocket for a few hooks, and drove in the nails.

The hammering, of course, caught us all off guard. Momma looked up at him, and Birdie and I watched from the bedroom doorway.

Hazel was still dragging on her cigarette, but didn't budge an inch.

Grandma turned her stiff neck just enough to see the picture over her head. She made a little whimpering sound, and then tears streamed down her cheeks.

All eyes were on Daddy, who stood back, arms folded, staring up at the portrait. "I figured this might make you feel safe, hanging right up over your head, watching out for you," he said to Grandma. "Besides, you don't want to look at that hole I blew."

47. Lang Syne

The air was bitter cold, but at least there was no breeze. The year before, the wind had been gusty, and they'd canceled the show for safety reasons. We didn't get there until around eleven-thirty, but we still had time to relax before the fireworks were to begin.

Most people didn't arrive until late anyway because of the cold. The Resort guests, staying at the Lodge there at the park, were standing out on their balconies where it was warmer. It was a fairly good turnout for the show; everyone sat on canvas or plastic, huddled together. Lots of folks brought along a thermos of coffee, tea, or some other hot drink.

Culler and I sat snuggled up together under a down blanket. We had our own thermos of mint-flavored hot chocolate. I was warm enough, though, just being next to him again.

I had called him that night and invited him over. He'd shown up with a kitten for Birdie, and Daddy let her keep it. She'd cuddled him in her lap all evening, and it made Heidi a little jealous; she kept whistling, growling softly, but didn't try to harm it.

"It sure is pretty out here at night," said Culler, leaning back on our blanket. "It amazes me just how clear it is in the country. You can't see all these stars in a city skyline."

"That's why I like it so much here," I said gazing at the sky. The air was incredibly crisp, even our whispering seemed loud. A soft chatter filled the night. Christmas lights draped from one light pole to the next, and the bright bulbs cast soft, colored shadows in the snow. The whole hillside glowed mysteriously.

The music began and a countdown to midnight. The first firework blasted, and the crowd oohed and aahed. Culler leaned over and kissed me. "Happy New Year," he said.

The show was beautiful; the lights and sounds around me were enchanting. Each time a spray of color burst into twinkling lights, the white ground below took on the same vibrant glow.

I was more absorbed in my own thoughts. With each boom, my heart thumped, but with anticipation, not fear. The feeling inside me seemed to reflect the magic light flaring above us.

When we got home, Culler walked me to the door. "Can I come in?" he asked. "Just for a minute. I have something for you."

I hesitated a moment, but it was cold so I unlocked the door and invited him inside. "What is it?"

"A Christmas present," he said, sitting down on the new couch. "I know it's a little late, but I wanted to get you something."

I plugged in the tree lights, pulled open the curtains.

The fireworks display had ended, but the bright moon sustained the romantic glow in the sky. I sat down beside Culler.

Then he reached into his pocket and pulled out a small box wrapped in green wax paper. "Here," he said. "Open it."

I unwrapped the gift, a small maroon velvet box. Inside was a pair of gold turtle earrings. I smiled, remembering the day I was wearing Birdie's green plastic ones, before I'd hooked Culler.

That seemed so long ago, the late summer. And now it was winter. Not only was a new year beginning, but a new life was starting for me. Soon, springtime would come, and the snow covering the lawn would melt. Sitting there next to Culler, admiring the earrings and everything they stood for, I could feel the cold layer around my heart melting too.

Culler was staring at me; I had left him for my thoughts.

"Do you like them?" he asked, an arm around me over the back of the couch.

"I love them." Carefully, I took them out of the box and tried them on.

"Now, whenever you wear them, you can think of me."

"I will," I said. "And everything the old tortoise has taught us, right?" I laughed.

"That's right," said Culler, "slow and steady." He hugged me close.

Inside me once again, a spark ignited.